OTHER BOOKS BY JORGE AMADO

Dona Flor and Her Two Husbands
Gabriela, Clove and Cinnamon
Home Is the Sailor
Jubiabá
The Sea of Death
Shepherds of the Night
The Swallow and the Tom Cat
Tent of Miracles
Tereza Batista: Home from the Wars
Tieta
The Two Deaths of Quincas Wateryell
The Violent Land

OTHER LATIN AMERICAN FICTION FROM GODINE

The Obscene Bird of Night
JOSÉ DONOSO

On Heroes and Tombs
ERNESTO SABATO

The Seven Madmen
ROBERTO ARLT

Two Crimes
JORGE IBARGUENGOITIA

PEN,
SWORD,
CAMISOLE

A NOVEL BY **Jorge Amado**

TRANSLATED BY **Helen R. Lane**

DAVID R. GODINE · PUBLISHER
BOSTON

AVON BOOKS
NEW YORK

PEN,
SWORD,
CAMISOLE

A Fable to Kindle a Hope

First English language edition published in 1985 by
David R. Godine, Publisher, Inc.
306 Dartmouth Street
Boston, Massachusetts 02116

in association with

Avon Books
1790 Broadway
New York, New York 10019

First published in Portuguese in 1980 by Distribuidora Record
Serviços de Imprentsa, S.A., Rio de Janeiro.

Library of Congress Cataloging in Publication Data
Amado, Jorge, 1912–
    Pen, sword, camisole.

    Translation of: Farda, fardao, camisola de dormir.
    I. Title.
PQ9697.A647F313   1985   869.3   84-48301
ISBN 0-87923-552-7

First edition

Printed in the United States of America

For *Zélia, reliving her childhood in Pedra do Sal.*

For *my sisters Fanny, Lu, and Misette.*

To *the memory of Afrânio Peixoto and António da Silva Melo.*

For *Alceu Amoroso Lima and João Condé, who know stories of those days.*

"... the glory that remains, ennobles, honors, and consoles."

> *(Machado de Assis,*
> *on the Brazilian Academy of Letters)*

"Quelle connerie, la guerre!"

> *(Jacques Prévert, "Barbara")*

"Heil Hitler!"

> *(A fairly common greeting at the time)*

"No pasarán!"

> *(Watchword of "La Pasionaria" during the Spanish civil war, adopted by the elderly Academician Evandro Nunes dos Santos)*

This fable tells how two elderly men of letters, Academicians and liberals, went to war against Nazism, dictatorship, and totalitarianism. Any resemblance to individuals, organizations, academies, classes and castes, personalities, and events in real life is due to pure and simple coincidence, since the story is the exclusive product of the author's imagination and experience. The only things that are not fiction are the dictatorship of the New State, with its National Security Law, its machinery of repression, its prisons full to overflowing, its torture chambers, and its obscurantism, and the Second Great World War, unleashed by Nazi-fascism, at its worst moment, when everything seemed lost and hope was dying.

The Execution of the Poet António Bruno, as a Result of the Fall of Paris, During the Second World War

THE SONNET THAT WAS NOT WRITTEN

The poet António Bruno died, the victim of a sudden heart attack—the second within a short time—on September 25, 1940. The luminous morning, with its clear, pure air and its pleasant temperature, had brought back the memory of a similar diaphanous morning, entering through the skylight, illuminating the Paris studio, enveloping—a transparent, rose-colored camisole—the naked body of the sleeping woman. A vision worthy of a sonnet, he had thought, but he had not written it, for the young woman awoke and held out her arms to him.

On remembering, he took up paper and pen, and in his elegant hand that was almost a decorative art he traced at the top of the page what was surely meant to be the title of a love-poem: "The Camisole." The memory suddenly became a sad one, a cruelly painful regret: ah, nevermore! The poet did not have time to write even one verse; he raised his hand to his chest, his head fell on top of the paper, and a chair in the Brazilian Academy of Letters became vacant.

He had had his first heart attack exactly three months before, upon hearing a news bulletin on the radio announcing the fall of Paris.

A HARD-FOUGHT, BLOODY BATTLE

"A battle, that's right, and what a battle it was!" Mestre Afrânio Portela said emphatically; with age, he had become dogmatic. At the time of the famous events, he had argued that the war being waged was worldwide in scope. We are all involved in it, he had said; the battlefield has no limits of any sort, either geographical or military; any weapon is useful and appropriate, and the least victory kindles a hope.

With the passage of time, this octogenarian with a captivating gift for words, a great talker, an incomparable conversationalist, tended more and more to exaggerate the importance of the events that had occurred and the lessons that had been learned from them, and began to claim, half seriously and half jokingly, that he had been an active member of the French Resistance, of the Maquis, a guerrilla leader—and it would appear that that was indeed the role he had played.

It was, moreover, the role the two of them had played— he and skeptical Professor Evandro Nunes dos Santos, his fellow conspirator and, according to Afrânio's own testimony, the more intrepid and implacable of the two of them in the second phase of the operations:

"I was satisfied at that point, thinking that we had already attained our objective, but Evandro wouldn't go along with that. With him, it was all or nothing."

Mestre Afrânio Portela never neglected to add that the battle, in which the international forces of Nazi-fascism and the national forces of reaction and totalitarianism had been defeated, was not only hard-fought, but bloody.

◼ THE HISTORICAL BACKGROUND

A mere election a battle? A contest, at most, confined to a single institution, limited to a strict number of voters, just thirty-nine of them—the thirty-nine living Academicians.

Without wishing to detract from the scope and the import of the election of a new member of the Brazilian Academy of Letters, a subject that attracted a great deal of attention in the press and in intellectual circles due to the undeniable, though much-debated, prestige of that institution, it must be conceded that it was an event of limited importance in an era of tremendous and terrible historical developments, since it occurred as the Second World War was raging, in the year 1940; that is to say, at the time when the victorious troops of the Wehrmacht had just overrun France, and the Luftwaffe was razing England's cities and countryside. For many, perhaps for the majority, the defeat of the democratic nations had become an irreversible fact, and their total collapse seemed imminent—a mere matter of days. Hitler had triumphantly announced a thousand years of Nazi domination, a reign that had already begun. A time of fear and despair.

A thousand years: how many generations of slaves? German planes filled the skies over London, dropping a continuous rain of bombs; invading German tanks swarmed over all the countries of Europe; Poland had been wiped off the map; no more Viennese waltzes were heard, nor was the imperial name of Austria uttered; the flag with the swastika waved atop the ancient tower of Prague, and on the breast of Jews the Star of David was a bloody flower. Blood and mud, terror and villainy, protectorates and protectors, the Gestapo, the SA and the SS, concentration camps, gas chambers, ignominy and death. A time of fear and despair. A time of hopelessness.

In Brazil, under the totalitarian constitution of the New State—the *Estado Novo*—martial law had been declared, a reflection of the Axis victories, and the repression had reached its high point of brutality and obscurantism. The idyll with Nazi Germany dictated government policy: total censorship of the press, the notorious National Security Law and the sentences handed down by its tribunal, no guarantees of individual freedom or rights; police power become absolute, with no restrictions whatsoever. In the prisons, in the correction colonies, in the basements of the various police forces—political prisoners and torture.

At precisely the same moment that the Academician

5

Lisandro Leite excitedly telephoned Colonel Agnaldo Sampaio Pereira to pass on the sad and happy news of the death of António Bruno the poet (a phone call that served as a call to arms), Elias the railway worker, also known as "The Prophet," a nom de guerre, was hanging suspended by his balls at the headquarters of the Special Police. The athletes of that shock brigade, bulwarks of the regime, wanted The Prophet, arrested two days before, to name names, to reveal addresses and contacts. Curiously enough, some verses of a recent poem, which he had read in a smudged mimeographed copy, had contributed to the prisoner's stubborn silence, sustaining him in the hours of cruel torture. They had not, however, sustained the poet António Bruno, who had written them; they had not lent him the strength to overcome his discouragement and despair.

In the face of such a pathetic panorama of events, how to take a mere Academy election seriously, how to see in it anything more than the usual idle intrigue and gossip? Illustrious electors, eminent personalities in the cultural life of the country, immortality, the title, the regalia of the Academician—all of this admittedly contributes to the fact that the contest for a seat in the Brazilian Academy of Letters is an event that attracts the attention of the entire nation, and on occasion gives rise to bitter competition. But that is a far cry from a battle without quarter between triumphant Nazism and the greatly weakened forces of democracy.

That is nonetheless what the election turned into. Mestre Afrânio Portela neither lied nor exaggerated when he spoke of a battle and of kindling a light of hope. As for the other elderly man of letters, the author of a number of seminal essays on Brazilian reality and the Brazilian character that were notable for his knowledge of the subject, for the originality of his thought, and for the boldness of his assertions, Evandro Nunes dos Santos, being a stubborn exponent of individualism, saw the battle through to the very end. He had a horror of any sort of arbitrariness or authoritarianism, to the point that he forbore to wear the Academy uniform, choosing to appear at its solemn sessions in an ordinary business suit. A suit that went very well with his "civilist" bias, his conviction that the military had no business running the country, and with his physique, that of a tall, very thin septuagenarian, with bony hands and bushy eyebrows.

A THUMBNAIL PORTRAIT OF THE HEROIC COLONEL

It was downright unpleasant when the colonel, who had begun to leaf through the galleys, lost his head and dropped the role he usually played. Up to that point, the atmosphere in which the interview had proceeded had been tense but bearable; it was scarcely worthwhile, naturally, to put on a show of cordiality, to exchange friendly greetings, courtesies, and smiles at a confrontation between the Chief of Security of the New State dictatorship and a lowly, despicable, subversive journalist who was suspected of belonging to the Communist party and was quite obviously a Jew.

His face distorted with rage, the yellow gleam of the fanatic in his eye, the colonel turned threatening and unpredictable. He shook the fistful of galley proofs in the thin face of the terrified young man on the other side of the table; on the other side of the trench, that is to say, inasmuch as the colonel's office was in fact a battle front. His voice rose in a shrieking falsetto:

"You shameless wretch! Do you dare claim this rag isn't Communist? What do you take me for? An imbecile?" Thunderous pounding on the table: a shell or a grenade.

Ordinarily, the colonel speaks in a resounding, emphatic, even voice, a commanding voice: both when he propounds truths that in his eyes are incontrovertible and when his words, in the midst of a heated discussion, hit his adversary square in the face like a violent slap. A calculated tone of voice and deliberate gestures, the pose of a leader. On occasion, however, the colonel loses his self-control, and then it's goodbye to the image of the bold, self-assured leader, tough and competent, intrepid. Of the imperturbable and heroic Colonel Agnaldo Sampaio Pereira, the famous (and infamous) Colonel Sampaio Pereira.

A man of action and a thinker, a battle-hardened veteran in the fight (in the war, he corrects himself, in the ceaseless war against the enemies of the Fatherland), the widely acclaimed author of some ten books, a well-preserved man in his fifties, dark-haired, with a slightly dusky complexion. A few moments before, on hearing the colonel proclaim the superiority of the Aryan race ("We Aryans will take over the reins of the universe and ride astride it. . . ."), the journalist Samuel Lederman, despite the uncomfortable position in which he found himself, instead of admiring and applauding the polished style and vigor of the phrase, could not help wondering, impudently and imprudently: What is the percentage of black blood in the blue veins of this noble equestrian of the universe? As for the colonel's powerful though hooked nose and the surname Pereira, did they not perchance betray traces of a New-Christian family background, of Semitic forebears, converted by force of fire and fetters by the Holy Office? ("You're diabolical, Samy," Da kept telling him, curling up at his feet.) A secret accusation, naturally, since it would have been pointless to discuss the colonel's quintessentially Aryan attributes.

Yes, because even if, as was amply evident, his Brazilian ancestry went back many generations and had included many mixtures of blood, it was with absolute conviction that he claimed he was Aryan. He had written a voluminous tome, *For an Aryan Civilization in the Tropics: An Essay on the Essential Brazilian Character*, praised to the skies by the rightist newspapers and adopted as a text in the public high schools and in the university-level course on Moral and Civic Education, thus guaranteeing the book many successive printings and the colonel fat royalties.

A number of women thought him good-looking, admiring his broad shoulders, his resolute stride, his well-groomed black hair gleaming with brilliantine, his dynamic silhouette beneath his impeccable uniform. At first glance, he was reminiscent of a certain North American actor, the number-one box-office star of the era. Moreover, there was something of the actor about him, for in his celebrated pose as an inflexible leader, possessed of a lively intelligence and perspicacity of judgment, intransigent, inhuman if necessary in the defense of his unshakable convictions, a certain role-playing undoubtedly entered the picture, apparent in the placing of his voice, in the orotund accent with which he uttered even the most trivial phrases, and in his inquisitorial eye, capable of reading the secrets of guilty consciences. This gaze cost him a real effort, constant attention, since by nature his eyes were round, habitually inexpressive, ingenuous, unspiteful.

Certain newspapers, on mentioning his name, preceded it with sonorous, martial adjectives: brave, dauntless, fearless. Especially in the days that followed the afternoon on which the then Lieutenant Colonel Sampaio Pereira, at the head of the battalions of Special Police and the shock units of the Brigade to Ensure Social and Political Order, confronted and vanquished, in the streets of Rio de Janeiro, capital of the Republic, a howling, threatening mob of agitators armed to the teeth with fierce rallying cries, shouts, and raised fists, demonstrating against Itamaraty's handing over of the property of the Embassy of Czechoslovakia to the authorities of Nazi Germany after the Munich Pact and the occupation of Prague. A historic defeat of the forces of subversion, which

9

put an end to mass demonstrations for a long time to come.

A man of action, and in addition a thinker with a vast corpus of theoretical works that had earned him honors and praise in the realm of letters: "one of the most prolific and active writers of his generation," "a seminal political thinker," "an essayist at the pinnacle of his powers," and so on. His books constituted a justification of dictatorships and propaganda in their favor, analyzed the decadence and corruption of the democracies, and denounced the monstrous peril that Communism represented.

He had written his first essays while still a member of the Chamber of Forty and an ardent militant of the Integralista party. When the 1937 coup dissolved political parties, he withdrew his support of Integralism, stating in an article: "The New State signifies the practical application of Integralist doctrines and ideas, thereby rendering a party structure unnecessary and, indeed, redundant and provocative." On the occasion of the attempted coup in 1938, Sampaio Pereira remained faithful to the government and did not hesitate to order the arrest of his former party comrades. His most recently published volumes were intended to provide an ideological basis for the New State, whose purity, totalitarian principles, and iron discipline were being threatened by the notorious inability of the Brazilian people to take great ideas seriously and to recognize great men, an explanation furnished the journalist Samuel Lederman by the author himself in the initial stage of the interview:

". . . Weaknesses, perversions, moral indolence, misfortunes owed to mixed blood . . ." The colonel had a horror of racial interbreeding.

As a second lieutenant, fresh out of the military academy, he had written Romantic verses and published them in a slim volume. Since the novice poet occupied no position of power at the time, the critics either ignored the meager volume or tore it to pieces. Even the learned João

Ribeiro, ordinarily so indulgent toward beginning writers in his weekly literary column, could not manage to find anything except "cheap rhymes and vulgar sentiments" in those pages. Years later, however, after Sampaio Pereira had abandoned poetry for the political essay, the same elderly critic lamented this fact: ". . . It would have been better had he persisted in massacring meter and rhyme, for in tawdry prose he now threatens the nation and the people, freedom and the future."

As was quite evident, along with his many unconditional, toadying admirers the colonel had detractors who could forgive him neither his public acts nor his writings. They accused him of being the grave-digger of democracy and of human rights, of dishonoring the uniform he wore by placing it in the service of a police state, of being the national leader of the fifth column, of being the official responsible for political repression and torture, of importing Gestapo techniques: they called him a candidate for the post of Hitler's Gauleiter in Brazil.

The colonel was equally proud of the praise he garnered and of the attacks against him. It was the "proven patriots, the very heart of the new Brazil" who lauded him and crowned him with laurel; the insults and calumny came from the "liberal and Communist rabble."

ORDERS FROM HIGHER UP

"Orders from higher up, my dear friend. Matters are out of my hands; there is nothing I can do . . ."

When the director of the DIP—the Press and Propaganda Department—announced to him that his review had been stricken from the list of permitted publications and expressed his regrets at not being able to help him, accompanying his explanation with a meaningful gesture, Samuel Lederman nonetheless did not admit defeat. He decided to go directly to Colonel Sampaio Pereira. The order had come from him, and he would do his best to persuade him to change his mind. ("You're hopeless, Samy. You're going to go to your death believing in miracles," and Da shook her curly chestnut-brown locks.)

"Our half-breed Goebbels is a beast," the director of the DIP opined, referring to the colonel. To do him full justice he added, with a certain note of fear in his voice: "A bloodthirsty beast. Watch your step, or you'll end up in prison." Samuca remembered the days he had spent in the basements of the political police during the raids of the year before: hundreds of people arrested when German troops entered Prague. He had found himself with more than fifty other detainees, all of them jammed into a cell that would have been overcrowded with only twenty, without a single washbasin or bed, taking turns sleeping on the damp cement floor, stomach-turning food dished out once a day, a permanent stench—the toilet facilities consisted of a kerosene can. Not to mention the perfectly audible screams of those tortured during their interrogations in nearby rooms. But even this painful memory did not discourage him. He had been a political reporter on a large daily paper, he had pull, he'd get to see the colonel.

"Just remember that the way things are right now, it's not going to be easy to get you out of jail," the director of the DIP had concluded.

The political duplicity of this official merits special mention. Though serving the government in such a vital post, he had inavowable yet evident sympathies for England and France, and he protected individuals as suspect as Samuel Lederman, editor-in-chief of *Perspectivas*, a monthly with an irregular press run, the last of the publications on the DIP permitted list to possess a vague leftist slant, and in the end definitely banned.

◼ THE COLONEL BEGINS TO WAGE
TOTAL WAR AND ESTABLISHES
CRITERIA FOR THE PLASTIC ARTS

This political duplicity proves that the New State was not that monolithic bloc, in the service of Nazi-fascism, that Colonel Sampaio Pereira dreamed of it being; vestiges of rotten liberalism were corrupting the state apparatus. The day was not far off, however, when the government would be composed solely of ardent totalitarian patriots, simon-pure Aryans. A great day, close to final victory: heads would roll, the blood of purification would flow freely. Inspired by this vision, as he stands in front of the blackboard on which a map of Europe is pinned, the colonel declaims:

"We shall exterminate the enemy, every last one of them. Mercilessly!" His gimlet eyes bore into the journalist. "Pity is a sentiment of weaklings, degrading." The ferocious colonel moves the pins with colored heads to the border between France and the Iberian Peninsula. "We have ended the first phase of the war, with total success; all of Europe belongs to us. The Führer, with his genius, planted the flags bearing the hooked cross on the summits of the Pyrenees. In Spain, we have the glorious Generalissimo Franco; in Portugal, our learned Dr. Salazar, a brain worth its weight in gold."

A balance sheet drawn up in the first phase of the interview. The editor-in-chief of *Perspectivas* was still optimistic. Before examining the galley proofs—all harmless material, Samuel had assured him—the colonel had attempted to demonstrate the futility of any opposition whatsoever to Nazi-fascism and unleashed total war, blitzkrieg. But despite the armies, the tanks, the infantry troops, the bombings, despite the dead, the prisoners, the work camps, the extermination camps, the victorious flags bearing the swastika, the journalist had not yet lost hope of a favorable outcome: in the face of such grandeur, what

danger could there possibly be in a small monthly, reduced to the publication of a few reporters' stories, some
cautious international pieces, on the New Deal in the
United States for example, and a handful of poems and
short stories? The journalist listened attentively; he did
not question the statements made by the colonel, who,
carried away by enthusiasm, proceeded to envision the
days to come, the imminent surrender of England, and
after that . . . A pause in order to give an even greater air
of solemnity to the absolutely certain information that,
who could tell, might well have come straight from the
German high command.

"After that . . . It will be the turn of Communist Russia. For our armored divisions"—he spoke of "our divisions" without even thinking twice about it: wasn't Brazil
the natural ally of the Third Reich in South America?—
"a stroll across the steppes, lasting two weeks at the
outside . . . Russia will disappear from the world, and
Communism will be wiped off the face of the earth!"

Having conquered the Soviet Union and freed the world
of Communism, the colonel sat down again, martial and
self-satisfied. He cast a triumphant glance across the table,
or, better put, the trench, so as to enjoy the spectacle of
the annihilated enemy, noting to his surprise that the
miserable Jew was not utterly undone. He caught a glimpse
of a mocking smile on the latter's unworthy lips, and a
hint of irony in his voice:

"A week, Colonel? That's quite a stretch of territory
to cover; Napoleon . . ."

"Shut your mouth!"

The gimlet eyes turned cruel and suspicious; the colonel's face suddenly froze. Samuel regretted having said
what he had, but it was too late. ("Ah, that disposition
of yours, Samy, is going to get you in trouble one of these
days," Da had predicted, kissing him on the eyelids.) After
a moment of painful silence, the colonel grabbed a handful of galleys, and the minute he began to glance through
them he was overcome with indignation.

"You're shameless! There's poison in every single line. . . ." His eyes lingered over the heads of the articles, the photographs; he read brief passages aloud: " 'Large landed estates, vestiges of feudalism, outlaws robbing the rich to help the poor'—Marxist preaching, do you dare deny it? Photographs of slums and blacks . . . Isn't there a single decent district in all of Rio that merits being photographed? Have all the whites suddenly disappeared?"

"A documentary piece on the samba . . ." Samuca tried to explain.

"Shut your mouth, I said. Modern art! Obscenities, degenerate art! The Führer, in his genius, banned such disgusting horrors. Things like that emasculate a nation. That was how France became prostituted, how it was transformed into a nation of queers."

Those powerful and violent nudes offended the aesthetic sensibilities of the dashing colonel. He rejected them with real disgust, sincere repulsion; they were the diametrical opposite of the beautiful. The colonel did accept the nude female figure, "when it is really artistic, painted with inspiration and feeling."

Samuel took advantage of this unexpected art criticism to recover from his fright, and was ready to resume the dialogue. But he did not have time to get a single word in, for the colonel lost all self-control and fell into a rage at the sight of a full-page photograph of the President of the United States, Franklin Delano Roosevelt:

"That's adding insult to injury! This is the last straw!"

"But, Colonel, he's the President. . . ."

"President? . . . A Jew in the pay of international Communism, that's what he is! Delano is a Jewish name, didn't you know that? Well, *we* know it!"

Revolted, he let go of the page showing the smiling face of the abominable statesman and grabbed up the last pile of proofs, but didn't have time to wax indignant over the "Song of Love for an Occupied City" by the poet António Bruno, because the phone began ringing. A private, personal line, the number of which was known to only a very few intimates and used only for extremely serious, urgent matters. The colonel laid the proofs down, lifted the receiver, wild-eyed and still beside himself, his voice breaking. Immediately, however, he cloaked himself in his very best image once again, his voice not only steady and calm but amiable, deferent, almost fawning. At the very least, it must be the war minister on the other end of the line, the journalist decided.

■ THE ACADEMICIAN LISANDRO LEITE, DISTINGUISHED JURIST AND GENEROUS FRIEND

He was mistaken. It was not the minister, nor the deputy minister, nor even a member of the military. The person who had sweated to get this call through was Academician, Justice, and Professor Lisandro Leite. The fat man with the head of hair like a lion's mane who bore all these titles had had the greatest difficulty obtaining the colonel's unlisted number.

"António Bruno died this morning, Colonel. But I was in court and the news has just reached me. . . ."

On hearing this sad (and promising) news, the colonel was unable to contain his excitement, to keep from smiling. But he immediately regained his composure, suppressed a smile, concealed his joy, and assumed the air of solemnity and deep regret that was the proper response to this unfortunate (fortunate, most fortunate) piece of news:

"The poet António Bruno? He's dead?"

"We've got our vacant seat, Colonel!"

"A great loss for Brazilian literature. An inspired bard. . . ."

"Doubtless, doubtless, a consummate poet," Lisandro Leite broke in, interrupting the eloquent epitaph. After all, he had not persisted, despite the rude refusal of corporals and sergeants to put him through to the colonel, he had not moved heaven and earth to obtain his private number merely to listen to platitudes; the time had not yet come for the colonel to deliver his Academy acceptance speech:

"Save those fine phrases for your speech, Colonel."

"What's that you say? The speech?"

"We have our vacant seat, Colonel!"

He announced the news with the emphasis of someone offering a rare gift of inestimable value. He had not gone to all the trouble he had merely to pass on the news of the death of a poet, a fellow Academician. A devoted and generous admirer of Colonel Agnaldo Sampaio Pereira, he had called to offer his eminent colleague and friend the vacant seat, immortality. "But you must act quickly, Colonel, you must not lose a moment's time, you must go into action immediately. Immediately!" he repeated.

A member of the Academy for more than ten years, Lisandro Leite, "a renowned practitioner of juridical letters," considered himself a specialist in elections to the Academy, familiar with the subtleties, the maneuvers, the strategic and tactical moves that were certain to lead to the victory of his favorites. A shrewd sponsor and supporter of various candidates, he inevitably gained a certain advantage from each election campaign. Backbiters, who exist everywhere, even in Academies of Letters, called the rapid advancement to highly-coveted vacant seats by the learned Professor of Commercial Law in the course of his career as a magistrate "getting ahead in life by climbing on the backs of the dead." If such comments reached his ears, they did not trouble him; he proceeded imperturbably on his way. A mild-mannered man affably exerting his authority, it was he who outlined the conduct to be adopted by the candidate hoping to win a seat.

"The Academicians must be apprised forthwith of your candidacy, and have it borne in upon them that this seat belongs by right to you, my illustrious friend."

17

Fearless, dauntless, aggressive when leading the troops responsible for repressing the country's vile and treacherous internal enemies, now that the hour has struck to attack, to begin the battle for immortality, the colonel is suddenly overcome with unexpected timidity. Assailed by doubts, he stammers:

"Go straight to the Academy? Right away? Are Bruno's remains being taken there? Hmmm . . . I don't know. . . . Isn't it better to wait till after the funeral? Doesn't that strike you as more seemly?"

The colonel's round, ingenuous eyes alight on the journalist, whom he has completely forgotten, an embarrassing witness. He puts his hand over the receiver and orders:

"Clear out of here!"

Samuel Lederman, Samuca to his friends, Samy to Da, his wife, presses his point—without hope; but duty calls, and must be fulfilled to the very end:

"And *Perspectivas*, Colonel? Is it off the list of banned publications?" ("Champion of lost causes, that's what you are, Samy": Da's faint voice.)

The colonel's gimlet eyes bore straight through him:

"What! Do you still have the nerve . . . ? Get the hell out of here before I change my mind and send you to the slammer."

Defeated, the journalist gathers the galley proofs together. The interview has not produced the hoped-for results: the ban on publication of *Perspectivas* still stands, and its editor-in-chief has escaped being clapped in prison only by sheer chance. From this day forward, Samuca will never allow anyone to speak ill of the Academy, an illustrious institution.

As he heads down the dark corridors, the useless proofs tucked away in the pocket of his suit coat, Samuel Lederman the little journalist is saddened by the death of the poet António Bruno, with whom he has personally spoken only once and whose ode for the city of Paris occupied by the Germans, a call to rebellion and hope, will remain set in type but will never be published. Like many other people, Samuca knows entire passages of the poem by heart and often calls them to mind. Little by little he overcomes his feeling of defeat; the dream that it is given all of us to dream is more powerful: someday, though deep in debt, attacked by the authorities, the banned monthly review will become a daily paper, alive and kicking, with important documentary pieces; famous collaborators, Brazilians and foreigners, will debate major issues, something unprecedented in the country's press. When Paris is liberated, and democracy reigns in Brazil. ("You're incorrigible, Samy. . . .")

▉ BRIGHT PROSPECTS AND AN EXCLAMATION IN LATIN

"Repeat, if you please, Judge. I didn't hear clearly. You were saying that . . ."

Free of the accursed Jewish spy, free to allow his face to express his uncontainable emotion, the colonel listens enraptured. He nods his head in approval at each phrase forthcoming from the expert electoral campaigner. "This is no time for protocol, my illustrious friend. The hour has come to attack. The most important thing is to not waste time, to advance, to occupy the position, to prevent anyone else from moving in ahead of us and sewing up votes. There will be a good many candidates. . . ." In order, doubtless, to lend greater weight to his advice and greater importance to his efforts, in order to impose his authority and make it appear indispensable, from the very beginning Lisandro is to picture the election, ordinarily a lively but peaceful contest, in terms of a heated battle. "Attack as soon as possible, my friend; that's the proper tactic so as to lay the foundations of a spectacular victory. *Alea jacta est!*"

The colonel doesn't argue. He repeats: *"Alea jacta est!"* And then: "I trust you implicitly, my dear friend. I appreciate your arguments. I shall do as you say; I place myself entirely in your hands."

The jurist, an efficient campaign manager, wants only one thing: to lead the colonel to victory. An easy task, moreover. There could not possibly be a candidate with greater prestige, enjoying the support of the regime's most powerful authorities. Clear sailing ahead . . . As clear as all that? There will be those who will choose to argue, turn up their noses, question the candidate's political views, but none of them will go beyond grumbling and grousing, and in the end they will all swallow the bitter pill and give him their vote. The election is already in his pocket. After getting him elected, helping him don the Academy uniform, delivering the traditional enco-mium to him in the formal reception speech—yes, because it would be unpardonably rude of the colonel to choose anyone else to receive him into the Acad-emy . . . The hall full of generals, ministers, perhaps even the head of state, ambassadors, ladies from the top drawer of society, elegant low-cut evening gowns, jewels, deco-rations and medals, all that luxury, that splendor (not to mention the photographers), and after that . . .

Ah! After that, receiving his rightful reward: the first vacant seat on the Federal Supreme Court, since, as the old saying goes, if you scratch my back, I'll scratch yours. You take the Academy, Colonel, and give me the Supreme Court.

He pours out a steady stream of ideas and suggestions over the phone, the sweat running down his face. "A master at chicanery," according to his colleagues on the bench. He reveals new perspectives, broader horizons, in an ingratiating, persuasive voice. The colonel is beside himself with enthusiasm:

"Of course. My candidacy will have the unconditional support of the Army. A hundred percent. The minister? He'll do everything necessary, everything. What's that? Yes, that's quite true; you're altogether right: my candidacy is an obligation imposed on me by the Army, which at present has no representative in the Academy. An absurd state of affairs, really. You're quite right, my esteemed friend: a duty imposed upon me as an Army officer."

The professor goes on, unearths the decisive, unanswerable argument implicit in the history of the Academy. What a brain! The colonel has the feeling that he's practically elected already.

"Right, Judge, absolutely right. I hadn't thought of that. . . ."

"Yes, there's no doubt about it, my illustrious friend. That chair belongs to the Army; it always has. Its founder, its first occupants . . . Your election will mean the resumption of a tradition that was broken with Bruno's election."

Tradition: a word dear to the colonel's heart. He is euphoric. Lisandro Leite concludes with one last auspicious prediction.

"The sole candidate? Do you think that's possible, my dear friend?"

"Come, come, my valiant colonel. Don't be naïve. In the present circumstances, both national and international, who in this country is going to have the courage to run against the omnipotent Chief of the Security Forces? Even sheer folly has its limits," Lisandro Leite opines, as he wipes the sweat away, smiles, and promises:

"I for my part will do everything possible, or even impossible, to bring that about. A sole candidate and a unanimous election, my noble colonel."

▉ COMPLETELY SUPERFLUOUS CONSIDERATIONS

Can there be any sentiment more powerful, ruler of the human heart, than vanity? Mestre Afrânio Portela said no, and proved it in the course of the electoral contest.

To take one's place in the Illustrious Company, to be one of the Forty Immortals, to don the Academy uniform with gold facings, one's hand resting on the pommel of the ceremonial sword, the two-cornered cocked hat tucked under one's arm, to settle one's fat and bones in the velvet chair—ah, to arrive there the most respectable citizens, the most powerful personalities, submit to anything and everything: the man with the violent temper becomes mild-mannered, the arrogant individual humbles himself, the penny-pincher turns into a spendthrift, becomes prodigal with bouquets of flowers and gifts. Any description of the phenomenon seems incredible; it has to be seen to be believed. It is a subject that lends itself to much cheap philosophizing and any number of amusing anecdotes. Unfortunately, we have neither the time nor the space to recount them here.

Take the example of Colonel Agnaldo Sampaio Pereira. Having the power of the military and the police at his entire command, ruler of the roost, lord and master of the blade and the rope, a man before whom even ministers tremble, he does not feel himself to be completely fulfilled, for he does not yet have an Academy chair. A long-standing ambition, dating back to the days of his first (and now disowned) verses, a dream that he has cherished his whole life long.

He had once confessed as much to Lisandro Leite, his helpful friend and a native son of the state where he too had been born. "One has to wait for precisely the right moment," the jurist had explained, stressing the difficulties of the undertaking. Every so often, the two of them had exchanged ideas on the subject. "The time is becoming ripe," the Academician informed his friend, referring to the latter's candidacy. Six months before, he had announced: "The present situation is ideal; we're holding all the trump cards. All we need is the vacant seat." The two of them had drawn up a list of Immortals, classifying them according to their age and the state of their health.

The final tally gave them reason to hope: a number of Academicians would not be enjoying immortality for very much longer. The great Pérsio Menezes, for instance, who was suffering from cancer.

Member of the Brazilian Academy—a chimera stubbornly pursued. A sign that even a warrior chieftain, a stoic Aryan in the midst of a battle to conquer the world, can cherish a dream with the same fervor as a lowly subversive Jewish journalist.

THE LIVELY WAKE

A disturbing feminine commotion. Oh, incorrigible Bruno, what has happened in your hands to the seriousness of death, the rigid reserve, the austere silence, the obligatory demonstration of grief?

On climbing out of their cars, the Academicians assumed the air of solemnity that the occasion demanded; but who can contrive to remain grief-stricken and grave if he is obliged to kiss the hands of charming ladies, to exchange frivolous remarks about this and that, to listen to amorous reminiscences, to recall passionate verses amid an elegant fashion parade?

A wake? The deceased was there, all right, on the catafalque erected in the foyer of the Academy. Looking much too handsome and nonchalant, despite the dignity of the full regalia, a dead man scarcely up to fulfilling the funereal role assigned him; a party to, if not directly responsible for, such a lack of grief and respect. Yes, because this farce had been foreseen and suggested by the poet himself, as might be seen by reading the "Testament and Wake of One António Bruno, Troubador and Bohemian, Dead Three Times Over from an Excess of Lovemaking," verses that had been written long ago but had endured, in which the bard makes mock of death and proposes a revel instead of a deathwatch over his body.

And that was what happened. Tears and laughter, more

laughter than tears, he had requested in the poem. Pretty, madcap women: "I want to hear the crystal of your peals of laughter." Party dresses: "I want to glimpse softness peeking out of low-cut necklines." The women who were there knew the poem, line by line; some of them could recite all of it by heart. "Come, all of you, the one who made me suffer and the one who merely smiled at me on the street. . . ." They had all come, and in their sighs there was, as he had asked, a licentious note, "the cooing moans of love on gala dawns."

The foyer full to overflowing. Academicians, writers, a handful of government officials, theater and radio people, diplomats, artists, working-class people, simple readers. On his arrival, Justice Lisandro Leite posed alongside the casket for the photographers, uttered a few (lapidary) phrases into the microphone of a radio station. He then disappeared through the door of the secretariat, taking the president of the Academy by the arm and dragging him off, eagerly whispering in his ear.

Amid the women's charms the feigned mourning, the mask assumed on the occasion of a death, faded away. Only real feelings remained: the love of the beauties on parade; the esteem of his colleagues, some of whom had been close friends; the admiration of readers, who were many, the majority of them young. Even that odor of wilted and crushed flowers, inevitable at every wake, a portent of the decomposition that is close at hand, had been banished by the rare, exciting perfumes.

A DRY LECTURE ON POETRY

Critics had offered many definitions of António Bruno's poetry. But the label associated with him ever since his first book, one taken up by the press and by the public, one dear to his heart, was "the poet of lovers." "All lovers read his verses; at eighteen we are all his readers, but women remain so their whole life long," one critic pointed out, in a long, glowing essay when António's *Selected*

Poems came out. Certain critics, who did not take kindly to popular works and authors, taxed his poetry with being facile and anecdotal, but readers found in it the revelation of a universe at once real and magical, in which the ordinary, day-to-day trivialities of life, apparently unimportant things—a little back street and the color of the sky, a cat in a window and a potted cactus flower—took on a new dimension, an aura of mystery.

A sudden, moving discovery: the street and the dew, the clouds and the twilight, the vast night, landscapes, objects, sentiments. Hungry lips, a heaving bosom, the brazen geography of a woman's body undressing, the ardor, the violence, the sweetness of love. Poetry with the taste and scent of woman, and at the same time full of Brazil: it celebrated her trees and her birds, her rivers and the sea, her animals and the ways of her people. But love was the major theme of his verse; in the poet's heart there was no room for hate.

A journalist, a civil servant in the ministry of justice, he never saved money or accumulated possessions, spending everything he earned and almost always more than that. When still an adolescent, not yet nineteen, he had gone on a vacation trip to Europe with classmates of his from the university, where he was studying law. It seemed absurd to him to spend just a week in Paris; he stayed three years. To force him to come home, his father cut off his monthly allowance; yet he managed to survive, in great spirits and gluttonous for everything that Paris had to offer. He confided to friends that he had practiced, among other professions, the honorable and gratifying one of gigolo, a paid dancing partner of elderly millionairesses, "adorable little old ladies." Frequenting the literary cafés, the bookstalls along the Seine, learning the subtleties of wines and cheeses, when he came back to Brazil he brought home with him in his baggage the manuscript of his first book of poems, *The Dancer and the Flower*, a resounding success.

He returned to Paris as often as he could. Already past forty, he had been able to stay two more years there, thanks to a certain minister of foreign affairs, an old friend from university days, who had secured him a soft job at the embassy, with vague cultural duties. The longstanding fascination he had felt for the city grew deeper than ever. To him, Paris was the greatest triumph of man, an incomparable city, the home of humanism, beauty, freedom. On his return to Brazil he devoted an entire volume of poetry to it: *Paris Love Paris,* prefaced by an epigraph from Jacques Prévert, who had become a personal friend: "Tant pis pour ceux qui n'aiment ni les chiens ni la boue."

A critic regarded as erudite described Bruno as the "Prévert of Brazil," a facile judgment, since Bruno's poetry lacked the social and political dimension so notable in the works of the French poet. Bruno had kept aloof from politics, even when a governor of his native state, wanting to exploit the poet's popularity, had offered to put him on the list of his party's candidates for a seat in the federal chamber of deputies. He refused, keeping his distance from any sort of political commitment. The establishment, in 1937, of the dictatorship of the New State distressed him, but he took no stand in protest. He was hard at work writing his Academy acceptance speech at the time. He had been elected some months before, defeating both a member of the federal legislature famous for his fiery oratory and a doctor known for his scientific achievements and possessed of literary ambitions, and thereby succeeding an elderly general, a passionate explorer of the backlands, the author of dull but authoritative studies on the languages and customs of indigenous Brazilian peoples.

On more than one occasion, leftist intellectuals criticized António Bruno for failing to take sides politically in his poetry, in a divided, unjust, and troubled world in which other poets experienced the bitter taste of exile or were shot to death by firing squads.

THE POET DESCENDS FROM HIS CRYSTAL TOWER AND IS EXECUTED IN PARIS

When, however, the Nazis let loose the dogs of war, Bruno the poet emerged from his cocoon, aware at last of the threat to his universe, to civilization, to freedom, to everything he loved. "I descended from the crystal tower; the crystal was cloudy, it kept me from seeing the world," he said in a sort of self-criticism delivered as a speech at the Academy. He began to follow events with mounting passion, vicariously living and suffering each detail of the conflict.

He never doubted for a moment that the Allied armies would be victorious. Not even when the Wehrmacht invaded France; French soldiers were invincible. The defeat took him by surprise; he had not been prepared for that. It was devastating. Everything collapsed round about him, expectations and enthusiasm gave way to utter discouragement, he saw himself surrounded by ruins, he lost, suddenly and completely, all confidence in the future and all his lust for life. The fall of Paris brought on a heart attack.

While still in the hospital, he wrote a heartrending poem. For the first and only time, the sweet saga of love was set aside in favor of a poem on war, verses full of fire and blood, of insults and imprecations, an anathema against Hitler and his followers. Broken by the humiliation and suffering of his beloved city, the home of civilization and humanism crushed beneath the Nazi boot, Bruno the poet nonetheless unexpectedly rose from his sickbed and, overcoming his despair and his lack of will to live, predicted and proclaimed the imminent and inevitable day of liberation, when Paris, happiness, and love would be resurrected.

Thus the "Song of Love for an Occupied City" ended with an impassioned appeal to pursue the struggle till victory was won. A strange breath of inspiration, an inexplicable ardor on the part of someone who had ceased to believe in life.

The truth of the matter was that the last part of the poem had been completely rewritten. In the original version, the poet had taken his leave of life and committed suicide, refusing to live in such a monstrous world. But when he saw tears in the eyes of the woman risking her safety and her honor to visit him, in secret and deeply distressed, bringing light amid darkness and driving back pain and death, António Bruno, who could deny her nothing, pretended to share her militant and stubborn certainty, crossed out the agonizing verses of despair and disillusionment, and composed new stanzas calling for resistance and celebrating victory. He was indeed the author of those sweeping, penetrating, epic verses, but the inspiration had come from the frail and fearless visitor who, in her charming foreign accent, had forced each word of them upon him. Bruno gave her the manuscript of the poem, and she typed, in secret, the first copies.

Submitted for publication to the literary supplement of one of the two great daily papers in Rio, it was banned by the censors (or by self-censorship on the part of the newspaper) on the grounds that it was "insulting to the head of a friendly nation." Despite the ban, in just a few days the poem was being widely circulated and was beginning to enjoy a vast popularity. Mimeographed copies of it passed from hand to hand; printed as a leaflet, it soon reached the most remote corners of the country.

Even the success of the "Song of Love for an Occupied City" did not contrive to lift the poet's spirits. The hope and encouragement voiced in the poem, which sustained thousands of Brazilians, did not sustain the poet's failing heart. When the director of *Perspectivas*, a review whose existence António Bruno had previously been unaware of, came to ask his permission to publish the accursed *engagé* poem, Bruno merely shrugged.

"Of what avail are verses against cannons and bestiality? Publish them if you like, if the authorities will allow you to. Poetry has no place in the world now. It will never have one again."

Ten days later, on a luminous morning, with the sun flooding the Paris studio lost forever, the poet fell, victim of an execution.

■ THE SIGH, THE ROSE, THE KISS, THE LADY IN BLACK, THE COLONEL, AND DEATH AT LAST

"If there were music, we could dance," Mestre Afrânio commented with a faint smile.

Listening without a word, the lady whose beauty had faded allowed a sigh to escape her lips, having suddenly remembered the masked ball. The eminent, notoriously ferocious Evandro Nunes dos Santos agreed, in the husky voice of the heavy smoker:

"It wouldn't surprise me if Bruno suddenly rose to his feet and called for champagne all round. I saw him do that in Paris more than once. . . ."

Two elderly men of letters, deeply moved. The crowd of women continued to throng around the casket where the poet and his legend as a bohemian without peer, as an irresistible seducer, reposed. So many women: blondes, brunettes, a redhead with freckles, elegant ladies in their forties and lasses in the flower of youth, adolescent schoolgirls in uniform carrying verses copied out in their math notebooks, the great actress and the little seamstress with a rose in her hand.

The timid little seamstress stepped forward and placed the rose on the brocaded uniform—"rose of copper, rose of honey, child-rose." The great actress leaned over the casket, her eyes wet with tears; she kissed the cold forehead, cast a long farewell gaze at the romantic profile, the "romantic profile of a Bedouin"—the poet had proclaimed himself the descendant of desert sheiks, and Moorish blood had in fact coursed in his veins. When his maternal grandfather, Fuad Maluf, set aside his measuring-tape and scissors, he composed poems in Arabic. Memories of days long past, of another farewell, made the bosom of the first lady of the theater palpitate, and she stepped away, suffocated by the devouring fire of her first passion, and, who knows, perhaps the only true one in her entire stormy love-life. She had been marked by it forever.

A group formed around the two friends. Evandro Nunes dos Santos took out his handkerchief, wiped his pince-nez and burning eyes. He recounted recent events (they had happened only a few years before, yet they belonged nonetheless to a bygone era):

"He received no more than a tiny salary from the embassy; he wasn't even an official member of the staff, but everyone treated him as though he were the ambassador himself. I spent three months in Paris at that time, and we went out together every day. I don't think I know anyone who ever loved a city as deeply; Paris belonged to him. An absolutely charming friend. . . ."

Still overcome with emotion, the great actress joined the group:

"I owe him my career. He was the one who got me on the stage; he was the most generous person imaginable. . . ." (She owed him far more than that. If she could, she would recount the details, and it would be a pleasure to do so.)

Mestre Afrânio agreed:

"The perfect friend. . . ." The smile on his trembling lips faded. "What killed him was the war—Hitler. Only last Thursday, he had heard from a French couple who were close friends of his. They were desperate: their only son, just twenty years old, who had been seized as a hostage, had just been shot to death by the Germans. 'I can't bear any more,' Bruno said to me."

He fell silent, reflecting how bitter life had become and how the horizon had narrowed. His eyes wandered over the crowd of people present, and it was then that he saw her arrive, dressed all in black, her face half-hidden by a mourning veil, looking more beautiful than ever before— she had come despite everything, disregarding his advice. She slipped unobtrusively over to the catafalque. Mestre Afrânio looked at her closely: rigid, tightly clenching her crossed hands with their long, slender, pale fingers before stealing off to take refuge behind some curtains. "She's a goddess, Mestre Afrânio, descended from Olympus. I don't deserve her, I'm only a mad minstrel. . . ."

Justice Lisandro Leite suddenly emerged from the secretariat, nervous and dripping with sweat, crossed the foyer, and went to the main door to look out into the street. The president of the Academy, Hermano do Carmo, joined the group and added his words of praise for the deceased to theirs. Then, amid the buzz of conversation at this lively wake, there could be distinctly heard the clear and melodious voice of the great actress reciting, very softly, verses of Bruno's, verses perhaps written for her. Lisandro Leite halted for a moment to listen to them, but in the middle of a stanza he hurriedly headed for the door again.

That firm, uniform, loudly resounding tread was unmistakable; no civilian had such a martial step. Colonel Agnaldo Sampaio Pereira, every inch of him on funeral parade, marched to the bier, loudly clicked his heels, stood at attention before the remains of the dead Academician, saluted him (and repeated the entire scene for the photographers).

"Good Lord," Afrânio Portela moaned.

Suddenly a silence, a chilly silence, fell. The voice of the actress broke off; the verses abruptly ceased. Standing at attention, the colonel remained motionless for a seemingly endless moment. Then, turning smartly about-face, he paid his respects to the president, repeated "A great loss to Brazilian literature" to the Academicians, greeted several high-ranking officials. At his side, triumphant and protective, Justice Lisandro Leite.

In response to a repeated sign from the jurist, and somewhat ill at ease, the president invited the colonel to come upstairs with him. They headed for the elevator, as Lisandro Leite rounded up two illustrious Immortals in passing. The other Academicians hesitated, not certain whether they should go upstairs or not. "We have a candidate," one of them remarked. Another added: "And what a candidate!"

"Good Lord!" Mestre Afrânio said again.

Evandro Nunes dos Santos put his pince-nez back on: "It can't be!" Rather than a negative statement, it was an anguished exclamation.

The lady in black came out from her refuge behind the curtains and, abandoning all circumspection, stupefied and indignant, walked straight over to the two friends: What did the presence of that individual at the wake mean? Was he perchance thinking of presenting himself as a candidate for Bruno's seat?

The foyer thereafter never regained the animated, almost festive atmosphere that the poet had called for, wherein grief and sadness were real and deeply felt and not just masks for the occasion, fake sentiments. The lively tumult died away: bursts of laughter, happy voices, irrepressible sighs, murmured love-verses were heard no more. The mad minstrel had fled his casket, in which there remained only the dead body of an Academician, ready for the cemetery. All that was left in the room now were words carefully weighed, solemn phrases, grieving faces, the corrupt scent of wax tapers and flowers, a chilly silence. The ritual of death had finally won out.

THE BATTLE
OF THE PETIT TRIANON

REPORT ON A DINNER WITH WINE OF PURE BRAZILIAN STOCK

The colonel had left the choice of the menu up to the eminent cultivator of juridical letters, a trustworthy gourmet who frequently dined out in restaurants—he enjoyed eating well and heartily, especially when he was an invited guest. But the colonel had insisted on ordering the wine, a red from Rio Grande do Sul.

"It's pure Brazilian stock, delicious."

For ideological and geographic reasons, Lisandro Leite had cherished the hope of imbibing a bottle or two of real Rhine wine, of noble and glorious German origin. Resignedly, he raises his glass of hundred-percent Brazilian wine:

"To the success of your candidacy."

"Thank you very much. What do you think of the wine?"

"Sheer nectar!" ("*Cheap table wine, terrible rotgut . . .*")

The colonel, in civilian clothes, seems to shrink in size and importance. Lisandro Leite, however, does not allow himself to be fooled by mere appearances; his host's attire does not diminish his power. He need merely glance over at the next table, strategically situated, where mighty champions are the guardians of the mortal body of their chief. In like manner, on the paths of the cemetery, late that afternoon, the jurist had been able to appreciate the importance and the extent of this power by observing the reaction of the Academicians to the news of the colonel's candidacy. Not a single one of them had dared raise his voice in open opposition to the colonel's pretensions, although a number of them had been unable to conceal their displeasure. A bunch of liberaloids! He and the colonel were going to have to take careful steps to avoid the possibility of blank ballots being cast, thereby compromising a clear-cut victory:

"You'll be the only candidate, that's certain. As for a unanimous vote, I'll fight as hard as I can to obtain one, catechizing the rebels, the BBC contingent."

"The *what* contingent?"

"Those who live with their ears glued to the radio, listening to the BBC broadcasts from London. I won't hide from you the fact that the Academy is crawling with them. But your prestige, my dear friend, and my experience . . ."

He reports, between mouthfuls, on the (positive) results of his first opinion-sampling. Sampaio Pereira lays down his knife and fork, the better to feast on the commendations and prognostications gathered by his friend as he made his way through the cemetery.

"And what about the president of the Academy? He struck me as being somewhat closemouthed this afternoon."

"As president, Hermano is obliged to be discreet; he's not in a position to proclaim his preferences from the rooftops. I had a long conversation with him before you arrived. 'In all truth, the Academy needs a representative of the Army,' he said to me when I informed him of your intentions. The fact that he invited you to go upstairs with him, accompanied by Academicians, meant, practically speaking, that you were publicly announcing your candidacy under the auspices of the president. A small task that I took upon myself. . . . And kindly note that there were at least three potential candidates present, and none of them was the object of such attentions. Not even Raul Limeira. . . ."

"The rector of the university?"

"His name has been mentioned for some time. There is no lack of strong candidates for the Academy. But leave it to me to clear the terrain. I'll personally take care of Limeira, who's assured of the next vacant seat after this one. Pérsio, poor thing, is on his last legs; he won't be with us long." He lowered his voice: "Lung cancer." The jurist had the list of the seats about to fall vacant at his fingertips; there was something macabre about this bulletin on the state of health of various Academicians. He ended his report in a confident tone of voice: "Afrânio Portela himself agreed with me that you're an unbeatable candidate. Even he, an irreconcilable enemy of the regime, who is not at all well disposed toward you."

"I can never thank you enough, Judge. Please be assured, however, that I know how to demonstrate my gratitude toward those with whom I am on intimate terms. . . ."

Apropos of intimacy, in the course of this "sumptuous and delicious *agape*" (in the words of the jurist, a competent judge in such matters), the candidate and his sponsor decided to put ceremony, degrees, and titles aside and simply call each other Agnaldo and Lisandro. As for gratitude, the Academician reaffirmed the absolutely disinterested nature of his help, motivated as it was only by the sheerest and most sincere admiration for the work of the writer and the most total and unconditional approval of the actions of the patriot. (Besides, there would not be a vacancy on the Supreme Court before the middle of the following year, when Justice Paiva, who, moreover, was a fellow Academician and a good friend, reached compulsory retirement age. According to Lisandro's calculations, this would be precisely the time when he, Lisandro, would be delivering the encomium in honor of the new Immortal at the solemn session at which the latter would be received into the Academy.)

At the wake and at the cemetery Lisandro had heard veiled, covert reservations concerning the colonel; getting him elected was going to be harder work than he had thought. The most important task: preventing anyone else from presenting himself as a candidate. In order for the colonel to be duly grateful to his friend, he must enter the Academy in triumph and not have to stoop to campaigning for votes:

"Next Thursday the meeting in memoriam will be held, at which eulogies for the deceased will be delivered, and after that the president will proclaim his seat vacant. Then the very next day you must send your letter presenting yourself as a candidate. I want your candidacy, my dear Agnaldo, to be a real triumphal march."

They drank another toast to that with the wine from Rio Grande:

"Pure Brazilian stock . . ."

"Nectar!"

At the next table the herculean gladiators were eating their dinner—paid for out of the budget for the fight against Communism. Lisandro Leite averted his gaze; to him the spectacle of all those muscles was not even aesthetically pleasing. Later on, using the requisite tact, he would have to advise the colonel to order his personal bodyguards to remain discreetly in the background. During the traditional formal calls on Academicians and the possible visits to the Petit Trianon, it would be wiser for him to leave his impetuous boys outside in the street. At the wake, they had rudely jostled the president as he was entering the elevator, and Ambassador Francelino Almeida, the *doyen* of the Illustrious Company, the only one of the forty founders still alive, a brittle skeleton, had been given such a violent shove by one of the brutes that he had been obliged to take to his bed. Francelino Almeida of all people, whom Lisandro had counted as a sure vote for the colonel.

◼ GRANDCHILDREN AND GRANDFATHER

Leaning on his cane, Evandro Nunes dos Santos crosses the garden, a sort of little park planted with fruit trees, and sits down on the bench underneath the mango. There, on the heights of Santa Teresa, the stars are shining brightly in the vast clear sky. Even the serene beauty of the night does not calm the elderly essayist's heart, however. Nor does the warm and affectionate presence of his grandchildren.

"Today, for the first time, I regretted having lived so long."

"He's talking and acting like a doddering old man," Pedro notes with alarm, his face hidden in the shadow. Isabel seizes her grandfather's hand and kisses it. She sits down on the grass at his feet, rests her head on his bony knees, tries to smile—what good are words? From the shadow, Pedro contemplates his stooped shoulders, his bowed head, his snow-white hair; the tormented phrase echoes painfully in the boy's ears, accustomed as he is to the fortitude of this grandfather who has always refused to let old age overtake him. His grandchildren can appreciate how grief-stricken he is; they too had loved the poet António Bruno. At the cemetery, Isabel, Bruno's goddaughter, had had to lean on her brother's arm for support.

Pedro remembers the time—he had been seven and Isabel five—when their grandfather took them to give a last goodbye kiss to their parents, Alvaro and Barbara, the victims of a stupid car accident. When the bodies of her only son and her beloved daughter-in-law were brought to her that morning, Anita, Evandro's wife ("wife, sister, mother, and mistress"), lost then and there all her joy in living, and though she lingered on for a few years longer, it was only in obedience to her husband's injunction: "We must live for the children." She lived long enough to see them into adolescence: Pedro was sixteen, Isabel fourteen. No longer feeling indispensable, Anita decided that her onerous task was done, and gave in to her cruel illness. "I'm going to die, my darling," she said to her life's companion.

Though he knew that her illness was incurable, that she was doomed to die, Evandro pleaded with her: "I don't want you to go before I do, I don't want to be an old man without a master." There is nothing sadder than a dog without a master, wandering about the streets in search of a kind word, an affectionate pat. What to say then of an old man without a master? Anita bade him remember the grandchildren, who no longer needed her but were still so dependent on him. "You won't be all alone. You have the children and your friends."

Anita had been right; he was not a sad, useless old man, a weary, lonely sheepdog. Besides his grandchildren and his friends, there was his work. He filled page after page in his neat, minute hand (he had never used a typewriter), analyzing the origins and character of the Brazilian people. In recent years he had published three books, crowning a body of work of exceptional significance. He broke with received ideas, destroyed preconceptions, advanced bold theories, revolutionized sociological and historical studies. Claiming allegiance to no ideology, a libertarian, almost anarchistic inspiration shaped his vision of life. Cynical, at times rudely outspoken, with an irresistible power of conviction and authority, he was feared by those who did not admire and love him. "Nobody ever knows what he may come up with or what he may do," they commented.

In the silence of the garden on this starry night after the poet's funeral, Pedro and Isabel do their best to raise their grandfather's spirits. Pedro's worried voice comes from the shadow:

"Bruno wouldn't like to see you this way, Grandfather...."

"That's true, my darling." Isabel had called her grandfather "my darling" ever since Anita's death, as though she had received him as an inheritance.

"It's not because he's dead. I'd been prepared for his death since his first heart attack. It's something else that's making me feel so downcast. . . ."

"What's that, Grandfather?"

"You two know how deeply this war affected him, how horrified he was by Nazism. To the point that when he lost all hope he died. Well, do you know who's going to occupy his seat in the Academy?"

"Has a candidate already presented himself?"

"Sampaio Pereira, that Nazi colonel. . . ."

"Who? Colonel Agnaldo? The king of the fifth column? That's too bitter a pill to swallow, Grandfather, that can't be."

"He's the one who's going to take over Bruno's chair. To think I should have lived to witness this infamy."

A shooting star falls through the darkness, and Isabel speaks up:

"He may want that, but you're not going to let him have it, are you, my darling? You're not going to let them do that to my godfather."

Pedro smiles, confident once more.

"Of course he's not going to let them. Grandfather will see to that."

He wasn't an old man without a master, a lonely, abandoned sheepdog waiting for death. He raised his head as Isabel repeated:

"You must do something, my darling."

The president of the Academy had said to him in confidence at the cemetery, "We can't do anything; the man is one of the masters of Brazil, who would dare to fight him, to oppose him?" Evandro Nunes dos Santos had left the graveside ceremony feeling demoralized, useless, and miserable. Pedro's firm voice:

"You've never run away from a fight, Grandfather."

He'd never run away from fights; he'd even caused

quite a few. Nothing could be done because nobody dared to do anything? You're wrong, Mr. President, there *is* going to be someone who will oppose this infamous candidacy, who will fight against this insult to the Academy and to António Bruno's memory. Without even seeking the support of his cane, he rises to his feet, bone-thin and majestic:

"You're right; something has to be done. I'm going to phone Afrânio this minute."

Isabel gets up to offer him her arm, but her grandfather has already walked on ahead. Pedro catches a glimpse of him striding on amid the shadows of the trees. How could he have taken him for a doddering old man? He picks up the cane that his grandfather has left behind.

▓ MESTRE AFRÂNIO CONSIDERS LEAVING THE ACADEMY

The sumptuous dining room, crystal chandeliers, porcelain bibelots, faience pieces, opaline vases, paintings by masters from the Academy of Fine Arts—everything obviously in excellent taste but just slightly old-fashioned. The servant removed the dishes left from the dinner served by candlelight. Saying not a word, staring out the window (through which he could see the headlights of cars moving along the roads of the Praia do Flamengo), Afrânio Portela had barely touched his dinner. Upset by this, Dona Rosarinho—Maria do Rosário Sintra de Magalhães Portela—nonetheless hesitated to suggest that he take his medication. In almost forty years of married life, she had seldom seen her husband so somber and downcast.

António Bruno had been more than just a friend. When he had arrived in Rio to attend the university, an adolescent with a passion for literature, he had appeared one night, without an invitation or an appointment, to show Afrânio, who was from the same state as he and had already earned himself a reputation as a writer, some poems and short stories of his own. The verses were good and the short stories wretched, Afrânio had opined, as Dona Rosarinho ordered one more place set at the table. From that night on and for more than thirty years, that had been Bruno's place; the childless couple had adopted the brazen apprentice poet. Dona Rosarinho had decided not to go to the wake or to the cemetery. She preferred to imagine him sitting there at the table, talking about Paris, celebrating his last and greatest love.

"Wouldn't you like me to give you . . ."

"Have them bring me a cognac; that's what I need," Afrânio said.

Slowly, he began to give her a detailed description of the wake and the graveside ceremony. By universal consensus, in all of Rio de Janeiro there was no one who was a more delightful raconteur. "He'd be an extraordinary novelist if he wrote with the same savor, the same charm he displays in conversation," a fellow writer with a sharp tongue had once snarled. Sheer spite, for Afrânio Portela's novels—though more or less relegated to the background in the midst of the great splash made by the modernist movement and the shock effect of the novels of the thirties generation—had earned the plaudits of critics who recognized and hailed in the creator of *Adélia* a penetrating and daring analyst of Rio society in the twenties. In an era poor in fiction writers, his works bulked large, thanks to their psychological acuity and the clarity of their language, both put to good use to create a most readable portrait-in-depth of the manners and morals of the so-called elite. He was the first writer in Brazil to use psychoanalysis to interpret the sentiments of his heroes, or rather of his heroines—a painter above all of women who are torn between their instincts and the prejudices of their milieu.

In only one book, his very first novel, had he recreated the scenes and the typical figures of the land of diamond prospectors and pilgrims where he had been born. A drama of primitive and elemental feelings, of violent love and wild country, an isolated work in a body of novels based on urban themes and set in elegant and frivolous social circles, that small volume little by little took on great importance. Dressed in rags, the innocent, wanton Maluquinha came to be more and more esteemed by readers, whereas the affected and complicated high-society snobs of his other nine novels languished, forgotten, in their adulterous alcoves.

The last one, *The Woman in the Mirror*, published in 1928, coincided with the appearance in Paraíba, in a shabby provincial edition, of *The Dregs*, by an unknown writer, José Américo de Almeida. Might this fact have contributed to Afrânio Portela's abandonment of fiction and his turning to the essay and literary history? A bold conjecture by an arrogant critic. It was more likely a simple coincidence, since the novelists from the northeast who had appeared in the wake of the writer from Paraíba had earned the warm praise and effective support of the author of *Flamingo Beach*. A volume on Castro Alves, studies of Gregório de Matos and Tomás António Gonzaga kept the name of Afrânio Portela before the public. Or Mestre Afrânio—"Master Afrânio"—as his colleagues and readers referred to him with friendly respect.

As Dona Rosarinho listened to the colorful description, her husband's recital of what had taken place became more forceful and mordant. She knew that beneath his outward appearance as a most erudite and highly cultured intellectual there beat the heart of a man from the backlands not easily discouraged. A pause before he announced:

"Prepare yourself now for a nasty piece of news."

Dona Rosarinho was surprised at the note of utter disgust in his habitually amiable voice. Something had happened, something capable of making António Bruno's absence an even crueler blow. Mestre Afrânio went on, and the refined lady heard the martial step, the clicking heels, and the repetition of the scene for the photographers. Because she had experienced them at first hand at her husband's side, Dona Rosarinho knew all about Academy intrigues. She followed each election closely, and had even influenced certain of them.

"A candidate, you think? Would he have the nerve to . . ."

"A candidate sure to be elected. Unbeatable, Lisandro Leite said to me at the cemetery, and he's right. Can you imagine Sampaio Pereira delivering the formal encomium of Bruno, of the author of the 'Song of Love for an Occupied City'?"

"How dreadful! That . . ."—she searched for an adequate word, without finding it—". . . is capable of wearing Army boots with the Academy regalia." Pensively, her eyes came to rest upon the outraged countenance of Mestre Afrânio:

"And how about you? What are you planning to do?"

"I'll cast a blank ballot, naturally. There are certain to be three or four of us who will. I won't go to the reception ceremony, and in fact I think I won't go back to the Academy at all after an election like that. It's too much for me. . . ."

Dona Rosarinho didn't have time to express her opinion on the subject, because the maid came in just then to announce that Senhora Maria Manuela was at the door, asking whether Dr. Portela could receive her.

"Will you come with me?" Afrânio asked his wife.

"No. She'll feel more at ease if I'm not present. Have you forgotten that, officially, I don't know a thing?"

THE UNUSUAL VISITOR

In Mestre Afrânio's vast study, whose walls were lined from floor to ceiling with shelves full of books, Dona Maria Manuela, pale and gasping for breath, refused to sit down. Her burning eyes stared at Bruno's old friend, his confidant, the one who always knew just what was going on. That morning he had heard her sobbing helplessly over the phone. He did not try to stop her from weeping, and if he searched for words of consolation, he did not find them. He waited till she had regained her self-control, whereupon he counseled prudence, even more necessary now that exposing herself to risks no longer made any sense. He promised to get in touch with her very soon; the two of them would share memories of laughter, charm, poetry.

"I've come to plead with you. . . . Tell me you're not going to allow . . . I wasn't able to keep him from dying . . . but you can keep his memory from being dishonored. . . ." She spoke in fits and starts; in her voice, vibrant with emotion, her Lisbon accent was more pronounced than usual. "I'm a foreigner, I know, but there are no more borders, there is just one war to be waged." She raised her proud head, her plea become an imperious demand ("a goddess descended from Olympus," a young woman of thirty in radiant flower): "A fascist cannot receive the inheritance that belongs to us. I came to hear from your own lips that that is not going to happen. A torturer of the people, a Nazi, succeeding António"— with a visible effort she suppressed a sob—". . . that's like killing him all over again."

Good Lord! To think that he had written ten books analyzing women's feelings. . . .

"How did you find out?"

"I had my suspicions at the wake; I even tried to have a word with you. I've just heard the news over the radio. I can't do a thing, but you can."

At the table after dinner, Mestre Portela had told Dona Rosarinho that he would stop going to the Academy, that he would never set foot inside it again if that individual was elected, as appeared to be highly likely. It had seemed to him to be an extreme decision, whereby he would be expressing the most violent protest possible. But here in his study now, hearing Maria Manuela, he realized that he had merely chosen to adopt a convenient, passive position that led nowhere. He was overcome with a sense of guilt. How could he have failed his friend so badly, leaving his memory at the mercy of assassins?

"I don't know if I can manage to prevent his being elected, but I promise you I'll do whatever is possible. . . ."

"And impossible."

"Very well: and impossible too. . . ."

The young woman, "Little Manuela," went over to the elderly man of letters, kissed him on the cheek, and headed for the door. Mestre Afrânio accompanied her to the entry hall. An absurd, amazing world—who could ever have imagined that the wife of the counselor of the Portuguese embassy, the daughter of one of Salazar's ministers, from a rich and influential family of bankers, was an enemy of the regime, a socialist sympathizer, destined to end up in prison, in a concentration camp? "I think she's more or less a Communist," Bruno had confided at the beginning of their affair. "Communist or not, she's absolutely adorable and utterly mad. I had a hard time persuading her not to leave her husband to come live with me. Can you imagine what a scandal that would have created, Mestre Afrânio? Just look at the mess I've gotten myself into."

On returning to the living room, Afrânio Portela said to Dona Rosarinho, who had sat down in front of the radio to hear the BBC News:

"She came to ask me . . ."

". . . the same thing I was going to ask you. To keep that butcher from being elected. I don't intend to stop attending parties at the Academy; I'm very fond of them. Now then, go phone Evandro, who wants to talk to you about that very thing."

She smiled at her husband, the very same conspiratorial smile as in the days when she had fallen in love with him, days when millionaire fathers were opposed to their daughter's marrying a poor devil of a writer without a cent to his name.

▓ AN OLD MAN WALKING DOWN THE STREET

You old fool, Mestre Afrânio Portela thought to himself as he walked down the street toward the Academy to meet another madman, Evandro Nunes dos Santos. Who was there who would dare take a stand against the DIP, the DOPS, the various police forces, the secret services, against the man who was the omnipotent head of National Security, the candidate of "the powers that be" in the country, of the established order, of the dictatorship of the New State, of the world's victorious warlords?

An old man out of his mind, yet he walked down the street with shoulders erect, a bright gleam in his tired eyes, a wicked smile on his lips. "There goes an old man who's happy to be alive," another man walking down the street remarked as he saw Mestre Afrânio Portela pass by.

▓ PRUDENCE AND TRUMP CARDS

As he waits in the president's office for Afrânio Portela, whom he has arranged to meet there, Evandro Nunes dos Santos launches into a long, bitter diatribe against the candidacy of Sampaio Pereira, setting forth the political and moral reasons that make it inadmissible:

"An affront to the Academy, an insult!"

"Do you think that I was the one who dreamed up this candidacy, or that I have anything at stake in it, that I'm accepting it with pleasure?" Hermano do Carmo is remembering his unpleasant experience of the evening before, when the colonel's two bodyguards had forced their way past him into the elevator, though he does not mention the fact so as not to add fuel to the fire. "What can I do to prevent it?"

The question hovers in the air, unanswered. Evandro Nunes dos Santos mutters that something ought to be done, no matter what. The president goes on:

"The rules stipulate that the candidate must have had at least one book published. The man has had several published, including a volume of poetry, did you know that? I hinted to Lisandro that a number of Academicians had thought of Feliciano, being convinced that the ideal candidate to replace Bruno would be another great poet. Lisandro answered me by citing the title of this book of verses and assured me that, poet for poet, his candidate was in no way the inferior either of Feliciano or of Bruno. It seems that they're Romantic poems, written in his youth. He even holds *that* trump card."

"A rather low one."

"But his other trumps make up for it. . . . You should have seen Lisandro taking them out of his vest pocket one by one: the Army candidate, one of the most important government officials, immense prestige, a crucial moment that doesn't permit playing around. Another weighty argument: this chair is reserved for the Army, it's always been theirs, from the very first to the next-to-the-last occupant, and the tradition must be reestablished. And so on and so forth. . . . I don't see any way out, old friend. If you find one, let me know. I don't see any. . . ."

"Listen . . . you yourself said: 'Get Feliciano to run. . . .' "

"Do you think he'll agree to be a candidate against Sampaio Pereira? I doubt it. Allow me to say, moreover, that this story of a chair that belongs to the Army is an argument that has merit. In principle, I'm in favor of the candidacy of an eminent figure from the Army. You yourself know that the Academy has always included and must continue to include representatives of all the various social institutions."

"Some representative. . . ."

"That depends on one's personal point of view, isn't that so?" The president has no intention of revealing his own.

Evandro Nunes dos Santos sips the last few drops of his cup of coffee and sets the empty cup down. Afrânio Portela is late for their meeting, and it appears to Evandro to be no easy task to undo this Gordian knot. On the other hand, he for his part has no fear of revealing precisely where he stands:

"That miserable scoundrel won't enter the Academy with my vote."

A CONSPIRACY AT THE ELEGANT TEA HOUR

Coming from different directions, Afrânio Portela and Lisandro Leite meet at the entrance to the Petit Trianon. The jurist's fat face is beaming with satisfaction.

"The news of Agnaldo's candidacy has already leaked out in the spoken and written media."

Jubilation in his voice as he refers to the omnipotent colonel by his first name, the proof of an enviable degree of intimacy. He does not reveal the source of this information, but the novelist has no difficulty guessing; like himself, Lisandro has lost no time getting down to work.

They head for the president's office together. The judge sinks into an armchair, and Mestre Afrânio hustles bony old Evandro Nunes dos Santos off with him, thus preventing the caustic essayist from "telling that fat toady a truth or two."

"We're going to go have tea at the Colombo. We'll be more at ease there to plan our conspiracy, far from Lisandro and close to pretty women to feast your eyes on, you old rake."

Having often dropped in at the Colombo with António Bruno, Afrânio attributes the latter's habits and appetites to Evandro. The poet's romantic idyll with the pretty little seamstress sitting watching by the window of the workshop on the third floor of the building opposite had inspired Afrânio's "The Five O'Clock Tea," a lighthearted yet touching short story, the novelist's one return to the realm of fiction, more than ten years after the publication of *The Woman in the Mirror*.

At the table of the confectioner's shop, Evandro, still in a bad mood, begins railing against the president, who "made no secret of his favorable reaction to the colonel's candidacy."

"Favorable? Despite the manhandling he got yesterday?"

"Manhandling? What's that all about?"

"I'll tell you in a minute. But first I want to know exactly what Hermano said."

"That he was in favor of an Army candidate. So as to reestablish the tradition."

"Did he refer to an Army candidate, or did he mention Colonel Sampaio Pereira by name? Agnaldo, that is to say, as Lisandro calls him, drooling."

"Hermano spoke in general."

"There's a vast difference, compadre." (Afrânio and Rosarinho had been the godparents of Evandro's son Álvaro.) "I'll let you in on a secret: I too am in favor of the candidacy of an eminent Army personality." He smiled wickedly.

Every once in a while his friend and compadre Afrânio manages to get on old Evandro's nerves, especially when an Academy seat becomes vacant. Though they almost always back the same candidates, their styles of campaigning could not be more different. Evandro openly champions his favorite and touts his qualifications, arguing and discussing, whereas Afrânio maneuvers discreetly, acts on the q.t., craftily pulls strings behind the scenes—and is regarded as the most redoubtable campaign manager of anyone in the Illustrious Company. Even now, in the face of the terrible threat of Agnaldo "Goebbels" Pereira's candidacy (the colonel himself, in a much-discussed article, had stated that he accepted with pride and honor the nickname of "the Brazilian Goebbels," which the enemies of the Fatherland had bestowed upon him in order to ridicule and insult him), Afrânio shows no signs of indignation. On the contrary, he appears to be enjoying himself, rubbing his hands together in great glee. Evandro replies impatiently:

"Explain to me, once and for all, what you have in mind, since mine's a total blank, except for my utter rage."

Mestre Afrânio obeys, giving Evandro an abundantly detailed account of the intense round of activities he has already engaged in. From time to time he interrupts his recital to greet an acquaintance or to call his old friend's attention to a woman walking past on the street who is worth having a look at. Like Lisandro, Afrânio hasn't lost any time. The evening before, immediately after his phone conversation with Evandro, he had telephoned a number of Academicians to exchange impressions. And that morning he had gotten up very early, left the house soon after, called on no fewer than four fellow members, and had lunch with a fifth, Rodrigo Inácio Filho. And the reason why he had shown up late for his meeting with Evandro was that he had gone to visit poor Francelino, likewise the victim of violent pushing and shoving the evening before. As a result of these phone calls and visits, he has been struck by certain obvious facts and drawn certain definite conclusions:

"There is a noticeable resistance to Sampaio Pereira's name."

"A general deep-seated aversion. . . ." Evandro too had contacted a fair number of Academicians.

"Let's not exaggerate, compadre. Let's be realistic. Reservations, some of them very grave ones, and an atmosphere of uneasiness do exist, I grant you. The man is looked upon with disfavor, and he has a terrible reputation. In his eyes, even Jesus Christ is suspect. Rodrigo told me that the censors banned the publication during Holy Week of the Sermon on the Mount in the *Revista dos Sábados*. The editor-in-chief of the review, Gil Costelo, complained to the DIP, convinced that it must have been banned because of the illustration accompanying it, a modernist drawing by Portinari. He was dumbfounded to learn that it was the Bible text itself that had been specifically prohibited. To save face, an employee at the DIP revealed that the order had come directly from Sampaio Pereira's office. Rodrigo heard the story from Gil himself."

"Who would possibly vote for someone like that?"

"Don't fool yourself. If we don't use our heads, he'll be elected despite all this. They'll vote for him holding their noses in disgust (as Alcântara remarked to me), but they'll vote for him. Lisandro's trump cards aren't a bluff, and he's by no means an idiot. The minute I found out about Francelino's accident, I went immediately to the poor old man's apartment. The first thing I saw as I came in was an enormous basket of fruit: apples, pears, grapes, and a fawning card, signed with Colonel Agnaldo Sampaio's name—in our Lisandro's handwriting. . . ." Afrânio smiles again. "If we're to win this game, Evandro, we're going to have to be fiendishly clever. Fiendishly clever!" he repeats, serious now. "We must find a candidate. . . ."

"We have Feliciano. There couldn't be a better one. A poet, universally praised, known by young and old alike, and a wonderful person."

"That's not enough, compadre. We need a candidate that the Academicians can vote for without fear. Without fear of reprisals. A candidate who can offer absolutely ironclad guarantees that those who vote for him will be safe from any attempted act of revenge on the part of Sampaio Pereira, a powerful and vindictive man. This eliminates any civilian, whoever he might be, from the very outset. We must come out for the candidacy of an Army officer, Evandro. A higher-ranking one than Pereira—a general, that is to say."

An inveterate believer in civilian power, the author of a book on the evils of militarism in the history of the countries of Latin America, a volume that has had an enormous impact all over the continent, old Evandro is immediately opposed to the idea.

"Don't hand me that business about a captive chair. . . ."

"It's not a question of that. . . ." Afrânio is no longer in a joking mood. "It's a question of keeping an individual who's committed to Nazism and everything it represents, who's involved in the torture of political prisoners, in censorship that has hounded writers and journalists—a man who is the very opposite of Bruno, who died because he couldn't endure such horrors—from succeeding him, from taking his place among us at Academy meetings; in other words, from becoming my colleague and yours."

There is a moment of silence as Evandro digests the novelist's words. Then he nods his head:

"Yes, you're right."

"Yes, that's true. I can't guarantee more than four or five votes for a civilian candidate—your vote and mine, Rodrigo's, those of . . ." He mentions two other names. "And that's it! Whereas with a general, if we do our work well, we can win the game. We urgently need a general, the author of at least one book, an adversary of Nazism and the New State, who's prepared to confront Colonel Sampaio Pereira. Right?"

"Right. What's going to be hard is to find one who fulfills all those requisites. . . ."

"We'll find one, I assure you. You, compadre, are a fanatic. As you see it, once a man has donned a uniform, he's lost his soul. But among Army men there are a great many good, honest, democratic sorts—the majority. Now, let me tell you the story of the manhandling. . . ." Even before he begins to recount what happened, he bursts out laughing. Mestre Portela finds life most amusing, and enjoys to the fullest all the choice things it has to offer him.

▨ THE GENERAL, AWAITING A
TELEPHONE CALL

Impatiently, General Waldomiro Moreira lays his newspaper aside, looks at his watch, gets up from his chaise longue, crosses the little garden, heads through the living-room door, notes the infraction of discipline. Just as he thought: Cecília is on the phone, flirting. That confounded dental surgeon! As if he didn't have enough annoyances to contend with already.

"Oh, come on, I don't believe it. . . ." The girl bursts into coquettish fits of laughter.

"Cecília!"

The coquettish laughter dies away at the sound of the general's imperious voice. Putting her hand over the mouthpiece of the phone, his refractory daughter begs:

"Just one minute more, Father."

"Hang up. This instant!"

"In just one little second, Father."

The obliging Sabença has agreed to telephone as soon as he has spoken with Dr. Félix Linhares and gotten his indispensable agreement. The meeting was scheduled to take place before lunch, at the Santa Casa, where the prolific author of novels based on Old Testament subjects fulfills his duties as a physician and deals with business having to do with the Rio de Janeiro Academy of Letters, of which he is president, having been reelected to that office for the fifth time by unanimous vote. At breakfast, the general had forbidden all use of the telephone after ten A.M. His wife and his daughter spend hours on the phone, Dona Conceição gossiping and complaining of the cost of living, Cecília swearing eternal love.

An admirer of the general's literary endeavors, particularly his campaign in favor of the purity of the mother tongue, Claudionor Sabença, the compiler of the *Anthology of Luso-Brazilian Literature,* of the *Selected Writings of Rio de Janeiro Authors,* and of textbooks on grammar (First, Second, and Third Year), had labored diligently to influence his fellow members of the Rio de Janeiro Academy, with evident success. They had turned out to be well disposed toward the general and receptive to his candidacy for a seat left vacant, especially since the reputation of the other candidate, Francisco Ladeira, owed far more to his venomous tongue than to the debatable value of his Parnassian sonnets. Pitilessly pressuring his colleagues in the lower depths of literature, the latter was still trying to get himself elected, and going about marshaling votes for himself with the most innocent air imaginable. It was nonetheless the president who would have the final word.

The prestige enjoyed in the world of medicine by Dr. Félix Linhares, whose practice had brought him great wealth and influence, guaranteed subsidies, favors, and funds that gave real weight to the Academy he headed, above and beyond the proceedings of that body, by assuring it a headquarters on state property and publication by the state printing office (invariably behind schedule, but free of charge) of the Academy's review, of Academicians' monographs, and even of their books—the *Selected Writings* edited by Claudionor Sabença, for instance. Not to mention the two public servants placed at its disposal: a clerk and a flashy, recently engaged, and morally very liberal-minded secretary. Small privileges, but nonetheless ones that made seats that fell vacant in the Rio de Janeiro Academy of Letters desirable and hotly contested: a limited immortality, confined within the borders of the state of Rio, but no less coveted for all that.

The general's nervousness and irritation stem from the ambiguous situation that has arisen, from the prolonged uncertainty. Besides having a poisonous tongue and being a bad poet, Francisco Ladeira was proving to be a shrewd operator as well. He had said dreadful things about almost everyone, yet had never once opened his mouth to criticize Dr. Linhares's biblical characters (though Heaven only knows they deserved it), an attitude that naturally the president had appreciated. Since he is powerless in the face of cabals and plots, the general's nerves are understandably on edge.

Having gotten his daughter off the phone, he returns to his chaise longue in the shade of the garden. Early in 1937, he had been on the point of presenting himself as a candidate; the ever-zealous Sabença had begun contacting various Academicians, but at that point more important politico-military interests had intervened, taking up all the general's time and energies. He had devoted himself, body and soul, to the electoral campaign of Armando Sales de Oliveira, an opposition candidate for the presidency of the Republic, with such fervor that his name had been repeatedly mentioned in the press as the probable future war minister if his candidate won. Dona Conceição, a woman of irrepressible enthusiasm and given to daydreaming, savored for several months the prestige promised by this rosy prospect. Alas, not many months, however, since in November of that year a coup d'état inaugurated the dictatorship of the New State, dissolved the Congress and political parties, put an end to candidacies and elections, and changed General Waldomiro Moreira's status from that of a future minister to that of an officer shunted off, with pay, to the reserves. He had thereupon donned the classic pair of lounging pajamas and returned, full-time, to peaceful and diligent pursuits in the field of letters.

He went back to writing a weekly column, "In Defense of the Portuguese Language," for the *Correio do Rio*, which he had given up during the presidential campaign. He had finished writing another volume, the third, of his *Stories of the History of Brazil*, accounts and tales of glorious military exploits, the recent publication of which had coincided with a vacancy in the Rio Academy, leading his friend Sabença to go into action again, with clear possibilities of success. If it were up to the Academicians alone . . . The meeting arranged for that morning between the general's campaign manager and President Linhares would seal the destiny of the ambitious candidate: either victory, or giving up seeking the vacant seat.

The church bell strikes noon: the end of the morning. Why hasn't Sabença phoned yet? A postponement of the meeting, or might the wary Linhares have decided in favor of Francisco Ladeira so as to remain safe from his epigrams and gibes? The general fears for his heart; the cardiologist has advised him to avoid stressful emotions.

He thinks he hears the phone ringing, and keeps himself from coming into the house on the run. Dona Conceição announces from the door of the living room:

"Telephone for you, Moreira." She always calls her husband by his last name, with respect and devotion. "He says to tell you it's the Academician . . ."

"It's Sabença, I know. . . ." He is already on his feet.

"No, that's not who it is. . . ."

"It's not Sabença? Well, who is it, then?"

"He says he's Dr. Rodrigo Inácio Filho, of the Brazilian Academy. He wants you to set a time to receive a committee of Academicians. . . ."

General Waldomiro Moreira hesitates, feeling uneasy. It must be a trick, the handiwork of that treacherous Ladeira, who relishes practical jokes in poor taste.

"The man's waiting, Moreira."

A trick, no doubt about it. With a set expression, the general marches to the telephone. If this is some sort of trick, let that scoundrel of a Ladeira beware: he'll pay dearly for it. No one can get away with making mock of a general of the Army, even one put out to pasture in the reserves, relegated to the sidelines.

◼ THE CHOICE, WITH NAPOLEON BRANDY

The one who remembered General Waldomiro Moreira's name was Rodrigo Inácio Filho, who had been advised of the scheme and had agreed to take part in it. And he recalled it just as Mestre Afrânio was about to admit defeat and concede that his old friend Evandro was right: a difficult task indeed, finding a general with a published book who was openly anti-Nazi, had no ties to the New State, and was prepared to run against Sampaio Pereira. Anti-Nazis, many of them, the majority; against the dictatorship, a fair number, but behind the scenes, not in public; with a published book, a mere handful. And among these latter, how many would agree to present themselves as a candidate, to confront the colonel's power and his wrath? In the novelist's study, sipping cognac (*grande fine champagne Napoléon*, French and worthy of great warriors), the two old friends eliminated possible candidates one by one:

"Please, Afrânio: a mathematics book . . . it won't do."

"That one will never agree to run against Sampaio Pereira. . . ."

"He'd be a good name to put up if only he were a general instead of a major."

Invited to join them, Rodrigo Inácio Filho, the most peace-loving creature in the world, appeared, all smiles, with the rosette of the Legion of Honor in his buttonhole, a fitting reminder of his participation in the Resistance. He kissed the noble hand of Dona Rosarinho.

"A recruit at your husband's command, madame. This whole thing is absurd, but it would please Bruno."

"Absurd? Why? What's absurd is the war," Evandro answered.

Dona Rosarinho picked up the bottle of cognac, poured the recently-arrived third Academician a drink, and challenged him:

"Put your hand in your vest pocket and pull out a general who'll fill the bill, Rodrigo. You know the requirements. . . ."

"I'm at your command, Rosarinho. I propose General Waldomiro Moreira."

"Waldomiro Moreira . . . I know that name. . . ." Mestre Afrânio searches his memory: "Good Lord, where have I heard of him?"

A few days before, Rodrigo had received a new book by General Moreira, the author of a good half-dozen weighty tomes. The general was by no means an unknown; he enjoyed a certain political and military, not to mention literary, renown, and his name had appeared frequently in the newspapers during Armando Sales's campaign, which was when Rodrigo had been introduced to him. They had met again on two or three occasions. At a banquet for the presidential candidate, they had found themselves seated together and had talked of literature and politics. The general was no admirer of the moderns, faulting them for their ignorance and their scorn for the proper use of their mother tongue, but on the other hand he was a battle-hardened democrat, the reason why the New State had transferred him to the reserves. He was an anti-Nazi and a supporter of the Allied Powers; one had only to read the commentaries on the war that he had been writing in the *Correio do Rio*. In them he tore Hitler to pieces: "A madman, a degenerate."

"So prejudiced he refuses to believe the Nazis are winning victory after victory, thereby denying the obvious."

"It remains to be seen if he'll agree to be a candidate."

Assigned the task of seeking more complete information, Mestre Afrânio returns twenty-four hours later in jubilation:

"There's no doubt about it: he's our man!"

In the same study, sipping the same martial Napoleon brandy, he sets forth facts regarding the general and lists his qualifications: the Constitutionalist Revolution, the

Armando Sales presidential campaign, retired from active duty by the dictatorship. Five published books: a trilogy of historical narratives, a volume of collected articles from his newspaper column dealing with linguistic problems, plus a brief treatise (out of print) outlining various aspects of the military campaign of 1932 on the Minas Gerais front. Regarded as a courageous and honorable man, though somewhat opinionated and headstrong. Pigheaded.

"Given the situation we're up against, that's a virtue."

"Do you think he'll agree to enter the fray?" Evandro asks.

"I'm convinced he will. . . ." Mestre Afrânio's eyes gaze fixedly at his fellow conspirators with that characteristic look of his of gleeful sarcasm: "I'll wager you can't guess what his greatest ambition of the moment is, what he's aiming at. . . ." A moment's suspenseful pause, a swallow of cognac: "Nothing more or less than declaring himself a candidate for a seat in the Rio de Janeiro Academy of Letters."

"That can't be true! You're joking!"

"It's the absolute truth. Can you imagine his reaction when we propose that he declare his candidacy for a seat in the Brazilian Academy? He's going to go out of his mind. Moreover, Sampaio Pereira can't do him any harm; they've already done all the bad things they could to him. He's our man. Rodrigo's hit the bull's-eye."

"And his books?" Evandro asks in a low voice. "What about his books?"

As proof of his devotion to the cause, Rodrigo had gone through the general's latest volume:

"It's mostly nationalist flag-waving, but it's readable nonetheless. He writes decently; grammar is one of his dogmas. A careful, solid style, do you follow me?"

"Careful and solid, eh? Classic Portuguese, you mean?"

"That's right. He's more suited to the Rio Academy, I grant you, but outside of him, I don't see anyone else."

"Nor do I," Mestre Afrânio agrees. "I'm going to spend

the rest of the day reading his books. I've managed to get hold of four of them, and Carlos Ribeiro promised me he'd get me the one that's out of print. Carlinhos was the one who furnished me with most of my information about the general."

He was referring to the celebrated Rio book dealer, the "old book peddler," as he was fond of describing himself. His bookstore, on the Rua São José, was a favorite haunt of Greeks and Trojans, academics and modernists, men of letters of the most varied talents and reputations, from every imaginable background, school, tendency, coterie, and sect. There was absolutely no one who was better informed than Carlinhos Ribeiro.

"What's more," Afrânio declares, his good-humored smile broadening, "I bought two copies of every volume, one for me and one for you, compadre. We need to be thoroughly acquainted with the works of our candidate in order to be able to sing his praises."

Old Evandro doesn't go along with that:

"Sing his praises, you say. I'm willing to do that if necessary. All's fair in war, and this is no time to have scruples. But as for reading him—no, that's asking too much. Nationalist flag-waving, a careful, solid style . . . I know what that sort of writing is like. The less of it I've read, the more I'll be able to praise it."

BELLES-LETTRES, A BALM

His dream of being named war minister shattered, shunted into the reserves until he reached compulsory retirement age, General Waldomiro Moreira decided to dedicate himself exclusively to literary endeavors and the glory resulting from them, modest but comforting. He suffered a military relapse, however, and came a cropper.

His polemical newspaper column devoted to the defense of linguistic canons resulted in a number of letters from a select group of discriminating readers and cordial relations with other fanatical defenders of linguistic purity, alarmed at the scorn for the most elementary rules of grammar, a scorn evident everywhere in modern literature, written "in Nagô, in Cabinda, in Quimbundo dialect." He was hard at work revising the third volume of his *Stories of the History of Brazil* when the war broke out in Europe, bringing on his military relapse.

The general took on yet another job. An authority on linguistic questions ("a competent philologist," in the decisive opinion of Rivadávia Pontes, the author of *Notes on Grammar*), he was also an authority on martial sciences, a student who had been awarded top honors by the professors of the French Military Mission, and invincible when it came to military tactics and strategy. Hence, in the very same *Correio do Rio* where on Sundays he taught his readers how to write well, he began to publish a daily column on the progress of the Second Great World War, a brief and categorical commentary entitled "The War Day by Day—Analysis and Predictions," signed "Gen. W. M."

The military strategist did not achieve the same success as the grammarian. Entrenched behind the impregnable Maginot Line, the general saw Hitler's Panzer divisions reduce his solid knowledge to dust. With a total disregard for the established rules of martial science, they belied each afternoon the analyses and predictions published that morning by the columnist. "Gen. W. M." began to lose ground with Gamelin and went under with Weygand, suffering one defeat after another—a hecatomb. Disillusioned, he took advantage of the censors' repeated scissoring out of the epithets with which he was avenging himself for the Führer's advance, and eventually gave up the column, to the relief of the editor-in-chief of the paper.

He took refuge once again in belles-lettres, which compensated for his disappointment, thanks to the gratifying reception accorded the third volume of his *Stories of the History of Brazil*, the object of a number of favorable reviews. The faithful Sabença had written a long article praising it highly, and the eminent scholar Altino Alcântara, of the Brazilian Academy, had written him a letter thanking "my esteemed colleague for sending me his new book, whose pages are not only evidence of a flawless style, but are vibrant with true patriotism as he brings memorable exploits to life once again." A phrase quoted in the "Books and Authors" section, by the promising Mauro Meira, in the *Jornal do Manhã*.

What proved more difficult to overcome was his paternal annoyance at Cecília's flightiness; she had abandoned her husband, a hardworking, upright Army captain stationed in Curitiba, to go live it up in Rio, a bigger pond. A man of honor faithful to his word, the general was indignant (though not surprised).

The vacant seat in the Rio Academy and the possibility of winning it were a balm that healed his wounds. The last echoes of the jeers at his war commentaries, which he had heard secondhand here and there (". . . they're enough to make you die laughing. . . ."—and they laughed uproariously in Colonel Sampaio Pereira's office as they read "The War Day by Day" aloud), painful thorns in his flesh, had died away. As for Cecília's loves (loves?—the general preferred not to call a spade a spade), he left them up to the mother of his wayward daughter to deal with: Dona Conceição do Prado Moreira, a stout-hearted woman whom he had married when, as a childless widower of thirty posted in Mato Grosso, he found his loneliness unbearable.

Dona Conceição also came from an old Army family. Her husband's authoritarianism did not upset her; she was used to such treatment. Before submitting to his despotic rule, she had had to bear that of her brother, in whose household she had lived until her blessed meeting with Moreira. Besides delivering her from spinsterhood, the marriage had freed her from the clutches of her terrible-tempered sister-in-law. As for Cecília, she had taken after her father: obstinate, headstrong, deaf both to reasonable arguments and to threats. But since the general was irreproachably virtuous, and Dona Conceição decorum personified, from whom had the daughter inherited her irrepressible ardor, her shocking sensuality, her unbridled lust? Heaven only knew.

Had the general received the phone call from Sabença as agreed, announcing the good news that he had secured the president's backing, he could have eaten his lunch in peace and then stretched out in the chaise longue for an afternoon nap. He would have told his friend to come by in the late afternoon, and the two of them would have planned the details of his election campaign and the reception to follow. All of a sudden, everything was changed. Instead of the unprepossessing Claudionor Sabença, the author of an anthology and of classroom grammar texts, a member of the Rio Academy, the person who had telephoned was the eminent Rodrigo Inácio Filho, author of *Memoirs of Another*, a masterpiece, and a member of the Brazilian Academy.

The general's heart signals what a shock the call was: that familiar stabbing pain. Dona Conceição brings him his pill and a glass of water:

"Why don't you lie down a while, Moreira, till lunch is ready?"

Served invariably at twelve-thirty on the dot, even lunch was late that day.

CONJECTURES, FEW IN NUMBER AND ABSURD

A committee of members of the Brazilian Academy of Letters! Dr. Rodrigo had been quite specific on the phone: he was calling to request that his dear friend General Moreira set an hour and a day, as soon as possible, for receiving a committee of Academicians. All this after recalling their meeting at the memorable banquet, the subjects they had talked about, thus dispelling any suspicion on the general's part that the whole thing was some sort of joke perpetrated by the spiteful Ladeira. But Rodrigo had offered no information as to the object of the visit, and the general had thought it impolite to ask. He had replied that he would be most willing to receive the committee, on any day and at any hour, and declared himself highly honored.

"A committee from the Brazilian Academy! Can you imagine, Conceição? Why the devil are they coming here?"

After giving him the pill, Dona Conceição tries to calm him down:

"Why don't you lie down while I go see about lunch?"

Lie down! As if that were possible! He refuses bed, armchair, chaise longue. The phone call must have been due to a misunderstanding. But what misunderstanding, exactly? And what if it wasn't one? For all he knows, they might be considering him for the Machado de Assis Prize, the supreme distinction awarded annually by the Academy, crowning a writer's entire *oeuvre*. There had been instances in the past where, if there was an impasse between two authors of equal merit, they had chosen a third, unexpected one. Well acquainted with what goes on behind the scenes in the world of letters, the general is familiar with the rules and traditions of the Illustrious Company. He knows that, in the case of the Machado de Assis, the writer who has been chosen is the object of a circumspect prior consultation, through the intermediary of an Academician with whom he is on friendly terms, who approaches him with all due discretion. He has never heard, however, of a case in which a committee visited a writer at his home to ask him whether he was willing to accept the coveted prize—a great honor accompanied by a substantial sum of money. Since it wasn't the Machado de Assis, then, what could it be? An enigma capable of driving the calmest of men mad. The general is faced with more than twenty-four hours of nervousness and anxiety, since Dr. Rodrigo has proposed that he receive the committee the following day, at six P.M. Twenty-nine hours of agony, then, to be exact.

The general paces up and down the living room, in cadence—tall, corpulent, red-faced, with close-cropped hair. Not even his pajamas hide the fact that he is a military officer; it is obvious in his every feature, his every gesture, in the authority that is an integral part of his personality. But why the devil should a committee of members of the Brazilian Academy of Letters be coming to see him at his house?

He knows of the death of the poet António Bruno and of the chair thus left vacant, but does not allow himself to imagine that any sort of connection exists between the announced visit, the sad event of the poet's death, and its possible joyous consequences for him. Such an impossible dream hadn't entered his mind. But willy-nilly that disturbing conjecture now suggests itself.

On learning of the phone call and the meeting that has been arranged, Cecília bursts into the living room.

"They're going to put you in the seat of the Academician who's just died, Father."

The general's heart leaps painfully.

"Don't talk nonsense."

"Well then, they're going to arrive with a list, collecting money for a bust of one of the Academicians. They spend all their time unveiling busts."

"A bust! You don't know what you're talking about!"

Dona Conceição calls them to come have lunch, half an hour late. Good Lord, what a day! General Moreira eyes his special diet plate with distaste; he has lost his appetite.

He puts down his fork to answer the phone: it is Sabença, calling at last to apologize for keeping him waiting and to inform him that the meeting with Dr. Linhares has been postponed. The president had been detained at the bedside of a patient and had not appeared for their

67

meeting at the Santa Casa. But his dear friend can rest assured, in twenty-four hours his candidacy will be official, having received the president's necessary backing. The general forces himself to conceal his nervousness, and thanks him with feigned effusion.

At the lunch table, Dona Conceição is discussing with Cecília the question of what to serve the important gentlemen, members of the Brazilian Academy. True Immortals, with the right to wear the full regalia of Academicians and be paid a token sum—the *jeton*—for every appearance at an Academy session. During the unforgettable first six months of 1937, the Illustrious General Waldomiro Moreira and his Esteemed Spouse had received an invitation to the solemn reception ceremony for Dr. Alcântara, the famous political figure from São Paulo, and had accepted.

"It was dazzling, my girl. It was like being at a royal court."

The Brazilian Academy of Letters. Yes indeed. It was worth wasting one's time, wearing one's nerves to a frazzle, fighting hard for a contested seat; but apparently this honor was not for the likes of Moreira, reduced to begging for help in getting a seat at a second-rate little academy, located in Niterói, with no ceremonial uniform, no token remunerations, no picture published in the newspapers. Such thoughts occur to Dona Conceição, but she keeps them to herself. Moreira is all upset today, and Cecília hasn't a brain in her head. But perhaps she's the one who's right: they're coming to touch Moreira for money, to ask for a donation to erect a bust to that poet who's just died— a skirt-chaser, according to everything she's been told. At the cemetery, a scandalous bunch of women weeping as they followed the casket. A good thing that Cecília had never met him.

"What shall I serve? Beer, guaraná punch? Should I order some little meat pies, some chicken croquettes?"

"It's better not to serve anything. Beer? Where did you ever get that idea?" the general snaps.

"A little fruit cordial, at least. Or tea. Isn't tea what they drink at the Academy?"

"Why not just serve them a little coffee, Mother?"

The general agrees with his daughter. With her suggestion to serve coffee and, in fear and hope, with her initial conclusion:

"They're going to put you in the seat of the Academician who's just died, Father."

Twenty-nine hours of waiting, including a sleepless night. If his heart holds up, it will prove that the family doctor and the cardiologist are nothing but charlatans.

■ THE CANDIDATE'S BALLET DANCE

The next day, at eleven A.M., General Waldomiro Moreira officially presented himself as a candidate for a seat in the Rio Academy of Letters. His letter requesting that he be placed on the list of candidates was handed to the dedicated Claudionor Sabença, who, after having obtained the approval of President Linhares at nine A.M. at the Santa Casa, took a streetcar to the general's residence in Grajaú to bring him the good news. In order to do all this, he had taken the morning off from work at the paper.

Eight hours later, at seven P.M., the general found himself a candidate for the Brazilian Academy, in response to the invitation of the distinguished committee of Academicians, and entrusted his letter requesting to be placed on the list of candidates to the novelist Afrânio Portela. The general had never dreamed that the latter was one of his readers, nor would he ever have imagined that the famous author of *The Woman in the Mirror* would prove to have such intimate knowledge of his entire body of work, as revealed by his exhaustive analysis of the gallery of exemplary figures portrayed in the three volumes of his *Stories of the History of Brazil* and of the problems dealt with in penetrating detail in his volume entitled *Linguistic Prolegomena*.

A longtime reader who had followed step by step, book by book, "your brilliant intellectual trajectory," as he put it, Mestre Afrânio gave the impression of having completed his reading of the general's *oeuvre* very recently, as demonstrated by the manner in which he flawlessly quoted long passages from memory, recalling specific images and repeating dialogues word for word.

"What an extraordinary memory, Mestre Portela!" Moreira, deeply moved, exclaimed ecstatically.

"I've read and re-read your work, not just once, but several times," Afrânio Portela replied, smiling shamelessly.

Evandro Nunes dos Santos carefully avoided his old crony's eyes: "War is war; everything's fair." He began to second his confederate's flattering opinions with a string of forceful adjectives: "Admirable!" "Masterful!" "Magnificent!" Coming from this old and redoubtable essayist, these epithets took on special value; they were priceless. The other three Academicians also contributed their quota of lofty praise. Overwhelmed, the general was at a loss for words to thank them. He realized how badly he had underestimated his own *oeuvre*.

At a certain point he summoned his wife and daughter to witness the infinite honor being accorded him by the illustrious committee, representing a powerful group of Academicians. The two of them were thus able to hear with their own ears the praise being heaped upon the books of their husband and father. Dona Conceição was deeply impressed, and Cecília was thrilled.

Forty minutes after the departure of the two large automobiles bearing off the Academicians, the general, having reached Sabença by phone, gave him back the vacant chair in the Rio Academy, requesting that the letter in which he had presented himself as a candidate be returned to him and promising Sabença exciting news. "Come over after dinner and I'll tell you everything. You've a great surprise in store for you, my friend."

"Do you mean to tell me you're no longer a candidate for the Academy seat?" Sabença didn't understand: after all that work to secure the president's backing, when everything was now all arranged . . .

"Yes, I'm a candidate for an Academy seat. What I'm not a candidate for is a seat in the Rio Academy. . . ."

"I don't follow you. . . ."

"You'll see what I mean when I've explained matters to you. Tell Linhares that I'm grateful for the invitation but that he's free to do as he pleases with regard to the vacant seat."

Invitation? Sabença thought to himself in surprise. But there wasn't any invitation. Only he knew how much effort he'd expended in convincing Dr. Linhares to allow the general to register as a candidate. Were it not for the respect that he felt he owed the general—rank is rank— Claudionor Sabença would have allowed a swearword to escape his lips over the phone. He didn't utter it, and hung up in a melancholy mood: all the trouble he had gone to in order to get the general on the list of candidates had come to nothing. But it had at least opened to him the doors of the cordial house in Grajaú where, "a butterfly of dreams, there flutters Cecília, kindling desires." From time to time, Claudionor Sabença perpetrates poetry.

▉ AN INITIAL TALLY OF STRENGTH

A week before, at the time of Bruno's wake, there had been two of them: Afrânio Portela and Evandro Nunes dos Santos. Then there were three, after Rodrigo Inácio Filho had been recruited: at the general's house five of them had made their appearance, the three already mentioned plus Henrique Andrade—the biographer of Ruy, Rio Branco, and Nabuco—and R. Figueiredo Jr., a dramatist whose plays, once eagerly sought after by theatrical companies, had disappeared from the boards with the proclamation of the New State. They dealt with social problems, and his heroes, whether Hellenes or inhabitants of Ceará, all cried out for freedom and defended human rights.

After sounding out the opinions of his colleagues, in the days that preceded and succeeded the meeting in memoriam for Bruno, Afrânio Portela's initial calculations had led him to conclude that they could count on eight certain votes for the general. Evandro swore that they could count on a dozen, but since the elderly essayist was easily carried away by enthusiasm, his calculations were not to be trusted.

As for the colonel, after counting and re-counting Portela concluded that he had fifteen more or less certain votes from the outset. If Sampaio Pereira acted quickly and decisively, he would be able to increase that number appreciably, thus assuring his victory. But it was also possible that he would gain only a few more votes and even lose some of those he was counting on as certain if General Waldomiro Moreira's supporters seized the initiative and acted even more quickly, decisively, and, above all, astutely.

Adding up the eight initial votes in favor of the general and the fifteen for the colonel, the total certain votes came to twenty-three. Hence, of the thirty-nine Academicians who would be casting their votes, there remained sixteen to be won over during the electoral campaign. An electoral campaign that was to become known as the Battle of the Petit Trianon when the facts entered the realm of legend.

"Lightning-blows and chicanery at will!" This was the order of the day proclaimed by Mestre Afrânio after his first tally of votes for and against.

In the course of the committee's visit to the general, one fact had surprised the novelist: the eagerness with which the candidate had agreed to confront Colonel Agnaldo Sampaio Pereira, as though this were his one and only desire. Undoubtedly, the two of them had accounts to settle. Curious by nature, Mestre Portela wanted to get to the bottom of the reasons behind the general's furious urge to meet his adversary face to face. The occasion to do so would be provided by the dinner party, when wine would contrive to breach protocol.

In order to draw up his battle plans and on the express orders of Dona Rosarinho ("I want to see what your general and his wife are like"), the Moreiras, husband and wife, had been invited to dinner at the Portelas', together with Evandro and Rodrigo Inácio. The invitation had not included Cecília, but she had taken it upon herself to join them. She was not about to miss the opportunity of seeing with her own eyes the "elegant mansion at Praia do Flamengo," so often mentioned by Jacinto de Tormes, Gilberto Trompowski, and other gossip columnists, still few in number but already influential.

Not to mention the fact that this Dr. Rodrigo, with his air of a Spanish nobleman, his graying temples, his carefully manicured hands, and his English blazer, had haunted, troubled, and cast their spell over Cecília's dreams for some time now. Ah, Cecília's dreams: if they were to be recounted here, they would transform this little Academic fable into a sensational best seller.

▓ INFORMATION INDISPENSABLE TO THE PROPER UNDERSTANDING OF THE STORY AND USEFUL TO ANY FUTURE CANDIDATE FOR ADMISSION TO THE ACADEMY

Now that the two candidates have officially registered, a few explanations are in order, otherwise it will be difficult for the reader to follow the march of events and understand all the details of the story. While contrary to the well-founded rules of effective narrative, this parenthesis describing procedures followed by the Academy may be excused on the above grounds, and may perhaps be of some use to a possible candidate for admission to the Academy by apprising him of the rules and customs that it is indispensable for him to be aware of.

Once an Immortal is dead and buried, the chair that he has occupied is declared vacant at the first session following his demise—the aforementioned meeting in memoriam. Four months later, the election of his successor is held.

During the first two months of the four that separate the funereal session from the festive one, anyone who so wishes may register his name on the list of candidates; the sole requirements are that he be a Brazilian citizen of the male sex (thirty-six years were to go by before women were allowed to present themselves as candidates) who has had at least one book published. Once this period of precisely two months has elapsed, the list of candidates for the vacant seat is declared closed. In the two remaining months, it is up to the candidates vying for the seat to solicit the votes of the Academicians, and up to each of the latter to choose the candidate whom he will honor with his vote.

In order to be elected, the candidate must obtain an absolute majority of the votes (one-half the total number, plus one) of the Academicians who are alive at the time, on one of the four rounds of balloting permitted by the rules at each election meeting. The vote is secret; the Immortals present place their ballots in a box in which they are burned after being counted. The absent members participate in the proceedings by sending in their votes in sealed envelopes, accompanied by a letter explaining their reason for being absent.

An Academician may abstain from voting or may cast a blank ballot. In the first case, though he does not acknowledge the intellectual qualities of the candidate(s), he nonetheless does not want to antagonize him (them) personally. The blank ballot, however, signifies a much more radical objection: it is proof of the Academician's aversion toward the person(s) of the candidate(s), whom he does not consider worthy of sitting with him as a fellow member of the Illustrious Company. An abstention does not prevent a vote from being declared unanimous, providing that a candidate has obtained all the other votes. A blank ballot, however, bars election by unanimous vote.

Once the election is over, the Academicians appear as a group at the residence of their new fellow member, where they find a table well laden with food and beverages, prepared by the candidate's family to celebrate his hoped-for victory. Following a most laudable custom, hospitality is also extended to the always considerable number of persons—intellectuals, politicians, government authorities, people from his home state, friends and admirers—who hasten to congratulate the brand-new Immortal. They toast him in champagne, whisky flows freely, and the reception lasts until late into the newly-elected Academician's night of glory.

Before going to the winner's to congratulate him, two or three Academicians take upon themselves the sad duty of presenting themselves at the residence(s) of the defeated candidate(s) to offer explanations, solidarity in his bitter hour of defeat, and the customary mentions of brighter future prospects: "... the next time ..." In the opinion of Rodrigo Inácio Filho, the arbiter of questions of decorum and propriety, decency demands that on these fatal missions of consolation the members of the delegation, out of respect for the feelings of the crestfallen family, not partake of the sweets, the canapés, and the drinks if perchance they find them still on the buffet table, laid out to celebrate the certain victory that has not taken place.

The Battle of the Petit Trianon lasted a little over two months. It ended, somewhat unexpectedly, ten days after the closing of the registration period for candidates seeking the seat in the Brazilian Academy left vacant by the death of the poet António Bruno. Only two contestants had presented themselves: Colonel Agnaldo Sampaio Pereira and General Waldomiro Moreira (by order of registration). No civilian had dared to do so; everyone had accepted the idea that the chair belonged by right and by tradition to the military. It had been wrongfully occupied by the poet António Bruno, a civilian and a bohemian, through the inexplicable negligence of the armed forces.

Events that took place later, during the period between the end of the Battle and the election date, had nothing to do with the full-scale combat planned and led by Mestre Afrânio Portela. At that point it was no longer an out-and-out war but rather guerrilla warfare, in which the novelist was merely a lieutenant, the supreme command of the resistance forces having been taken over by old Evandro Nunes dos Santos, who was determined to prove that there was no such thing in the Academy as a captive chair, reserved for this or that confraternity, of whatever nature.

In the course of the two months and ten days of stubborn fighting to conquer the Petit Trianon, the hostilities as a whole were divided into three separate phases.

During the first twenty days, the initiative was taken by the forces that had rallied round General Waldomiro. The impact caused by his candidacy—either a pleasant or an unpleasant surprise for the majority of the Immortals, who had been convinced that Colonel Sampaio Pereira would be the sole candidate, without opponents— and the lightning campaign that was then unleashed, in accordance with battle orders issued by Mestre Afrânio, had enabled the general to occupy a number of important positions and gain new supporters, including deserters from the enemy camp. The enemy, confident of victory, had neglected to campaign; the colonel was so certain that nothing stood in the way of his peaceful march to glory that he had postponed beginning the traditional ceremonial visits to the Academicians until his return from an inspection trip to Santa Catarina, in the south of the country, where intolerable events had occurred, and to Rio Grande do Sul, where the situation was disturbing. Afrânio Portela took advantage of this fact to launch a swift attack.

This initial advance of the Moreira candidacy was followed by a vigorous, violent reaction on the part of the forces faithful to Colonel Agnaldo Sampaio Pereira. Once he had recovered from the shock of seeing the sole candidacy that he had envisioned come a cropper, Lisandro Leite called upon external allies for massive support—extremely influential allies, capable of changing the course of the battle, inflicting a humiliating defeat on the general, reducing the number of votes in his favor to a mere meaningless half-dozen thanks to the pressure they could bring to bear on those electors still wavering.

How to respond to this attack mounted with the aid of foreign intervention, coercion, and subornation, the arms of the now-furious Lisandro characteristic of the second phase? Mestre Portela did not hesitate. He resorted to every manner of ruse and intrigue ("Chicanery at will!"), using and misusing ridiculous farces and outlandish tricks.

In the final period, during the last twenty days of the stupendous battle, a stalemate was reached, or appeared to have been reached, amid the reigning confusion. The military maps of both armies—their printed lists of Academicians, with their names, addresses, and phone numbers, scribbled all over with kabbalistic signs—revealed identical conquests: some ten names at the least figured on the lists of both adversaries. Sure votes for the colonel, according to Lisandro; certain votes for the general, in Portela's opinion. At this point in the battle, in their offensive and defensive maneuvers, the two camps used lures and traps, false rumors and insinuations, stratagems ranging from intimidation to outrageous flattery.

Just as the rude combat reached its height, the Battle of the Petit Trianon came to a sudden and definite end. Rather than a cry of victory, what was heard in the victors' camp was a sigh of relief.

✠ THE EVENTS IN SANTA CATARINA

Intense and constant support from the outside furthered the colonel's candidacy. But at least once the general too enjoyed the benefit of it—the ease with which he was able to maneuver in the early days of the battle stemmed from events in Santa Catarina. Support that was accidental but nonetheless effective, inasmuch as Colonel Sampaio Pereira was obliged to abandon matters having to do with the Academy election and turn his attention to other fronts that had been placed under his direct responsibility, since, as the reader already knows, the colonel was one of the bulwarks of the dictatorship and one of the principal props of the alliance (in full force, though not official) between the Third Reich and the New State. Unwittingly, Captain Joaquim Gravatá, a native of the northeast transferred to Santa Catarina, played an important role in the Battle of the Petit Trianon in its first phase, and thereby made it possible for the general and the sponsors of his candidacy to move freely.

Once the dictatorship of the New State had been installed, political demonstrations of any sort were prohibited anywhere in the country, and all political parties were outlawed, regardless of their nature or ideology. Going beyond other totalitarian regimes, the New State even dispensed with the classic single legal party. An Army officer brought up to love his country, Captain Joaquim

Gravatá was extremely sensitive to any possible threat to its territorial integrity and its national honor. He had served in the Amazon jungle, a vigilant sentinel standing ready to repel any attempt by perfidious neighbors to violate our frontiers. A patriot who had proved his worth in the far north of the country, in Santa Catarina he showed himself to be an inflexible defender of the law.

In the inquiry that was opened following the events that took place there, an attempt was made to identify his respect for the letter of the law with political idiosyncrasies, but the proceedings were eventually shelved for lack of evidence when, after Pearl Harbor and Stalingrad, the Second Great World War took a new turn, abolishing infamous alliances and sending Captain Joaquim Gravatá to the battlefields of Italy, where he won medals and stars on his epaulettes.

Having been transferred directly from the half-breed settlements along the Amazon to the post of commander of the company garrisoned in Blumenau, a city colonized by Germans, Captain Gravatá thought that he had landed on foreign shores. Not so much because of the white skin of the Aryan inhabitants, their blond hair and their blue eyes, or the disquieting predominance of the German language over Portuguese, but more particularly because of the complete scorn for and frequent disobedience of the laws laid down by the government—whether good or bad, it was after all the government of Brazil, an independent country, situated in South America.

Brazilian and peaceful until just a few short years before, during the war Blumenau had taken on the appearance of a bellicose German colony. A native of the state of Sergipe, with no prejudices against racial intermarriage, and uncompromising with regard to the question of national sovereignty, the captain was horrified at what he saw and heard in Blumenau. Noisy political demonstrations were constantly being held in clubs, schools, churches, streets, and squares. Parades marched through the city celebrating victories of the Nazi armies, bearing flags and emblems with swastikas and portraits of the Führer. Paramilitary marches, with young men dressed in uniforms of the SS and the SA, brown shirts and black shirts, goose-stepping, arms raised in salute to their Leaders, and shouting "Heil Hitler!" On platforms in public gardens and parks, fanatical, aggressive speeches were delivered that sounded even more insolent in Bavarian dialect.

Yet all political demonstrations, either in private or in public, were prohibited by law, as were any and all party activities, without exception. Nonetheless the German National Socialist party, with headquarters in Berlin, acted openly in a city that, in the opinion of Captain Joaquim Gravatá and the troops under his command, should remain Brazilian. Determined to impose respect for the law, the officer sought out the prefect of Blumenau so as to act in concert with him. The former prefect had been replaced at the beginning of the war, and the new one had taken on in addition to his official duties that of local leader of the Nazi party. He smiled at the naïveté of the bothersome half-breed captain: decrees concerning political gatherings were not aimed at the joyous celebrations held by the German community to commemorate the victories of the Wehrmacht, and as for the National Socialist party, since it was German and Nazi, the prohibitions established under Brazilian law did not apply to it. He smiled again, considering the subject closed. The captain liked neither the explanations nor the smile and went into action.

He seized flags, swastikas, various emblems, enormous quantities of pamphlets and other publications in German, posters with slogans, countless portraits of the Führer, and a fair number of weapons. He closed the headquarters of the party and pocketed the key. The prefect riposted with a public march; the captain broke it up and clapped some of the more hotheaded demonstrators in jail.

The echo of these events in the country's press was almost nil. There were brief items in one or two newspapers, but the censors prohibited forthwith any mention of the events that had occurred or their consequences: the hasty visit of Colonel Agnaldo Sampaio Pereira, the immediate transfer of Captain Gravatá, the charges brought against him by a military court, the return of the swastika to the sound of trumpet flourishes, arms raised on high, speeches and shouts of "Heil Hitler!"

As the colonel reestablished law and order in Santa Catarina and then proceeded with his inspection tour of Rio Grande do Sul in order to forestall similar episodes, strengthening the Germano-Brazilian alliance by his very presence, the general stepped up his visits to the Academicians. He recited to each of them a carefully rehearsed speech: a writer and a military officer holding the rank of general, a historian and philologist, presenting himself as a candidate for a chair traditionally occupied by members of the Army, come to seek the support of the illustrious Immortal, as confirmed by his vote.

In the eyes of certain Academicians, the general's candidacy was a welcome development: without it they would have been obliged to vote for the Nazi they detested. In the eyes of others, it was an embarrassment: had it not existed, the colonel would have been the only candidate, and, having no other choice, they would have been able to vote for the prestigious leader with a clear conscience, without fear of criticism, reproach, malicious insinuations.

In order to prevent Captain Joaquim Gravatá from being accused of having played a role in this curious, hotly-contested election without having had the slightest connection with it, mention should be made of the fact that the name of the poet António Bruno was not unknown to him. He had read, deeply moved, a dog-eared hand-written copy of the "Song of Love for an Occupied City," and in it he had found encouragement and a call to arms. On arriving in Blumenau, another occupied city, he had made up his mind to liberate it.

Because of the secrecy surrounding Colonel Sampaio Pereira's movements—he had left Rio de Janeiro for an unknown destination, on a mission having to do with national security—Justice Lisandro Leite was not even able to prepare him for the news that he was no longer the sole candidate. He tried, to no avail, to find out where to locate him, how to get in touch with him. Before his sudden departure, the colonel had telephoned him:

"I must leave town for a few days on urgent business. The visit to Ambassador Almeida will have to be postponed until my return."

"Set your mind at rest. I'll explain things personally to Francelino. When you get back, my dear Agnaldo, we'll draw up a schedule for the courtesy visits. A sole candidate enjoys certain advantages: he needn't hurry to make the rounds." In order to reassure him further, he added: "I'll be here on the spot, mounting guard. . . ." Rash words.

Once he had delivered to the Academy secretariat, immediately after the meeting in memoriam for Bruno, the colonel's letter requesting that he be placed on the list of candidates for the vacant chair, Lisandro Leite had relied on the fear reigning throughout the country: no one would dare present himself as an opposing candidate, thereby offending the government, defying the ruling powers. In the early days preceding the election, after the court of appeals adjourned each day, he had been in the habit of dropping by the Petit Trianon, exchanging politenesses with the president, checking that there were no new developments worth noting. Later on, reassured, he decided that he could relax his vigilance and visited the Academy less frequently, using the time instead for telephone conversations with his fellow Immortals, holding out to them the promise of an era of official benefits for the Illustrious Company as a result of the election of Colonel Sampaio Pereira.

Faithful to his word, at the end of the afternoon on the day of his dear friend Agnaldo's departure, the justice headed for the apartment of Ambassador Francelino Almeida, whose only servant was an elderly maid-of-all-work whom he referred to as his housekeeper. Lisandro was going to see him in order to present the colonel's apologies and set a new date for the latter's courtesy visit, during which the candidate personally informs the Academician of his intentions and requests his support. The dean of the Academy, the only one of the founding members still alive, Francelino was traditionally the first one to be honored by the visit of candidates seeking election, as a token of their respect and esteem.

In the living room where the housekeeper had left him waiting, Lisandro's eyes fell upon a magnificent basket full of exotic fruit, tins of English biscuits, Swiss chocolates, bottles of Port and Portuguese tonic wines. Lying alongside it on the table was the tag of Ramos & Ramos, the most elegant and most expensive purveyors of delicacies in the city, and a card that had been removed from its envelope: *To the illustrious Ambassador Francelino Almeida, eminent practitioner of letters and diplomacy, an expression of the profound admiration of General Waldomiro Moreira.* The jurist knew the general by name, and that handwriting by sight, inimitable hieroglyphs traced by the Machiavellian Afrânio Portela. He was utterly taken aback. What was the meaning of such a sumptuous gift basket, such a princely present? He too had sent a gift basket to Francelino, a less spectacular one bearing the tag of a cheaper shop, and had signed the accompanying card with the colonel's name. That Portela was not only diabolical, but a plagiarist to boot!

Francelino Almeida, ingratiating, obliging, pleasant company, had come to occupy important posts in the course of his career as a diplomat: Brazilian Ambassador to Belgium, Sweden, Japan, Secretary General of Itamaraty, the office of the head of state. The Academy had been of great help to him in reaching such heights. Though he had been only twenty-eight years old, with scant literary baggage—a slender volume of short stories and a laudatory little study of the works of Machado de Assis—his name had figured among those of the forty original members of the Illustrious Company. At the time, this had occasioned neither surprise nor discontent, since the newborn Academy was penniless, unknown, without permanent headquarters of its own, and did not yet pay token emoluments. Thirty years later, Francelino filled out the sketchy bibliography of his works with a volume of his impressions of Japan: *The Land of the Rising Sun: Landscapes and Customs.* A bachelor, he had left behind him in all the countries to which he had been posted a reputation as an inveterate admirer of the fair sex.

Sir Anthony Locke, His Britannic Majesty's Ambassador at the court of the Mikado, repeatedly mentioned Mr. Almeida, his incomparable fellow explorer of the nightlife and the erotic rites of the Orient, in the scandalous book of memoirs that saw print after he had retired from active service. For half a decade the two of them had been the most dazzling ornaments of the entire diplomatic corps accredited to the Japanese court, acquiring a notorious popularity in dubious and lively pleasure haunts—until the transfer of "Mr. Almeida, King of the Geishas," so sorely missed by the English lord, to another post. In Francelino's book on Nipponese customs, there was no mention whatsoever either of Sir Anthony Locke or of Japanese nightlife, despite the fact that age had not made Francelino impervious to the charms of the female sex. Quite the contrary.

Having been informed of the arrival of his confrere, Francelino Almeida came to join Lisandro in the living room, preceded by the housekeeper carrying a tray on which were two wineglasses, a bottle of port, and a little plate of English biscuits. The dean of the Academy heard and graciously accepted the apologies extended on behalf of the colonel.

"We'll set a date whenever he likes. Not tomorrow, however: I've already set the afternoon aside for General Moreira's visit. I'm going to tell you something, my dear Lisandro: the very best thing about the Academy is the elections. The candidates are so nice, so . . . flattering. If it weren't for the elections, who would pay any attention to an old man like me, a retired ambassador who receives a mere pittance every month from Itamaraty, in devalued currency that's worth practically nothing? Nobody, my dear friend. But the moment there's a vacant seat, just look what happens: in fewer than ten days I've received two baskets of fruit, wines, and delicacies, all imported, all of the very best quality." He dipped his English biscuit in the port to soften it.

"Does that mean that General Waldomiro Moreira is also a candidate?"

"Didn't you know? He's just submitted his name. A strong candidate, my friend."

He didn't say one word about the general's beautiful secretary, who had arrived, immediately after the basket, to set a day and a time for the courtesy visit of the new contender for Bruno's seat. Friendly and relaxed, she had stayed on to have a lively chat with him, and in the course of the conversation she had hinted at how bored she was by young men: all of them were scatterbrained and discourteous. The diplomat Francelino Almeida, on the other hand, was that rara avis, courtesy itself.

Lisandro bade him goodbye, promising to telephone as soon as the colonel returned, and rushed to the Academy. The colonel's status as the sole candidate was past history.

"What wouldn't I do for him?"

" 'Rose of copper, rose of honey, child-rose,' " Mestre Portela remembered with a tender smile as he sat at the table in a discreet corner of the milk bar. The young woman blushed: the long, straight hair of an Indian, the full lips of a black, the green eyes of a white.

"He kept on sending me roses, even after it was all over between us. There will never be anybody like him."

Afrânio Portela explained the situation to her, the need to safeguard Bruno's memory, the importance of the dean of the Academy, one of the founding members, the only one of the original forty Immortals still alive. His whole life long, Francelino Almeida had endeavored to please only powerful men—and women. Colonel Sampaio Pereira was powerful, extremely powerful.

"Seduce an old man?" Rosa exclaimed in surprise. "At his age does he still have an eye for women?"

"An eye for them? That he certainly does have. I'll testify to that."

At the door of the Academy, a few months before, he and Bruno had followed Francelino's gaze—a doddering oldster whose eyes had lighted up at the sight of a young woman's brown leg. The poet had defended the dean of the Academy when Portela had ventured an ironic comment, confessing that when he, Bruno, grew old and lost everything, when he had become nothing but "a decrepit old gaffer," he intended to sit in the sun on a park bench, eyeing women and happy to be alive. The two of them, Mestre Afrânio and Rosa, fell silent, both lost in memories, he remembering his friend and she her lover.

Rosa drained her glass of milk. At the age of eighteen, almost a child still, she had seduced a mature man, thirty years older than herself, with whom she had fallen passionately in love, just seeing him from the window of the workshop where she sewed dresses for rich ladies from high society.

Rosa had read "The Five O'Clock Tea," the short story, at once touching and amusing, written by Afrânio Portela and inspired by her love-affair with Bruno. The story had struck her as being a nice one, romantic but entirely false. Based on true facts—the asking of her hand in marriage, for example—it nonetheless was a story that was the precise contrary of what had really happened. In the novelist's version, the plot centered on the encounter between a dissolute Don Juan and a naïve young girl who had lost her head and was a mere toy in the hands of her seducer. The contrary, the opposite, the reverse of reality. But who would believe in the naked and cruel truth, even if Rosa were to reveal it? Despite his fame as a writer with a profound understanding of the feminine soul, not even Afrânio Portela could bring himself to admit that a humble little adolescent seamstress had acted as she had. Even Rosa herself didn't know why she had behaved as she had, and didn't try to explain. It had not been madness, much less lust. Merely love, the midday sun, and the full moon.

A surprise, a blinding light, a sudden violent storm inundating the earth, rending the sky with flashes of lightning. Daring that knew no bounds, the shamelessness of a gypsy—who could possibly have imagined her capable of such bold, fearless passion?

Serene and indifferent to the flattering compliments, the propositions, the supplications, the cheekiness of young men, Rosa had made her way down the suburban street. Zecão, the center-forward of the Madureira Athletic Club, invited to try out for the prestigious Botafogo soccer team, stopped hanging round the entrance to the little back street waiting for her to pass by. Puffed up with pride, putting on airs, the neighbors decided, seeing the grave, absorbed expression on her face, the faraway look in her eye as she thought of the gentleman seated at a table at the Colombo. More handsome than any leading man in the movies; there was no comparison. She had no idea as yet that he was a famous poet. She first fell in love with the man himself. The revelation of his poetry came later: God's gifts were too bountiful.

I look at him so intently that sooner or later he is bound to raise his eyes and discover me sitting there next to the window, my sewing needle flashing in and out. It had happened: the poet had looked up toward the third-floor balconies of the building opposite and spied the girl smilingly staring at him. He had stopped and watched her for a moment, trying to catch a clear glimpse of her from so far away.

In his hand the little glass of cassis. He slowly set it down on the table. Then he turned away to go on with his conversation with his friend. The woman on the balcony must be young and pretty.

He didn't come every day, nor did he always come on the same day of the week. She sat waiting for him next to the window, nervous, distracted from her work, the needle pricking her finger. One afternoon as he got up to leave, the indifferent onlooker cast one last glance at the atelier, perhaps by chance, who knows? Rosa waved goodbye to him, smiling, and he waved back. The following day, growing bolder, Rosa threw him a kiss with the tips of her fingers. A proper young girl, she wore almost no makeup or any sort of finery; she had just turned eighteen and had never had a serious sweetheart. He was the one who kindled the fire that consumed her, leaving her dazed. From a distance, like a bolt of lightning that falls on the forest and sets it ablaze.

Suddenly an entire week went by without his appearing. It was just after she had received some extra money from doing sewing that she'd taken home with her to finish, and she bought his book. Madame Picq, the dressmaker, on discovering the object of her apprentice's glances, had told her who Bruno was: "Un poète célèbre, ma petite. Toutes les femmes veulent se coucher avec lui."

Rosa saw the volume in the window of the nearby book-store, a re-edition of *The Dancer and the Flower*, asked the price, and worked twice as hard. At public school she had not been an outstanding student. Now, with no effort, she learned entire poems by heart, repeated whole stanzas, and translated Madame Picq's phrase: ". . . Every woman wants to sleep with him." Oh dear! Rosa thought of nothing else, and on reading the verses discovered that the handsome cavalier was a devil-may-care troubadour, an incurable bohemian, a divine lover. In order to be worthy of him, she broke the bonds that held her fast within the limits of routine, and the well-behaved, docile suburban girl turned into a self-confident, brazen vamp.

When Bruno appeared again and raised his eyes to the distant balcony, Rosa signaled to him and bounded down the stairs, waving the book in her hand. She arrived at the bottom all out of breath, and found herself face to face with the poet, who was not only surprised but open-mouthed with amazement: he had not dreamed that she was so beautiful. He was pleased every time he talked with a reader of his from the popular classes; he was proud of the fact that his poetry was known and loved not only by a snobbish elite but also by simple people such as this charming seamstress. An adorable little angel.

He was alone at the table; his friend had not yet arrived. He invited her to sit down, to have something to drink, tea or a fruit cordial; he was sipping his invariable cassis, a habit acquired in the bistros of Saint-Germain-des-Prés. The girl refused, looking straight at him. "My name is Rosa Meireles da Encarnação, but just put Rosa." Bruno took his pen and began to write in that hand of his that was almost calligraphy.

"To Rosa . . ." He stopped writing, and asked her jokingly: "With what?"

"With a kiss."

Bruno smiled in amusement. Rosa's eyes followed his

carefully manicured hand across the white page as it traced those perfect lines. Everything about him was perfect. His voice was warm, affectionate:

"Why won't you sit down?"

"Not here," she heard herself say.

"Where, then?" he asked, half in surprise and half in jest.

"Wherever you like."

"And when would that be possible?" Still more or less jokingly, but intrigued nonetheless.

"Today, if you like. I leave the workshop at six."

A very young girl, in a dress she'd made herself at home, simple but attractive, a pattern she'd invented herself. She was young enough to be his daughter, and she was obviously poor. She suited the poet's tastes, yet he did not feel he had the right to profit from the situation, to take advantage of the sentiments of the young girl who had found his verses moving. If she were older, or a high-society debutante, he would not have hesitated. But she was only a naïve youngster, at his mercy, an apprentice dressmaker obliged to earn her daily bread. Splendid mixed blood; too bad circumstances made her untouchable. There were plenty of equally beautiful women in elegant salons—rich and idle women.

"I can't today, darling, I've a dinner engagement," he said apologetically.

"Tomorrow then. At whatever time you like. I get off at six, but I can miss work. Tomorrow, all right?" The sparkling green eyes, the parted lips, the straight black hair, everything about her demanding a time and a place.

Bruno was no longer amused. He had never seen, in the world in which he had lived and loved, such boldness, so determined a young lady. He gave in. Why not, since she had offered herself? There would always be time to back out.

"All right then, tomorrow. When you get off work at six, I'll be waiting for you at the door of the bookstore."

He handed her back the autographed volume. Rosa wanted one more thing:

"May I return the kiss?" Her full lips burned the poet's Arab face. There were ties of kinship between the two of them. Those linking Africa and the Middle East.

Remembering the scene now, Rosa asked herself: What image was the real one? The bold vamp who had been born of passion or the girl she had been before that, reserved and serious? It was funny: Afrânio Portela had recreated in his story the Rosa of before, the innocent, quiet, modest young girl from the suburban whistle stop of Madureira.

She was the first to utter the word *love*. She was obliged to seduce him, since the conquistador who had had countless love-affairs, the libertine Don Juan, taking her to be an ingenuous, romantic adolescent who had fallen under the spell of poetry, had been perplexed, not knowing how to go about things in such a way as not to disillusion her or hurt her or cause her irreparable harm, ruining her future, making her unhappy. He took her for walks, to discreet restaurants to eat choice dishes, he showed her the most charming corners of the city, he gave her books— his own and those of other poets—he brought her roses, he murmured verses in her ear beneath the trees in the Botanical Garden on a petty-bourgeois Sunday that could have been a picture-postcard, he kissed her fingers with the needle-pricks, her dark face, her green eyes, and confessed to Mestre Afrânio that he was having a ludicrous and sensational romance, different from all the others that he had had before, a platonic love, made up of poetry and chastity.

But Rosa was a fire already set to blazing, and even though she loved Bruno's every word, every gesture, his least little caress, his fingers lightly touching her hair, his lips brushing the nape of her neck, she was not content with so little. She offered him her mouth, and the poet rediscovered what kisses were—perhaps because he had always taken the initiative before, whereas now it was she who kissed him. Rosa had made up her mind to be his woman, not just a mistress.

Unable to bear any longer the limits he imposed out of kindness and prudence, Rosa asked him to take her to see the house in Santa Alexandrina, which had been photographed in a recent article about him in the *Revista dos Sábados:* the walls covered with paintings, the exotic objects he had brought back from his travels, the angel hanging from the beams of the ceiling, the creepers climbing up the façade of the house, the rose garden, and the poet lazing on a step of the rustic staircase at the entrance.

"Aren't you afraid?"

"Just eager."

They crossed the garden hand in hand, he invented verses ("the snails and lizards salute you"), he tried to get her to sit down in the living room in order to explain a surrealist painting to her; but she had come with her mind made up, and headed for the bedroom—there would be time for paintings later.

Surely—he thought when Rosa took him by the hand and the two of them tumbled onto the bed together—oh surely she's already slept with other men and I'm just an old fool dreaming of virginities and virtues. He was mistaken once again: Rosa was a virgin, and she possessed among many other virtues those of courage and integrity.

A dazzled faun, the poet went down into the garden that surrounded and hid the house and picked all the roses, a great armful. A statue of copper, stretched out naked on the recently-stained whiteness of the sheet, Rosa appeared to be praying, thanking God. António Bruno plucked the petals from the roses and dropped them one by one on the body that surpassed everything he had imagined.

Perhaps Bruno never managed to understand her, to accept her entirely. The love that Rosa gave him (and that he returned), at once passionate and sweet—"There isn't a sweeter creature in this world," Mestre Afrânio said when he came to know her—totally lacking in any petty self-interest, left him with a gnawing sense of guilt. The fact that Rosa never asked him for anything did not change reality: she was still a poor, humble little seamstress, a naïve adolescent, destined before she met him for marriage, children, a home, a quiet and decent life. By making her his mistress, changing her destiny, he had become the one responsible for the uncertain future that awaited her in her dishonor.

On the day when, after several months had gone by, he looked at another woman and desired her, he felt obliged to offer to marry Rosa so as not to leave her lost and forsaken.

Rosa refused his proposal. As transparent as water, a man incapable of shams or subterfuges, Bruno could hide nothing from her. Rosa knew, without asking a single question, why he had proposed to her, and answered no. "I was your woman, and that's enough for me. You weren't meant to have a wife; you'd be a bad husband." Before that almost imperceptible shadow of boredom turned into indifference and the time of lies began, she left. She went out of Bruno's life as she had entered it, without explanation.

Even after they had separated, he continued to send her roses on each anniversary of their first meeting, each anniversary of his unexpected possession of her in the bed covered with rose petals and stained with blood, each anniversary of the last night, so sweet and passionate, so perfect and so equally unexpected. It was for Rosa that he wrote the oddest and most extraordinary, the most abstract of his poems, the series he entitled *The Ethiopian of the Amazon*: "Everything about you was a dark miracle."

Neither a sole candidate nor a unanimous election. Lisandro Leite worriedly scratched his head, buried his fingers in his lion's mane: how would the colonel react when he found out that the two most pleasing prospects held out before him recently by his enthusiastic campaign manager had come to nothing? In his eagerness to be the principal, if not the only, beneficiary of the victory of the influential bigwig, the jurist had refused to share the responsibilities of Sampaio Pereira's campaign, taking care of all the details himself. As a result, he alone would be obliged to suffer all the consequences of the fact that his optimistic initial predictions had failed to come true. That confounded Portela! While Lisandro was neutralizing Rector Raul Limeira, persuading him to wait for the next chair to fall vacant—something that could happen at any moment: Pérsio no longer left his house, the doctors had decided not even to operate on him; the cancer in his lung had metastasized and was now incurable—that devil of a Portela had dug up a general, the author of several books and a real go-getter with the constitution of an athlete. He had been running from one Immortal to the next, determined to get the courtesy visits over with as soon as possible.

"A redoubtable adversary in court": the jurist deserved the reputation he had acquired. He searched for and found a convincing argument to prove that the existence of another candidate was a development that had a definitely positive side to it. He put his theory before Colonel Agnaldo Sampaio Pereira on the latter's return from his trip to the south, where he had crushed base enemies of the Fatherland—in other words, enemies of the dictatorship and of the Führer.

Battle must be joined on every front. Perfidious enemies had also infiltrated the Illustrious Company. They had encouraged General Waldomiro Moreira to present himself as a candidate in order to give the Academicians a choice, thinking that they could thereby make inroads in the overwhelming vote for his dear friend. Utter nonsense, since they would not manage to make the slightest dent in the colonel's solid position, to threaten his election. On the contrary, their plot would backfire; not only would they fail to achieve their aim, but with the registration of the new candidate the colonel's most stubborn adversaries, such as Afrânio Portela, Evandro Nunes dos Santos, and R. Figueiredo Jr., would not be tempted to cast blank ballots. By voting for one of the two contenders, the Immortal gives proof of a mere preference, whereas a blank ballot signifies out-and-out personal aversion, an insulting rejection. The danger of humiliating blank ballots being cast had disappeared.

"Coming from the enemy, that's not humiliating; it's flattering," the colonel retorted, taking issue with Lisandro, displeased at the latter's news and not at all convinced by his explanation.

"Naturally, if you have any way of putting pressure on the general, your comrade-in-arms, to withdraw his candidacy, I for my part will do my best to win some of those Francophiles over to our cause and to persuade the most intolerant of them to abstain rather than cast blank ballots," Lisandro said.

"Put pressure on Moreira? There's no use even trying. He can't stand me. He thinks I had a hand in his being shunted off into the reserves, and, as a matter of fact, he's right. But will anyone really vote for that wretch? A numskull, who had his military column in the *Correio do Rio* politely taken away from him because he was so inept. An insignificant liberaloid. Nothing but a windbag."

"Doubtless. He won't get more than seven or eight votes. Not even ten."

"As many as that?" the colonel frowned.

"We can win two or three of them over. I'm already working on it."

"We must. Eight votes for 'Maginot Line' Moreira? Intolerable. I'm counting on your ability to do what's necessary, Judge."

The colonel was so disappointed that he hadn't even addressed him as Lisandro. The jurist was distressed by the colonel's loss of confidence in him as revealed by his calling him by his title rather than by his first name, but he did not lose heart. He had to find a way of regaining the colonel's trust and getting back on intimate terms with him.

"Leave it to me. I'll spare no effort. I'm an old hand at this and know what to say to each one of them. Now, if you agree, we'll try to set up a schedule for the first visits. To tell you the truth, your trip caused us to lose precious time, and we must now make up for it, my dear Agnaldo."

"You're right, let's go to it, Lisandro my friend."

The justice breathes easily again, opens his briefcase, takes out of it two lists with the names and addresses of and pertinent information concerning the Academicians, and hands one of them to the former sole candidate.

"Prepare to attack, Colonel!"

■ AN ORDER OF THE DAY

Annoyed at the news of General Waldomiro Moreira's candidacy, Colonel Sampaio Pereira became even more irritated in the course of his first five visits to various Academicians. For a candidate who had begun his campaign without an opponent and with the prospect of a unanimous election, the overall picture of the battle now looked dim and nebulous. He did not fear defeat; victory appeared to be assured, but it was not going to be the joyous march to glory to the thundering applause of the Immortals that he had envisioned. From all indications, the vindictive Maginot Line Moreira would receive more than ten votes. The figure might even be as high as twelve or fifteen. He needed to have a serious discussion with

Lisandro, to decide on a new plan of action, to launch an offensive that would rout the enemy once and for all. From what he had heard, Moreira, that insolent braggart, had already been going about proclaiming victory.

Of the five Academicians the colonel had visited, two of them had assured him of their unconditional support, to which one had added precious and precise information.

Following Lisandro's advice and leaving his overzealous young bodyguards (handpicked from members of the Special Police) in cars parked on the street, the colonel, in uniform to emphasize the military nature of his candidacy, after offering the customary polite formulas and compliments, had delivered his speech, just as General Moreira had done. Their two speeches had points in common (as well as perceptible differences in form, since one of them had been influenced by Afrânio Portela and the other by Lisandro Leite). Both of them set forth their identical literary and military status, both of them writers and both high-ranking officers competing for a chair traditionally occupied by representatives of the Army. Sampaio Pereira added that he had presented his candidacy at the behest of his comrades-in-arms, headed by the war minister, to whose authority he, a field officer in the regular Army, was subject. He reminded them, finally, of a secondary, though important, detail with regard to any candidate aspiring to deliver the formal encomium of a lyric poet in the course of his acceptance speech. A political essayist, whose voluminous writings—twelve volumes—qualified him to seek a seat left vacant by the death of António Bruno, he was basically a prose writer, but he was also a poet. The author of a book of Romantic verse, he considered himself "an apt epigonus of my late lamented predecessor."

One of the two Academicians who had assured him of their vote proved to be a warm admirer and a clever schemer. He thanked the colonel for having sent him the twelve volumes of his essays (they had also been sent to all the other Immortals, with carefully chosen auto-graphed dedications, after the colonel had registered as an official candidate), the majority of which he already in fact possessed, being a faithful reader who agreed heartily with the ideas of the eminent thinker. The Aca-demician in question then hinted that the manner in which the colonel's campaign was being conducted did not strike him as being as effective as it might be. Their friend Lisandro, helpful and hardworking, deserving of the highest praise, had nonetheless made a number of mistakes—serious ones!—and neglected important as-pects. He had spent too much of his time worrying about Raul Limeira, who had never had the slightest intention of presenting himself as a candidate, instead of covering the military sector, the really dangerous one. "Who rules our country at present? Answer me that! The military, thank God, who are saving us from anarchy, imposing order, and bringing decency to the country." Hence only another military candidate could take votes away from the distinguished colonel. No, the general wouldn't win, but he was going to draw votes, a certain number of votes, that would have been his, Sampaio Pereira's, if Lisandro had not done his best to monopolize the campaign, leav-ing no place for other admirers of his illustrious candidate who were also eager to work for his resounding victory.

The colonel listened attentively. He respected plotters and informers; he depended on them in his daily fight against subversion.

"The success of my candidacy lies in the hands of all my friends, not just Justice Leite, to whom I am grateful for all he has done but whose abilities, I confess to you in all frankness, I am beginning to doubt. What do you advise me to do, my dear friend?"

"A few notes from the minister sent to various Aca-demicians, and to those known personally to him a tele-phone call. Who can resist a request from the war minister?"

Two other Academicians promised the colonel their vote, and two refused to do so, for the very same reason and almost in the same words: they were sorry, but he had approached them too late. They had already promised their support to another eminent military officer who like himself was a writer—General Waldomiro Moreira. On each of these two occasions, Sampaio Pereira felt as though he had been slapped in the face. He cut these two visits short, visibly irritated, trying his best to control himself so as not to show any signs of coldness or displeasure as he bade the two Academicians goodbye. He made no attempt to conceal his displeasure from Lisandro Leite: the names of those two had not been on the list of the eight who, according to the jurist, were the only ones likely to vote for the insolent Maginot Line Moreira.

In an order of the day, less cordial and affectionate than the judge would have wished, the colonel commanded him to throw the external allies into the fray. To rouse the war minister, the Army chief of staff, various officials; to make promises and, if necessary, to hint at reprisals.

◼ THE DIPLOMAT

Two votes for, two against, and one hinted at but not definite: that of Ambassador Francelino Almeida, the first Academician he had visited, in accordance with tradition.

The aged diplomat had received the colonel with extreme politeness: biscuits and sherry. He had thanked him for the basket of fruit (fortunately, Lisandro had informed the candidate of the step he had taken after the latter's nervous bodyguards had handled the fragile Immortal so roughly), had praised him in the most glowing terms, but had not definitely promised him his vote. On the other hand he had not refused it either, nor had he spoken of a prior commitment of his vote. He had launched into a vague, meandering conversation that might mean either yes or no, thus obliging Sampaio Pereira to come straight to the point:

"I hope I may deserve the honor of your vote."

"You deserve much more than that. You may rest assured that you're already in the Academy; you're certain to be elected. You don't need my vote." He inserted his Turkish cigarette in a long ivory cigarette holder. Such refinements were not at all to the colonel's liking.

Ambiguous language, typical of Itamaraty—who could understand it? In the habit of calling a spade a spade, the colonel felt lost in the face of this frail little man who hopped from one subject to another and got him all confused. Though he had already been visited by Moreira, Francelino didn't once refer to the general or even mention his name. What could this silence mean? The devil only knew. A difficult dialogue, a maddeningly elusive conversational partner, who skirted the real subject and instead praised the sherry and the biscuits, waving his cigarette holder. Interrogations of subversives were much easier and more stimulating; the colonel could demolish their subterfuges with a few clever arguments. Francelino very courteously saw him to the door:

"You can start composing your acceptance speech. Do you have Bruno's books? A master-poet. Crazy about women!" he said, clacking his tongue.

His manner suggested that he was prepared to vote for him, but why hadn't he come right out and said "My vote is yours"? Lisandro tried to calm the colonel, whose feelings had been badly hurt, and personally vouched for the ambassador's loyalty. He always talked that way, in the most ambiguous manner, allowing one only the merest glimpse of his real thoughts, a habit he had acquired in the course of his diplomatic career. But Lisandro had no doubts: at no time had Francelino Almeida ever refused his support to a candidate favored by the state. What reason would he have for voting for General Moreira, who could offer him nothing except the basket of assorted wines and delicacies, sent, moreover, by Afrânio Portela? It was doubtless magnificent, but not enough to make the astute diplomat switch his vote.

Even so, to lay his doubts to rest and following Lisandro's advice, the colonel decided to dispatch immediately to the ambassador's apartment a dozen bottles of champagne (to be charged against the budget for the fight against Communism).

"I know of a very good champagne from São Paulo. The brand name of it is . . ."

Reminded with a wave of nausea of the wine of pure Brazilian stock—*sheer nectar!*—Lisandro vetoed that idea.

"Wherever it's from, São Paulo or anywhere else in Brazil, it's best not to send it. Don't forget that Francelino spent thirty years abroad in the diplomatic corps."

"And so . . . ?"

"It's advisable to send him French champagne."

Colonel Sampaio Pereira shrugged indifferently. The budget for the fight against Communism was practically unlimited:

"Choose the brand yourself. Those are the sort of refinements that lead to decadence and cause the race to degenerate."

A MEETING OF THE GENERAL STAFF BEFORE LUNCH

The alarm was sounded by Henrique Andrade. A liberal politician by vocation and by family tradition—his father had been a state governor, a senator, and a minister—on holiday despite himself due to the dissolution of the federal legislature, enjoying a lofty literary reputation, the author of the biography of the Baron of Rio Branco was one of the Academicians who would not vote for Colonel Sampaio Pereira under any circumstances. He had been a member of the committee that had invited General Moreira to present himself as a candidate, comporting himself at the meeting with characteristic prudence, eloquent in his appeal to the general and sparing of his praises of him. Possessed of countless connections, even among his adversaries he had the reputation of being one of the best-informed men in the country, capable of distinguishing between the true facts and the rumors that were the common currency of the day. There were people who swore that even at this early date Andrade was conspiring against the New State, in collusion with conservatives, liberals, and leftists. A native son of the same state as Afrânio Portela and a devoted friend of his (Afrânio had been of great help to him when he had been competing for a vacant seat in the Academy, against two other strong candidates), Andrade had phoned Afrânio to propose a meeting of the general staff of the resistance in order to pool their information and analyze the difficult state of affairs confronting them. Dona Rosarinho, who was most interested in participating in the plot, organized a Sunday lunch in the mansion at the Praia do Flamengo—a typical Bahia repast of Afro-Brazilian dishes in honor of the author of the *Life of Ruy Barbosa*—to which only the men were invited. If their wives had come, Dona Rosarinho would have been obligated to keep them company in the living room after lunch and would thus not have been in on the latest news of the election.

Even Evandro Nunes dos Santos, the perennial optimist, appeared to be worried. Lisandro Leite had taken it upon himself to drop in on the Academicians before the colonel's visits to them, bearing letters from the war minister and other military and civil authorities in support of Sampaio Pereira's candidacy. And in addition to Lisandro, two other scoundrels, the scum of the earth—the elderly essayist frequently abandoned Academic language when referring to his adversaries—had taken on the same task. They had obtained certain positive results: Marcondes's vote, pledged to Moreira thanks to Evandro's efforts, would now be going to the colonel. Marcondes had received an impossible request—a request? an order, a threat!—from the minister of agriculture, in whose department he had been given a seat, with a fat salary, on a vague and folkloric Commission for the Development of Goat Husbandry. More or less against his will the minister had informed Marcondes, his good friend and efficient collaborator, that if he were still determined to vote for the general, an uncompromising enemy of the regime, such an attitude would be regarded as a hostile act against the government. In such a case, the minister would not be in a position to keep him on as a special advisor of the commission to whose effectiveness he had contributed so much (by his absence, no doubt). Thus backed into a corner, Marcondes had capitulated; he could not let this hircine windfall go by the wayside. He was nonetheless honest enough to come to Evandro to set forth his reasons for backtracking.

"The government has decided to regard Sampaio Pereira's election as a closed question," Henrique Andrade explained. "The New State cannot permit any opposition; it wants to control everything. The Academy is no exception, precisely because of the prestige it enjoys and the repercussions caused each time a new Academician is chosen. Do you know how many requests Bayma received to back Pereira in less than a month? Five . . ."

The colonel and his lieutenants had moved heaven and earth. Just the evening before, in the Bishop's Palace, Andrade had heard the cardinal himself describe the visit paid him by Lisandro in an attempt to persuade him to use his influence with certain Academicians, those most loyal to the Church. The prelate had refused to collaborate—not that he held Colonel Agnaldo directly responsible for the torture of political prisoners, for the invasion of private homes in the dead of night, the raids on public and private libraries, the book-burnings in public squares, the endless series of brutal repressions. Only the night before, he had received a message from the Archbishop of Recife and Olinda, informing him of most unfortunate events that had taken place in Pernambuco. This being the case, he had chosen to keep his distance from the Academic dispute and not bring his religious authority to bear. According to Henrique Andrade, the minister of foreign affairs was also unwilling to take part in the blitz-krieg. The chancellor, as was common knowledge, had disapproved of the violence of the security forces and detested Colonel Sampaio Pereira, who had bugged the office and home phones of the minister. The minister, moreover, had submitted his resignation in protest against the government's policy of rapprochement with the Axis powers.

"Fortunately, General Moreira is not a man who will back down. On the other hand, what a third-rate pen-pusher you've turned up for us, my dear Rodrigo . . . ," Andrade concluded.

"Find me somebody better if you can. His books aren't works of genius, I grant you, but he's a good solid sort. He's got guts and lots of good points in his favor."

"The best point in favor of our ineffable general is his daughter," R. Figueiredo Jr. opined. "If Dona Rosarinho will allow it, I think the young lady could be of great help to us, providing she's willing to lend a hand. She's per-fectly charming, and gives every appearance of being most generous with her favors."

"Don't be rude, Figueiredo," the mistress of the house interrupted. "Leave the girl alone. Third-rate pen-pusher or not, the general is our candidate, and I didn't invite you to come here to malign him. What I want to know is what you're going to do to defeat that . . ."—she could never find the right word to describe Colonel Sampaio Pereira, and had to borrow it from the vocabulary of her old friend Evandro.

"What are we going to do? Dreadful things!" Mestre Portela announced.

In the face of the threatening prospect confronting them,

when in this second phase of the Battle of the Petit Trianon the adversary seemed to have all the advantages, Afrânio Portela proclaimed that it was necessary to use every possible weapon at their disposal, from well-founded accusations to sexual subornation. Figueiredo Jr.'s proposal had merit. He, Portela, had already . . . thought of it. Except that they would use more capable, experienced, and less preoccupied feminine collaborators than the general's daughter, who was all involved in a grand passion at the moment.

"How do you happen to know so much about the girl's private life, Afrânio?" Dona Rosarinho asked in amazement.

"My Secret Service. . . . I must be up on everything concerning the candidate and his family. You can't imagine the things I know. . . ."

The time had come to abandon all scruples, for it would be shameful, immoral, degrading, insulting to award a seat in the Brazilian Academy of Letters to a Nazi, to a man who was a party to, if not directly responsible for, the public burning of books, the bringing of Gestapo experts into the country to train the national police in methods of torturing political prisoners. They had to defeat him, by any and every possible means, in order to prove that decency still existed in the country, that the Academy had remained independent and honorable. All this was no joke: freedom and men's lives were at stake.

Evandro, who was about to go off on a trip to Recife, where he was scheduled to deliver a lecture at the law school, wanted to know what events in Pernambuco the cardinal had been referring to.

"I've heard talk of arrests, of the banning of a theatrical performance," Henrique Andrade informed him. "But I don't know any of the details. Nor do I know whether Sampaio Pereira had anything to do with what happened. Evandro can make inquiries on the spot and enlighten us."

The meeting of the general staff, with its exchanges of opinions and its resolutions, took place before lunch. After the *vatapa*, the *caruru*, the *efo*, the *frigideiras* and the *moquecas*, it would have been impossible. The resistance commandos were busy digesting.

✠ THE EVENTS IN PERNAMBUCO

With the exception of the dramatist Aristeu Arabóia's proclamation broadcast over Radio Olinda and the edition of the *Luzeiro de Caruaru* that was seized, the events in Pernambuco had no repercussions in the country's spoken and written media. Despite the cultural importance of the signers of the manifesto, or because of it, the censors banned not only its publication and distribution but also any reference to the events that had brought it about. The weekly of the city of Caruaru was so modest in size and circulation that the functionary on duty at the DIP (the state Press and Propaganda Department) had neglected to notify the editors that the manifesto had been banned, and hence the *Luzeiro* prides itself even today on having been the only newspaper to publish the protest by the intellectuals, and on the front page at that, since one of the signers of it was the publisher and editorial director of the paper, the folklore specialist João Condé. The editor was seized and the functionary officially warned. If the *Luzeiro* repeated its offense, it would be permanently stricken from the list of permitted publications; if the functionary repeated his error, he would become the victim of the implacable Article 177 of the new constitution, whereby any civil servant, without exception, could be summarily retired or dismissed, for reasons of national interest.

It all began when Lieutenant Alírio Bastos, known as "Bulldog," and soldiers from the military police destroyed the shack in which a puppet show was being held, on the outskirts of the city of Recife, in a poor district inhabited by both working-class people and peasants. The little popular play told the story of the trials and tribulations of a family of poor half-breed wretches whose life was made miserable by the greed and lust of a rich and depraved owner of a sugar refinery, the lord and master of a huge landed estate who was aided in his evil designs by the militia and by the Devil. The militiamen forced Joãozinho Bloated-Belly, the head of the family, to work far into the night cutting cane, while Satan did his best to make pretty Chica, Joãozinho's decent wife, fall into the arms of the lascivious landowner. With the appetites of starvelings and iron stomachs, the little swollen-bellied children of the couple staved off their hunger by eating lumps of dirt. Joãozinho, Chica, and the little urchins could count only on the protection of the Virgin and the cunning of the cane-cutter.

Though the refinery owner was possessed of a far greater fortune and a great deal more power, the unlettered author of the play had cleverly shaped his plot in such a way that it was Joãozinho who won in the end. As crafty as they come, Joãozinho tricked the militiamen and was granted a great miracle by the Virgin, his patroness and protectress: the concupiscent owner of the sugar mill contracted an incurable venereal disease and was left impotent; the soldiers, real machos, began to talk in a simpering lisp and roll their eyes, transformed into definite queers; and Beelzebub, a turncoat by nature, dragged his former allies down into the depths of hell. The miserably poor audience laughed and clapped their hands, discovering hope and art in the burlesque farce and the rustic marionettes. Dozens of other puppet shows were put on, on simple little makeshift stages made of crates and cardboard boxes, in Recife, in the neighboring towns, in sugar mills and factories, offering, for next to nothing, reality, miracles, lessons.

No one ever found out who had denounced them, but Lieutenant Alírio Bastos, Bulldog, famous and feared for his evil temper and known to be a pimp—whores in that wretched neighborhood worked for him—turned up with four of his men, and they knocked the little theater to pieces with their truncheons, thrashed the owner and his assistant, a father and son, and gave the audience a good drubbing as well. The puppeteers were taken to the military barracks and worked over some more there—a severe beating—so as to teach them to respect a uniform. The assistant they thrashed within an inch of his life wasn't yet fifteen.

Let go after a few days in jail, the puppeteers went to complain to Aristeu Arabóia, the author of plays that had been successes both in Brazil and abroad, inspired by the popular farces of the northeast: he lived side by side with mimes, ceramists, poets of the puppet-strings. They told him their story and showed him the marks left by the recent beatings they had received. The writer didn't hesitate; he spoke out immediately on a very popular radio program with a wide audience, sharply criticizing the actions of the military police and Bulldog.

Arabóia's indignant condemnation produced immediate results: Radio Olinda received a warning from the DIP, the program in question was suspended, and throughout the state of Pernambuco, especially in Recife, Olinda, and neighboring towns, the military police unleashed a lightning campaign against puppet shows and puppeteers: little stages bashed to pieces, puppets seized, puppeteers put to flight.

Aristeu Arabóia, a cheeky and obstinate man from the backlands, resolved to brave the storm head-on. He got together with the director of the Amateur Theater of Pernambuco, Waldemar de Oliveira, a figure respected in all circles, and decided to put on a benefit performance for the persecuted puppeteers, bringing to the illustrious stage of the Teatro Santa Isabel the crude puppets and their stories to make an audience laugh and cry, along with a one-act play, *God's Puppet Show*, that Arabóia had written especially for the occasion. The box-office receipts would be turned over to those whose pitiful little stages had been smashed to bits by the Glorious Brigade.

In view of the lofty reputation of these two men of the theater, the local censors hesitated: should they permit the performance or prohibit it? Unable to decide, they solved their dilemma by handing the case over to the federal censors, who in turn brought the subject to the attention of the highest echelons of the National Security apparatus, inasmuch as members of the military had been involved in the affair. The matter ended up in the hands of Colonel Sampaio Pereira, who immediately realized that the puppet show was revolutionary propaganda for international Communism, and that quite obviously the planned benefit performance was of a highly subversive nature. He ordered the censors to forbid it and the DIP to issue yet another decree prohibiting all mention of it in the press and on the radio.

The bureaucratic mills ground extremely slowly, and meanwhile the organizers of the performance went ahead: the house was completely sold out, the date was set, everything was ready. If Rio had not answered, it was because it had found the performance unobjectionable. The head of the state board of censors finally arrived at the same conclusion and gave it his stamp of approval.

Every seat in the Teatro Santa Isabel was filled and the curtain about to go up when the soldiers surrounded the building, bayonets at the ready. The spectators were forcibly ejected, the puppeteers run out of the theater at saber-point. After being taken to local National Security headquarters, Arabóia and the director of the Amateur Theater finally learned, after much argument, that the chief of police had been carrying out an order from Rio, issued by Colonel Sampaio Pereira. By him personally. The order, moreover, specified that those responsible for the performance were to be dealt with in accordance with the National Security Law if they offered the slightest resistance. They should consider themselves lucky to have escaped being tried in court. What they did not escape was being given an official police record, being photographed with a number on their chest, and being fingerprinted.

These Pernambuco intellectuals proved to be stubborn cases. Far from admitting defeat, Arabóia, with the collaboration of other suspects, drew up a manifesto addressed to the entire nation, signed by writers, artists, musicians, theatrical performers, university professors, people of the most varied political and religious persuasions, ranging from a renowned sociologist, the glory of the nation, to the author of a widely praised book on Eça de Queiroz, a notorious Communist. The manifesto, describing in detail the acts of violence unleashed against the puppeteers and the theatrical personalities who had supported them, mentioned only two names: that of Lieutenant Alírio Bastos, the Bulldog of the Glorious Brigade and a well-known panderer, and that of Colonel Agnaldo Sampaio Pereira, a tyrannical government official.

Although the manifesto had seen print only in the *Luzeiro de Caruaru*, it was widely circulated in secret. A number of the signers were arrested; the authority on Eça de Queiroz had a bag already packed with his toothbrush and his pajamas, since they'd come to haul him off to jail so many times before. Private houses were searched, books seized, an inquiry opened. The walls of the manor house inhabited by the master of Brazilian studies, a scholar whose renown had spread to the United States and Europe, were defaced, daubed with the crudest insults imaginable, aimed at the man whom many people regarded as the highest expression of Brazilian culture; the one figure comparable to him was the nuclear physicist Pérsio Menezes, another genuine national glory.

After delivering his lecture at the law school, Evandro Nunes dos Santos had been invited to lunch by the sociologist, who apprised him of the events that had taken place in Recife. Evandro was indignant on learning of the insulting graffiti scrawled on the walls of the sociologist's house, and secured a mimeographed copy of the manifesto, in which he found the name of Colonel Sampaio Pereira, an Academy candidate, mentioned. When he returned to Rio he had more copies made, which were distributed to the Academicians on Thursday, the day of the week on which their meetings were held, following a tea.

THE CAMP FOLLOWER

Maria João puts the last finishing touches on her makeup before starting to get dressed to go on stage:

"I was a real devil. . . ."

" 'I *was*,' you say?" A smile of affectionate irony appears on Mestre Portela's lips.

"I tormented him so one night, by making him jealous, by recalling certain things, by hinting at others, by letting names slip out, that Bruno all of a sudden slapped me in the face."

"You must have gone a long way to get Bruno that upset."

"Too far. . . . He gave me that slap when I told him he had a vocation for being a compliant cuckold. I went on from there to outright name-calling: a spineless deceived lover, a meek billy goat easy to cheat on, a dish-mop. He, poor dear, was sorry he'd cuffed me and was trying his best to control himself. But when I screamed at him in French, 'Cocu, roi des cocus!' António grabbed me, and what a thrashing I got! I couldn't say at what point the blows turned into caresses; it was a glorious night. Dawn found us swearing to love each other forever. The next day I was red all over from my poet's hands and mouth."

She rises to her feet, her half-open dressing gown revealing her beautiful firm breasts; she has never worn a bra. She begins to put on her costume for her role as Hedda

Gabler. Ibsen's play, in a translation by R. Figueiredo Jr., had opened two weeks before.

"For Bruno, Mestre Afrânio, I'd be capable of selling myself to the Devil—or to Barreto the Creep, which would be much worse."

Known in theatrical circles as "The Creep," old Stênio Barreto, a filthy-rich businessman, collected actresses, paying a stiff price for them. He had feathered the nest of an impressive number of them, both Brazilians and Portuguese. Maria João had turned down all his propositions, out of sheer contrariness or in the hope that he would raise his offer to unimaginable heights—who knows? As a matter of fact, The Creep had gone so far as to offer her a five-room apartment in Copacabana if she would spend a weekend with him in Petrópolis.

Mestre Afrânio hands her the list of Academicians:

"The names marked with an *X* are ours: their votes are certain. The ones marked with an *N* belong to the enemy: they can't be budged. The ones that are unmarked are still undecided. Among these latter, by making a great many promises and granting just a few intimate favors, how many votes can you deliver for General Moreira?"

Half Hedda Gabler and half naked (she was worth a five-room apartment, and the price was cheap at that, he decided, with the eye of a connoisseur), Maria João studied the list of names:

"I can guarantee you two. No, wait. Three. Too bad that Rodrigo's already on our side. I'd enjoy taking up with him again. Our affair was all too brief."

"He's ours, no question about it. So much so that he's keeping Moreira's dotty daughter occupied full-time, thereby preventing her from working for her father. That's how these great aristocrats are, Joãozinha, terribly selfish. What three do you have in mind?"

Knocks on the door of the dressing-room; Dona Maria João is to go on stage in five minutes. Finishing dressing, she points to the names with the tragic finger of Hedda Gabler, heading for the dense fogs of Scandinavia.

"These three here . . . Paiva, that old dear, is marked with an *N*, he's in the other camp, but if I ask him nicely . . . Don't you want his vote?"

"Of course, but even though I know you're irresistible, I doubt that you'd get it."

"Do you want to bet?" She bites her finger. "That sweet little old man's a lamb, he eats out of my hand, he'll do anything for me."

"You're a real devil."

"This whole thing is going to be a sidesplitting farce."

The merry laughter of a child—who would ever believe that she is forty years old? Love is the very best tonic there is, Mestre Afrânio thinks as Hedda Gabler majestically goes out of the door of her dressing-room to make her entrance on stage. Not only does she still have the slim, svelte body of a young woman, but, more impressive still, she radiates an irrepressible *joie de vivre*.

THE GREAT ACTRESS

The election of the Queen of Mid-Lent took place at the Teatro São José. In addition to the poet António Bruno, the jury was composed of the president of the carnival association that went by the name of "The Devil's Lieutenants," the impresario Segreto, Jota Efegê, a newspaper columnist whose specialty was carnival festivities and associations and popular dance-halls, and the star of the Brazilian theater of that day, Itália Fausta, at the height of her fame.

As he approached his thirty-fifth birthday, António Bruno too was at the height of his glory. The success of his first book had been repeated on a greater scale when three other volumes of his work appeared: *The Ugne Sonnets* and *The Barcarole of the Antónios*, both of them poetry, and an anthology of little essays that had previously been published in newspapers. Hailed enthusiastically by the majority of critics: "A major young poet, an incomparable master of the sonnet," "A lyric bard who has brought new life to the art of song and lyric poetry," "Birds, trees, women, and love have been reinvented by António Bruno in verse that is at once spontaneous and deeply felt," "Little journalistic essays that are poems celebrating the everyday," and so on. There was no lack either of harsh attacks on the poems and newspaper pieces: "Saccharine and repetitive," "Heedless of the new directions being taken by poetry," "Sentimentality for ladies' maids," in the opinion of pedants and of critics consumed with jealousy at someone else's success. In addition to all this immoderate attention, Bruno's books also won him a most faithful audience and went through many editions. His poems were recited on stage by famous stars at benefit performances, by students at literary soirées, and by female admirers at festive family gatherings.

To augment the meager salary he earned as an editor at the ministry of justice, Bruno engaged in a number of other activities: he gave lectures in clubs and salons, wrote articles for newspapers and magazines, composed numbers for musical reviews, the lyrics of songs. An unknown composer barely twenty years old, Heckel Tavares, asked him to write some verses for a melody that he had just written: there thus was born "Corrupião" ("Oriole"), an immortal song in our national repertory. Leopoldo Froes announced that he would soon stage a play by Bruno, a comedy dealing with life in Rio, not yet written. Success for the poet and success for the man, whose "romantic profile of a Bedouin" was reproduced in photographs, drawings, oil paintings, caricatures. Damsels and matrons, adolescents and "Balzacian" women of thirty heaved a sigh on contemplating him in the pages of *Fon-Fon*, his chin resting on his hand, a faraway look in his eye, wild locks à la Mascagni. It was the year 1921; the First Great World War was a thing of the past; the country was preparing to celebrate the Centennial of Independence.

Ah, what a coveted title: Queen of Mid-Lent! In addition to the gilt crown, the velvet mantle, and a ring set with an aquamarine offered by Ouvidor, the jewelers, for the winner it meant above all enormous publicity in the papers, interviews, articles, and the passionate envy of her contemporaries. Hence there were a great many contestants, involved in such a hard-fought campaign one would have thought that it was a Brazilian Academy election. Among those competing were legitimate theater actresses, music-hall stars and chorus girls, and unknown and eager girls from amateur theatrical companies hoping to earn themselves a title so as to become professional actresses and embark upon a fascinating—and poorly paid—stage career. Poorly paid, but with compensations: success, popularity, fame. And to counterbalance their miserable salaries, there were men such as Sténio Barreto and other Creeps, prodigal little old millionaires.

Under pressure from the impresario, three of the other four jurists decided to elect the lively and piquant Margarida Vilar: perfect legs, long red hair, a warm voice, the star of the revue *Misses, Maxixe, and Hot Pepper Stew*, which had had a run of more than a hundred performances. But during the parade of contestants Bruno's eye had fallen on one of the eager unknowns, and it was as though he had been struck by a bolt of lightning. Nothing like that had ever happened to him before: an instantaneous passion, mad, uncontainable. Tall, haughty, elegantly thin, ethereal, so blond and with such pale opalescent skin she seemed translucent: where had he seen her before? In a painting, surely, but in what museum? What Renaissance master had foreseen her and painted her portrait centuries before? A come-hither look, a promise of surrender in her night-dark eyes, in her lips where the mystery of sex begins, in her bold hips and provocative breasts. Bruno felt his mouth grow dry and his stomach contract the moment he laid eyes on her: the *femme fatale*, in the flesh.

They had reached an impasse because of the poet's

dissenting vote, but they were all good friends and affable sorts, and in order to make Margarida Vilar's election unanimous they decided to create the title of Princess of Mid-Lent and award it to the anonymous contestant.

Bruno did not know her; if he had seen her before it had been in a painting or in a dream, and he knew nothing about her: her age, name, profession. On being questioned by the jury, she stated that her name was Lúcia Bertini, from an Italian family, undoubtedly related to the great Francesca Bertini, since she had come from the same village in which that incomparable movie actress had been born; twenty-one years of age (only those who had reached their legal majority were eligible to compete for the title and to participate in the ceremonies of the coronation ball); possessed of some experience in the theater, obtained when she had resided in the town of Campos and been a member of the Fénix, an amateur company. She had come to the contest accompanied by a cousin, a dour individual seated in one of the last rows of the orchestra.

Bruno's interest, and the title he offered her in the name of the jury, left her dazzled. On seeing him come on stage with the other members of the judges' committee, she had immediately recognized him from the photographs of him that had appeared in *Vida Doméstica* and from a caricature of him in *O Malho*, in which the poet, pen in hand, was writing in his meticulous calligraphy the title of a book—what was it exactly? *The Barque? The Barque* of what? *The Barcarole of the Antónios?* That was it, a funny title, what did it mean?

Once the tumultuous deliberations of the jury had ended and the winners had been proclaimed and applauded, Bruno tried to leave with the Princess, in the hope of satisfying, that very night, the hunger that was devouring him. But Her Royal Highness, very chaste and dignified, refused. She had to go home with her cousin:

"My father's very strict. He only allowed me to come if I was escorted by my cousin, and he doesn't know that

I came to be a contestant. If he'd known, he might well have beaten me and locked me in the house."

The two of them agreed to meet the following day, in an ice-cream shop, on the Largo da Carioca. The dishes of spumone (she had a terrible sweet tooth), the whispered words, honeyed words so nice to hear, the poem born of his sudden emotion the night before on first laying eyes on her, the poet's Bedouin handsomeness, his legend won her over completely, leaving her so eager she was panting for breath. She confessed to some of her first lies. She had not lived in Campos, she had never appeared on the stage, her name was not Lúcia Bertini, nor was she of Italian descent; she had borrowed her name and her Italian blood from neighbors. Her real name was Maria João, one chosen by her father, a Portuguese who was dead now.

"A horrible name, don't you think so?"

"There's no more beautiful name in the world. I'm going to call you Joãozinha, whether you like it or not."

She had no will of her own at that point, she wanted anything and everything Bruno wanted, she had never dreamed she would meet him in person, much less be kissed by him in the dark of the Iris theater—kisses as endless as those in the film on the screen—or feel the poet's hands caressing her free breasts underneath her blouse. There thus began that mad passion, amid a furious whirlwind of desire and jealousy, enveloped in a permanent aura of lies, with constant scenes and all sorts of outrageous behavior in public. Their affair lasted nearly two years, and during all that time Bruno never managed to separate reality from sheer fabrication, to make out the precise boundaries between appearances and truth.

The cousin wasn't her cousin at all, but rather a clerk in the grocery store left the family in his will by her Portuguese father and run by his brother and partner. It brought in very little money and it was all that she, her mother, and her younger sister had to live on; when it came to dividing the profits, their brother-in-law and uncle had applied his own arithmetical rules. As for her age, she gradually proved to be younger and younger, till finally she turned out to be just over seventeen. The fake cousin had been the second man to possess her, preceded by a real cousin, a boy of fifteen, younger than she was. Once he had had her, the youngster wanted them to get married; can you imagine! She told her whole story in abundant detail, without the slightest modesty, and talked endlessly. When she had nothing left to tell, she made up stories.

At the Grand Coronation Ball held in the hall belonging to "The Devil's Lieutenants," she had created her first scandal. After being proclaimed and crowned Princess of Mid-Lent (a smaller crown than the Queen's, a bright satin mantle rather than the Queen's regal heavy velvet one, and only a small turquoise ring offered by the aforementioned Ouvidor Jewelers), she had crossed the ballroom floor on António's arm, receiving as great an ovation as the Queen. The poet felt his heart pounding: Maria João had been born for applause and self-exhibition.

"I too have a present for you, my Queen of Sheba, but I'm not going to give it to you either here or now."

Suspended from a heavy chain, a heart-shaped reliquary, a solid gold jewel, Portuguese and very old, that he had discovered in the shop of a reliable antique dealer (he had never lied to a customer) and thief who charged exorbitant prices: in order to buy it Bruno had had to borrow money from Afrânio Portela.

He opened the jewel-box and showed her the splendid piece. Though she knew nothing of the value or quality of jewels, Maria João possessed an innate sense of taste, recognized what a first-rate piece it was, appreciated its beauty, and was certain that it had cost a fortune.

"For me? I can't believe it!"

She wanted to wear it then and there, but he wouldn't let her.

"At my place, when you're naked. I want to place it on your breasts; it's my wedding present to you."

118

"But then nobody's going to see it. . . ."

"I'm going to see it: isn't that enough for you? Just once, you'll wear it only for me. After that, you can show it off wherever you please."

She smiled then and bit her lips, foreseeing the scene. She closed her eyes and they stepped out onto the ballroom floor, an inseparable couple.

"I want a portrait of you to put in the reliquary."

A marvelous dancer, with all the refinements he had learned in Paris cabarets, Bruno found in Maria João a conscientious pupil, able to follow him in the most daring variations. Half furious and half proudly disdainful, she carefully watched the look in other women's eyes as the poet danced by. A number of the more brazen ones dared to smile at him.

During a brief intermission by the jazz band, as the musicians downed steins of beer to quench their thirst, the Princess of Mid-Lent took advantage of the pause to go to the rest room. When she returned, the dancing had begun again and Bruno was whirling about the floor to the rhythm of a fox trot, cheek to cheek with the dazzling Queen Margarida. Her fury getting the better of her lofty disdain, the submissive Princess suddenly turned into a harpy and swooped down on the couple. Before Her Majesty realized what was happening, her royal crown had been snatched from her head and her regal mantle was dragging across the floor, for Maria João had flung herself upon the great music-hall star and grabbed her by the hair—Margarida Vilar was particularly proud of the coppery reflections given off on stage by her bright red locks when the spotlight played on them. They had never gleamed more brightly than on the night of the Coronation Ball.

"Don't make a play for him, you old witch, you shameless hussy. He's mine and nobody else's."

That was very nearly the end of the Mid-Lenten Ball. To get Maria João out of the hall, Bruno had to resort to brute force. She reacted by biting his hand so hard she drew blood:

"Let me go! I don't want to have anything more to do with you. Stay here with that tramp and give your present to her; I'm going home."

They went to his place: the bed of wild excess and lust. The heavy chain around her neck, the reliquary between her breasts, a filigree heart. The translucent opalescent skin, the belly like an expanse of ripe wheat, pure gold, all of her.

A dawn of howling wolves, of bites and love-marks, voracious assaults, close combat. When morning finally came, she said:

"Forgive me, my love, but that's how I am. What's mine is mine alone; I don't share it with anyone. Send me away now, if you like . . ."—she smiled and stretched—"only I won't go, I'm never going to leave here."

He had had and had awakened many passions, but never one this violent and devastating. It lasted nearly two years, and at times he thought he'd go mad. Maria João was the only woman he ever beat, and he did so in a raging fury. The sentiment that dominated all the rest, jealousy poisoned their idyll. An insane jealousy that she felt and made a show of at any and all times and places. A jealousy on Bruno's part that she deliberately provoked to test his love for her. Repeated rows that grew more and more frequent, becoming a daily occurrence; storms that ended in the furious assault of bodies damned to desire.

Maria João made terrible scenes. She could not bear to see him speak or laugh with another woman. At the same time, she would casually mention the names of men, hint at propositions she had received, hide blank pieces of paper to make him think they were compromising letters, notes arranging a love-tryst. And who could count the times she repeated the scandal of the Mid-Lenten Ball?

Bruno's passion burned itself out in jealousy. Two women in the same marvelous body: Maria João, the sweet, affectionate young girl in love; and her antithesis, the intolerant, uncontrollable witch whom he baptized Mary John. Both of them incomparable in bed.

Mary John was the title of the verse play that Bruno finally wrote for Leopoldo Froes's repertory, on the condition that Maria João play the title role. Before that, he had secured for her a few parts, singing and dancing in music-halls, under the name of Lúcia Bertini. Generous, incapable of holding a grudge, Margarida Vilar gave her more than one opportunity, and the two of them became friends. Despite her beauty, her magnificent body, her charm, Maria João lacked certain qualities required for that type of theater; one day, in the depths of despair, Bruno exclaimed:

"You're a born actress, that's what! I'm going to write a play for you, Mary John."

He had not been born a dramatist, but he was a born poet. What saved his play was the verse and the interpretation of the title role by the actress making her debut, creating with extraordinary talent the contradictory figure of the sweet and delightful young Brazilian girl whose head has been turned by American movies, imitating Hollywood poses and mannerisms. António Bruno never again wrote for the legitimate theater, and Maria João never again appeared as Lúcia Bertini in small parts in music-hall reviews on the Praça Tiradentes. A star had been born, a great actress, a new Itália Fausta.

She and Bruno remained friends. On two different occasions they took up their affair where they had left off, but each time it lasted only a short while.

▨ WEAR AND TEAR

Arduous, depressing, exhausting, the electoral campaign was reaching the end of the first stage: the two months allowed for candidates to register. The Battle of the Petit Trianon grew more violent, but no one foresaw its surprising dénouement.

Accustomed to commanding and to being obeyed,

Colonel Agnaldo Sampaio Pereira was irritated to discover that there was both overt and covert resistance to his pretensions to immortality. The triumphal march announced by Lisandro Leite had gradually turned into an obstacle race. Terribly wearing.

During the calvary of the ceremonial visits, forced to be humble and obsequious, he found himself obliged to listen in silence to the same insulting refrain repeated ten times over:

"I'm extremely sorry, Colonel, but I've already pledged my vote to someone else. To a comrade-in-arms of yours, it so happens, another illustrious representative of the Army, General Waldomiro Moreira."

The words differed, the content remained the same: a prior commitment to that beast of a Moreira. He discovered that two Academicians had lied when they stated that they had promised their vote to Maginot Line, since he had not even visited them yet. Clear proof of the opposition to his own name and to what it represented. A slap in the face repeated ten times, a number that spoke volumes and a fact that revealed a grave state of affairs: the tentacles of the country's enemies had reached as far as the Illustrious Company.

Inasmuch as the Brazilian Academy of Letters was an assembly of notables—not only from the literary world but also from other sectors of Brazilian life, from jurisprudence to politics, from the clergy to the armed forces, from diplomacy to medicine, from the sciences to journalism—representing a conservative tradition, the colonel would never have imagined that it could be so profoundly influenced by the diffuse, decadent forces opposed to the triumphant, life-restoring ideals symbolized by those glorious figures, the Führer and the Duce. The Academy was proving to be infested with the rot of liberalism, infiltrated by Communists. He was being accused, he discovered, of belonging to the fifth column. Very well then; he would take the necessary steps to

inject pure and healthy blood into the sick bo
Company, renewing it seat by seat as vacancies of the
The next Immortals would be handpicked.   ed.

It was quite true that fifteen of the Academicians
he had visited had promised to vote for him, and tw
three among them had joined Lisandro in actively ca
paigning for him. Two other members who were not
Rio (one of them was retired and living in Minas, and the
other was the Brazilian ambassador to Mexico), and would
not be able to be present in person on the day of the
election, had sent him their letters to be forwarded to the
Academy; to these he was to append, in a sealed envelope,
their ballots for the four rounds of voting. Moments of
intense pleasure when, on the advice of the jurist, he
himself had typed in on the ballots his full name and
surname, preceded by his military rank. But, everything
considered, he had been forced to swallow all sorts of
affronts and insults—toads and snakes, as the saying went—
in order to assure his victory.

Twenty-five solid votes at this point: fifteen in his
favor, ten against, and fourteen that might go either way.
No, not fourteen—thirteen, since Afrânio Portela, the
instigator of the general's candidacy, was Sampaio Pereira's number-one enemy. A tap placed on the novelist's
phone had revealed how intensely he was campaigning
each and every day among his fellow Academicians in
order to prevent "the Gestapo from entering the Petit
Trianon," his actual words. Along with Lisandro the colonel analyzed, one by one, the thirteen names in exhaustive detail, in a subjective probability calculus. In the
expert opinion of the jurist, all of them, without exception, would vote for his dear friend Agnaldo. But his dear
friend Agnaldo no longer blindly trusted in his dear friend
Lisandro's legendary experience and predictions. The
colonel was so downcast that he even placed old Francelino Almeida in the doubtful column, despite the basket of fruit and the (French) champagne.

irty-nine Academicians, he had only three left
Of the had gone through the prescribed ritual with
to vithers, and it had not always been an easy or a
all task. He had had to make a special trip to São
plo court the vote of Mario Bueno, the poet who had
n the *Book of Psalms*, and another to Belo Hori-
to pin down the vote of the former head of the
o do Brazil—a retired university professor, the au-
of volumes of short stories with very few pages and
en fewer readers, a hemiplegic. He had brought the
ralytic's letter back with him in the pocket of his uni-
orm jacket. The São Paulo poet had accorded him very
little time, but with great courtesy had guaranteed him
his vote, which he would be sending directly to the Academy. Mario Bueno always cordially received all candidates, without exception, and solemnly promised each of
them his vote, telling them in each case that he would
submit it directly to the Academy; it was thus never
discovered which name he had actually voted for. Knowing this, the colonel placed the bard on the list of those
whose votes were in doubt, despite Lisandro's assurances.
The visit to the ambassador to Mexico, Renato Muller
Vieira, was made via Western Union, in a warm and lengthy
cable (the budget for the fight against Communism paid
for such minor expenses: correspondence, travel fares,
hotels, a splendid wedding present for the daughter of one
of his fifteen solid supporters). The colonel received a
most cordial reply and the precious letter for the election
via the diplomatic pouch. Renato Muller Vieira, a poet
and novelist, whom the colonel did not know personally
and whose abstruse books he could not manage to get
through, the idol of the younger generation of academic
critics, proclaimed himself an unconditional admirer of
Sampaio Pereira's: "Your imperishable body of work and
your magnificent example inspire Brazilian youth at the
dawn of the new world that Schopenhauer dreamed of."
An enthusiastic expression of loyalty, compensating for

the hostility and the antipathy shown by certain base Moscow fellow travelers.

Two of the interviews he had were extremely unpleasant, devoid of the slightest civility, depressing. Most discourteously, Evandro Nunes dos Santos had not invited him to his house to receive him, meeting him instead at his publisher's, José Olympio. The elderly essayist heard him out in silence, his face a blank, declared himself a firm supporter of another contender, and held out only his fingertips as he bade him farewell. As for R. Figueiredo Jr., he had had the nerve to ask the colonel straight out his reason for seeking the vacant seat. Knowing the ideology that the colonel embraced and the nature of the functions that he fulfilled within the regime, Figueiredo could not quite understand why he was interested in membership in the Brazilian Academy of Letters. The one direct reference that any of the Academicians had made to his well-known fascist views and to his status as head of the security forces of the nation, the dramatist's spiteful question had stuck in the colonel's throat, as hard to swallow as a monstrous toad. He now had only three visits left to make: to Hermano do Carmo, the president of the Academy, to the illustrious dying Academician Pérsio Menezes, and to the novelist Afrânio Portela.

He would not even have visited the unbearable Portela, a decadent liberaloid and the instigator of Maginot Line's candidacy, had it not been for Lisandro's thoughts on the subject. His failure to call on him would appear to be an act of reprisal. Since the Immortals were extremely sensitive, they might well consider it an intolerable breach of protocol, insulting to all of them. Lisandro's dear friend Agnaldo, though certain to be elected, should not create problems that might reduce the number of votes he received. Moreover Portela—a social parasite, a *bon vivant*—would, unlike Evandro and Figueiredo, be courteous and, who could tell, perhaps even affable.

At the church of La Candelaria at Sunday Mass, Sampaio Pereira had run into Hermano do Carmo, who had agreed to set a date to receive him; he had not yet done so. He was extremely polite and respectful, but had impressed the colonel as being too discreet. A discretion stemming from the very nature of his office, Lisandro had explained: the president of the Academy was obliged to observe the rule that forbade him to divulge his personal choice before the vote was taken. But despite his reserve and his silence, he always made his preference known, in a curious way. How was that? Whereas he received the other contenders in the morning, serving them nothing but a cup of coffee, he invited the candidate for whom he intended to vote to his home for dinner.

Pérsio Menezes, the internationally renowned researcher who had begun his scientific training under the direction of Marie and Pierre Curie and had been one of Einstein's collaborators at the Princeton Institute of Advanced Studies, a professor of Superior and Celestial Mechanics, a member of the Radium Institute at the Sorbonne, a surrealist poet in his spare time, married to the concert pianist Antonieta Novais, had likewise not answered the colonel's request to set a date for a visit. This was due to the state of his health, Lisandro explained. Suffering from an advanced case of cancer, he spent day after day under the effect of drugs to dull his pain and heavy doses of morphine. He had ceased to appear at the Academy several months before, and received only his closest friends. But why then had he received Maginot Line? Because the general had asked to be received by him before the colonel had, and the eminent scientist was punctilious when it came to questions of etiquette. He would receive Lisandro's friend Agnaldo as soon as he felt better; those had been his very words to Lisandro, who had managed to speak to him on the phone the evening before, when he had called to arrange the date. Moreover, Menezes had added a phrase that to all intents and purposes amounted to a declaration in advance of how he planned to vote: "I am determined to receive him," he had said.

Confident of victory, the colonel at the same time felt demoralized, as though he were being slowly drained of all his strength. Resistance, pitfalls, traps, words with double meanings, insults, affronts—all terribly tiring, exhausting. Had he not so eagerly coveted the title, the chair, the Academy regalia, immortality—more eagerly than ever now that the election had turned into a battle without quarter—he would have abandoned the fray, given up: overcome with anxiety, humiliated, his self-confidence badly shaken, his nerves in tatters.

Subversives and suspects paid dearly for the fears and forebodings assailing Colonel Agnaldo Sampaio Pereira. It was on them that he worked off his yearnings for revenge upon the sinister band of conspirators within the Academy who were plotting his defeat, upon those who were refusing him their vote in favor of a good-for-nothing, upon those who were offending him by their coldness, their irony, their aversion, and upon those, the worst of all, who, proclaiming him the victor, already elected, held back, leaving him in doubt, utterly confused, lost amid brilliant, meaningless small talk. Pounding on the desk, shouts, threats, fierce orders to his henchmen—the prisoners who passed through his hands in those days tasted bitter bread kneaded by the Devil, traversed the descending circles of hell.

■ THE COUPLE (AND THE DAUGHTER)

"You're worried, Lisandro. Why?" Dona Mariúcia's calm and pleasant voice asked affectionately.

Everyone was always surprised when Justice Lisandro Leite introduced his wife. He was fat, sweaty, carelessly dressed, an effusively friendly extrovert and at the same time calculating and shrewd, different in every way from his chic, slender wife, meticulously coiffed and made up, still attractive, always coolly smiling and gracious. They had five children: four sons, all with professional degrees—two attorneys, a doctor, an engineer—and all of them married, and a daughter, Pru (Prudência, a name she despised), unmarried, a fourth-year law student, as pretty as her mother and as exuberant and outgoing as her father. A grandmother with seven grandchildren, Dona Mariúcia, elegant and serene, did not look like a woman who very soon would be celebrating her fiftieth birthday.

She got along well with her husband, invariably siding with him even when, in conversations with Pru, she seemed to disagree with his opinions and the positions he had taken. They had traveled a long road together, the first steps of which had been very difficult. Lisandro had had to fight like a lion to ensure that his wife and children did not lack at least the essentials. A passionate husband, a devoted and kindhearted father, concerned about his children's future, he had worked tirelessly, faced hardships boldly and courageously, forgetting ethics and scruples so as to assure his family's well-being and give his children a good start in life. All his sons, thank Heaven and thanks to the maneuvers and diligent efforts of their father, were well established now, and leading settled lives. The only one of his children left at home, still a student and dependent, was Pru. Dependent only in a manner of speaking: she allowed her parents to provide her with food, clothing, and shelter, but her dependence ended there, for as far as all the rest was concerned Pru, rebellious and strong-willed, would not brook the slightest interference from her parents. She was determined to live by herself, on her own, as soon as she could afford to do so, and had begun clerking in a law office, where she did not earn a salary but was gaining experience and fulfilling what she regarded as a duty: the law office specialized in the defense of political prisoners brought before the Tribunal of National Security.

Lisandro sat down at his wife's side:

"It's this confounded election. I thought it would be easy to get Agnaldo elected, but I was mistaken."

He had been grateful to Mariúcia ever since the long-ago days when they had fallen in love. Fat (with hands that were invariably sweaty), hairy, badly shaven, inept at sports, a poor dancer, a young man who had little success with girls, even today he had no idea what had made her say yes when he had proposed to her at his graduation ball. He could scarcely believe that the popular instructress—she was teaching at the time at the local public high school—really wanted to marry him. She had not been prompted by ulterior motives, since Lisandro came from a family even poorer than her own, and in order to pay his expenses at the university he had had to take a job (until he received a scholarship) with a clothing store, dunning customers who hadn't paid their bills; and he managed to collect. He regarded himself as being in debt to his wife all his life.

"Lots of members against him?"

As a general rule, Dona Mariúcia took no interest in the contests for vacant seats in the Academy, despite all the time and hard work that Lisandro devoted to them. She received the candidates cordially when they came to make their traditional visits, and she appeared at the Petit Trianon on solemn ceremonial occasions and at the festive tea just before Christmas, when she socialized with the wives of the other Academicians. Her circle of close friends was made up largely of the wives of magistrates and relatives—her own and those of her daughters-in-law.

"Quite a few, more than I thought. And clever rascals. . . . Afrânio Portela, do you remember him? A man of great distinction. . . ."

"I know, and most likable. I've read some of his novels, and was very much taken with them. *Adélia* is a lovely book."

"Likable, you say? Compared to him, Machiavelli's a mere schoolboy. Do you know what he's done?"

"Tell me." She reached out solicitously for his sweaty hand.

"Not content at having dug up a general to compete

against Agnaldo, he's talked Maria João into helping round up votes for him."

"The actress? And is it working?"

"I need only tell you that Paiva, our dear friend the Supreme Court justice, a sure vote of mine, as docile as a tame ox, is trying to slip the halter. I've never seen such a thing; it's an insult to the Academy."

Dona Mariúcia laughed:

"I could swear that you're up to the same sort of tricks. Is there any danger of your candidate's losing?"

"No. He's going to win."

"Well then, why are you so worried?"

"Because I wanted him to win by unanimous vote. Then that scoundrel of a Portela turns up with a general to ruin the party."

"It's the same old story every time: A terrible battle."

"It's my belief, Mariúcia, that in all of Brazil there's nothing more eagerly coveted than the ceremonial uniform of the Academy. The Academy is the ne plus ultra, there's nothing comparable to it. There are just forty of us, the elect of the gods, the Immortals."

"And you got in there, Lisandro. I was so proud. But was it all that difficult? I don't remember now."

"The circumstances were favorable. I was a kind of compromise candidate, but even so I had to do my share of creeping and crawling. Paiva was a great help to me."

He fell silent, remembering the battle of ten years before. He had been considered the weakest of the three candidates; no one believed that he'd be elected. Ah, the Academy costs blood and sweat! But the uniform cures everything, heals all wounds. He gazed tenderly at his spouse:

"You're the wife of a member of the Brazilian Academy of Letters."

"Many women envy me and don't hide the fact: 'Your husband's an Academician, isn't he? How chic!' It makes me feel as proud as a peacock."

"You should see Agnaldo, Colonel Agnaldo Sampaio Pereira, whose name makes half the world tremble, one of the most powerful figures of the New State, offering cases of French champagne to old Francelino, a retired ambassador without a cent to his name."

"And why is it you're sponsoring that colonel's candidacy? I've read things about him that make my flesh creep. In those papers that Pru brings home, hidden in her purse."

"I've told you before: Pru's involved with Communists. And one of these days she's going to get caught. I don't even want to think about it. Imagine, a daughter of mine in jail! I'm paying for my sins."

The manifesto signed by the intellectuals of Pernambuco, a copy of which Lisandro had found in his drawer at the Academy, had also turned up at home, lying on top of the desk where he reviewed court trials; it had been put there by his daughter to criticize her father's attitude. Pru had also brought home António Bruno's poem on Paris and had written in the margin: *A Nazi cannot succeed the poet of freedom.* The rebel, accusing him! But who was going to get her out of jail if, someday . . . To think what would happen if the colonel suspected . . .

"Let Pru lead her own life, the way I let you lead yours. But explain to me why you're so upset over this candidacy, why you're sponsoring it, if this colonel isn't even your friend?"

"He's the one who gives the orders, Mariúcia. The only ones above him are the war minister and The Man. It's Agnaldo who chooses and nominates. I owe you a great deal, I owe you too much, my darling. You're already the wife of an Academician, and I want you to be the wife of a justice of the Federal Supreme Court as well."

Slender, elegant, still attractive, desirable, Dona Mariúcia laid her head on her husband's shoulder:

"I understand now. You're doing it for me." She offered him her lips.

"Good news, my dear Lisandro."

"Tell me, my dear Agnaldo."

"I've just received a phone call from Carmo. He'll receive me tomorrow."

"The president? Perfect! Anything else?"

"He invited me to dine at his home, along with my wife. He asked me not to divulge the fact."

"Didn't I tell you? A dinner invitation is a guarantee of his vote."

"That's what everyone says, as a matter of fact. I wanted to let you know immediately."

"I'm much obliged. Do you know what day it is tomorrow?"

"Tomorrow? Let me see—Thursday."

"Not just any Thursday. The registration period ends tomorrow. As of Friday, no one else can present himself as a candidate."

"I wonder if the president has already received Maginot Line Moreira."

"I know for certain fact that he hasn't yet received General Moreira." Even when speaking of an adversary, Lisandro didn't dare skip the rank-designation preceding the name of a field officer, much less call him by a disparaging nickname, God forbid. "Keep me informed of all the enemy's maneuvers. The general will have to be content with just a cup of coffee."

"Can we meet day after tomorrow so I can tell you how the dinner went?"

"Certainly. Just set a time. I'm always at your disposal; I'm your orderly, Colonel."

"Supreme Commander, rather, my dear Lisandro."

Federal Supreme Court.

█ AN ANNOUNCEMENT

The meeting having been called to order and the minutes read, on that Thursday exactly two months after the meeting in memory of the poet of the *Ugne Sonnets*, the president announced to the distinguished Academicians present (and ordered that those absent be informed by letter) that the registration period for candidates to the seat "left vacant upon the death of our late lamented comrade António Bruno" was now officially ended. Two writers fulfilling the official requirements had presented themselves as candidates: Colonel Agnaldo Sampaio Pereira and General Waldomiro Moreira, both of whom had had a number of their works published. The election would be held in two months, on the last Thursday in January, 1941, which happened to be the last meeting before the Academy adjourned for its annual recess.

█ THE DINNER

That evening, in their modern house in Urca, the president of the Academy and his wife received Colonel Agnaldo Sampaio Pereira and his wife, Dona Herminia, for dinner. Dona Herminia appeared to be older than her husband, whom she addressed as Sampaio; saying almost nothing, answering in monosyllables when the president's wife attempted to engage her in conversation, she nonetheless spoke up after dinner to praise the various courses that had been served. "Everything very good," she said.

The dinner began quietly, but later on the conversation became very animated. Hermano do Carmo told stories about his life as a journalist. He had begun at the very bottom, as an errand-boy, delivering copy and taking corrected galleys to the print shop, at the *Folha do Comércio*, a publication of which he one day became the owner-publisher. Before being elected president of the Academy, he had been president of the Brazilian Press Association.

Despite the president's effort to avoid controversial subjects, how to keep the conversation from turning to talk of the war? The lady of the house having alluded with admiration to the resistance of the English to the Germans' monstrous aerial bombardments, mentioning the name of Churchill, the colonel was unable to contain himself, and between the marinated raw fish and the roast beef with vegetables he assumed command of the Luft-waffe, wiped London off the map, and then occupied England and clapped Churchill in prison.

Over coffee, they returned to more pleasant subjects; the timid voice of Dona Herminia was heard praising the fish, the meat, and the desserts. Though mad about sweets, she nonetheless could not eat very many of them; she was too fat already. She added an unexpected detail, and Sampaio confirmed the fact: only dogs liked bones.

When the couple had left, the president's wife asked her husband:

"Is he going to be elected?"

"Yes, unfortunately. Luckily, however, I'll no longer be in office when he takes his seat." Half sternly and half smilingly, he said accusingly to the imperious white-haired lady: "You brought up Churchill's name on purpose, didn't you? Troublemaker."

"Why did you invite him to dinner if you're not going to vote for him?"

"I'm not? How do you know?" She too learned how her husband intended to vote only when he informed her of the name of the candidate he'd invited to dinner.

"How do I know? Because it's not possible for a decent man to vote for that bastard of a little Hitler. Did you take a good look at his wife? A woman to him is an inferior being, fit only for fattening up and taking to bed."

"With my vote or without it, he's going to be elected. By an eight- to ten-vote majority, approximately." He put his arm around his wife's waist. "Within the week, next

Tuesday, General Waldomiro Moreira and his wife will be coming to dinner."

"The other candidate? That's a new development! What does it mean?"

"There's no need for you to loot the wine cellar. French wine is expensive and hard to get. Serve the same Chilean wine you did tonight."

The face of the president's wife lit up.

"Ah, I get it," she said with a beaming smile. "If you invite both candidates, it means you're going to cast a blank ballot."

"Soothsayer."

Hand in hand, they went out into the little garden where the jasmine was in flower, perfuming the darkness.

■ COURSES, LECTURES, AND CAMP FOLLOWERS

In 1940, the series of lectures delivered by Academicians, constituting the annual course offered by the Brazilian Academy of Letters on aspects of the nation's literature, dealt with the subject "Poetry in the Abolition and Republican Movements." The audience ordinarily consisted largely of young people, the majority of them students, along with a handful of friends and admirers of the lecturer of the week. The most famous Academicians managed to fill the hall and change the usual makeup of those in attendance, attracting university professors, publishers, writers, booksellers, and society matrons.

From the moment he had registered as a candidate for the seat left vacant by António Bruno, General Waldomiro Moreira had not missed a single lecture. He always sat in the first row, his pad of paper and pen conspicuously in view, taking notes, accompanied by the indefatigable Claudionor Sabença. Having gotten over his bitterness at the general's barefaced phone call, whereby he had let it be known that the Rio Academy of Letters could go to blazes, the infatuated Sabença had gone on to share the dramatic events of the new and glorious candidacy of the author of *Linguistic Prolegomena,* serving as the general's efficient, unpaid secretary. In return he continued to frequent the hospitable house in Grajaú, and carry on his discreet courtship of Cecília, now definitely separated from her husband. Speaking of Cecília, the general's charming daughter enhanced by her presence the lecture on Luiz Gama, delivered by Rodrigo Inácio Filho, applauding with such enthusiasm as to arouse both apprehension and jealousy on the part of the faithful Sabença. He had been placed on her reserve list for the moment, but at the same time his attentions had not been scorned. Cecília was not one to send a suitor packing, even in circumstances such as the present ones, when she was living on intimate terms with immortality in a deluxe bachelor apartment. But such gifts of fate, alas, habitually lasted only a short time. She knew how to awaken a man's interest, make herself desirable, an appetizing conquest, but because she was both dull and peevish she did not contrive to keep the initial flame burning; her impassioned lover very soon became disillusioned, and the idyll soon faded, an ephemeral flower. Unable to bear being alone, she then called upon her reserve supply of suitors. She had lost one of them, the dental surgeon, who had caught her *in flagrante,* kissing Rodrigo in the Immortal's limousine. His prejudices and vulgarity had been amply revealed in one last telephone call—to insult her (to call her by her rightful name, as he had put it) he had used the crudest term imaginable.

Observing the general taking quantities of notes, leading the applause when the speaker delivered himself of his most high-flown turns of phrase, leaping up from his seat as though shot from a gun in order to be the first to congratulate the orator, praising him for his erudition and his syntax, old Francelino Almeida recalled for a group of his colleagues, among them Afrânio Portela and Henrique Andrade, an amusing episode in which he and Lisandro Leite, who at that time was a candidate for an Academy seat with scant chances of victory, had been the principal figures.

It had happened in the days when, on Fridays in the late afternoon, the diplomat had been giving a series of lectures at the Pen Club on classical Japanese culture. A dry subject, a small audience that became even smaller at each lecture. The majority of those who had turned up had been dragged there by Lisandro Leite, who had rounded up students of his who were in danger of failing his course in commercial law and, by holding out the promise of better grades in the next exams, assured the presence and the applause of a good dozen listeners for the discourses of the ex-ambassador to the Celestial Empire on the Kojiki, the Manyo-shu, the *monogataris*, the *nikkis*, and other similar abstruse subjects. At the next-to-last lecture, apart from Lisandro and his blackmailed students, the only people who had appeared were the president of the Pen Club and the doorkeeper, both of whom were obliged to be there as part of their appointed duties. The audience filled only the first two rows of the small auditorium. On the evening preceding the last lecture, the Academy election took place, and Lisandro won on the third ballot, to the astonishment of many of the members. Among those who voted for him was Francelino, who had not been impressed by any of the three candidates, none of whom was outstanding, and had finally decided to cast his vote for this assiduous candidate who had faithfully attended each and every one of his series of lectures. And so it happened that at the very last lecture, the only people in the audience were the president, the doorkeeper, and four mere warm bodies, janitors and custodians of the building, hastily rounded up by the veteran doorkeeper. Lisandro had decided that it was no longer necessary for him to put in an appearance and had passed on the word to his students that they needn't appear either.

"I want to see how this general behaves after the election. If he wins, we'll lose a member of the lecture audience. But he has a number of strong points in his favor, despite the fact that the other candidate is a big wheel in the government. It's going to be a close race, don't you think?"

The group was dispersing, and Francelino Almeida bade them goodbye:

"I'm much obliged to you, my dear Henrique, but I'm not going to ask you to drive me home today. I have an engagement downtown."

"With a lady-friend?" Henrique Andrade asked jokingly.

The old man ignored the question:

"I find this general most likable."

General Moreira's most attractive asset—the reason why the dean of the Academy was finding him more and more likable—a dressmaker by profession, posing as the general's secretary, was at the very moment headed for Cinelândia, where she had a rendezvous at the Brasileira with the ex-ambassador to Japan and Sweden, a charming conversationalist with many stories to tell about certain curious aspects of life in the Orient and in Scandinavia, a most flirtatious gentleman, with hands that trembled slightly but were nonetheless graceful and bold.

"My camp followers are undermining the enemy forces. . . ." Mestre Portela commented as he got into Henrique's car. They were going to dine that evening, with Dona Rosarinho and Dona Julieta Andrade, at the Urca casino, where Carlos Machado's fabulous orchestra, the "Brazilian Serenaders," and the extraordinary young "Grand Othello," a real genius, were appearing.

■ THE INVITATION

This time, in his office and working headquarters, Colonel Agnaldo Sampaio Pereira is not seated on one side of the desk with his enemy opposite him in the trench, being ground to bits. Candidate and sponsor are sitting talking together on the big leather sofa in one corner of the room. On the wall are maps of Europe and Africa, the pins with black heads advancing across the sea toward the British Isles. In Africa, they dominate the desert. This front-line command post smells of war.

"Before you tell me how the dinner went, allow me to pass on a piece of good news to you, my dear friend: Pérsio's secretary telephoned me and asked me to tell you that he's awaiting your visit next Monday at six P.M."

"Where?"

"At his home. He no longer goes to the Institute of Physics, where he ordinarily received his visitors. He lives in Cosme Velho."

"I know. His address is on the list."

"He's going to hand you his vote personally—the most coveted vote in the Academy. I once heard a candidate say that since Pérsio Menezes had voted for him, it mattered little to him that he'd lost the election. Agnaldo, my dear friend, you're going to be the last candidate to receive this consecration from one of the greatest men in the world of science, a genius. Future historians will mark that fact." Lisandro gives the colonel time to contemplate the full significance of the vote of the dying scientist and the historic visit about to take place thanks to his, Lisandro's, diligence. "Now, the dinner . . ."

"Not yet. I too have a piece of news to announce to you, my dear Lisandro." The colonel rises to his feet, martial and solemn; following his example, the jurist too rises to his feet, all excited. A presentiment, a sudden hope: could it be the invitation so eagerly sought? The colonel's emphatic voice sounds celestial to his ears: "I want you, my faithful friend, to be the one to deliver the reception speech for me when I'm admitted into the Academy. And I won't take no for an answer."

"You want me to receive you, my dear friend? You can't imagine how happy I shall be to fulfill that duty that does me such honor. I am deeply moved. Allow me to embrace you, my dear Agnaldo!" He allows a tearful note to creep into his voice. He has raised his children, and made his way in life, climbing step by step to the heights he has now attained. At that instant he catches a glimpse of the supreme peak that he will soon reach, thanks to the campaign and the reception speech. Bruno has passed on at precisely the right time.

After the embrace sealing that friendship, in life and in death, and once they are seated again, Lisandro says:

"What a coincidence: without in the least expecting this great proof of esteem and confidence that I have just been privileged to receive from you, I began, merely for my intellectual pleasure, to reread your incomparable body of work, to study it, with the intention of writing an essay about it. In my speech I shall use the notes I jotted down in order to assign it its proper place in contemporary Brazilian literature. The one book I'm lacking is your volume of poems; I couldn't even get a secondhand copy of it at Carlos Ribeiro's."

"Sins of my youth, Romantic verses. You need only refer to the book in passing, merely mention the title. I'll see if I can find a copy to give you." He has no intentions of keeping this promise; Romantic verses, long since outgrown, do not befit a leader of his stature. Lisandro manages to control his emotion:

"And the dinner? I know that you didn't speak of the election. The subject is taboo for the president. But the invitation to dinner is tantamount to a declaration of how he is going to vote."

"That's true—we didn't speak of the election or of his vote. I followed your instructions to the letter. He told how he'd been a newspaper copyboy before becoming the owner of the paper. And then his wife began to sing the praises of—guess who! That cursed English dog who answers to the name of Churchill." He smiles in self-satisfaction: "I then gave her a lecture on the war. . . ."

"You discussed the war?" Lisandro says in alarm. "We'd decided you were to avoid political matters."

"Don't worry. Everything went very well; she held her tongue, and didn't say a word in reply. And bear in mind that I wasn't the one who brought the subject up. We must reeducate such people, my dear Lisandro."

The jurist swallows his objections and criticism; the harm is already done, the mistake made, and there is no point in arguing about it now. Churchill, de Gaulle, the Maquis in France, the stoic English people, the dauntless citizens of London, all those people are fighting for the general and threatening the colonel. Nonetheless, as he calculates the votes at the end of their conversation, Lisandro predicts that Sampaio Pereira will win, by a vote of twenty-eight to eleven. He will secure him an even wider margin if he can, to thank him for the invitation he had so eagerly awaited. As a matter of fact, he has already written the speech, a long-winded piece of oratory, a masterpiece of bootlicking.

"Even if it's only twenty-seven to twelve, it doesn't matter. What's really important is to have more than twice as many votes as Maginot Line. Otherwise I'll feel as though I've lost."

▚ PREROGATIVE

On Sunday, his day off, Lisandro was busy polishing the reception speech when Sampaio Pereira phoned. From the colonel's tone of voice, Lisandro realized that he had already heard the bad news. That proved to be the case.

"I've just learned that the president invited Moreira to dinner. What kind of business is that? It's intolerable!"

"Churchill, my dear friend. . . ."

"What do you mean by that? It was his wife who started it. . . . I consider Carmo's attitude really unbearable. He's making mock of me, holding me up to ridicule. It's a dirty, lowdown trick."

At the mention of the president's lowdown trick, the colonel felt as though a monstrous toad were stuck in his throat. It was promptly joined by a poisonous snake squeezing the breath out of his chest, a rattlesnake with a deadly bite.

"Keep calm, hold your temper, we'll talk it over. Even if he doesn't come through for you, we'll still have twenty-seven votes against Moreira's twelve, three more than twice as many, not counting the fact that Pérsio's vote is worth any five others."

Lisandro had learned, two days before, of the president's odd invitation to the general, and had concluded that the discussion about the war at dinner with the colonel had led him to switch his vote. Lisandro's dear friend Agnaldo refused to accept the fact that a candidate for the Academy cannot have a personal opinion, much less express it. It is incumbent upon him to listen, and if he is unable to agree and applaud he must remain silent and smile. He must never argue or answer back. Being the possessor of a vote, the Academician is always right. This is one of the prerogatives of Immortals.

❦ FUNERAL MARCH

Surprised, the poised and well-dressed young girl—a servant? a secretary? a relative?—halts at the door for a moment to watch the commotion being caused by security agents as they leap out of cars and occupy the area in front of the house. With a gesture of her hand, she invites Colonel Agnaldo Sampaio Pereira, his uniform covered with decorations and medals, to follow her down the hallway plunged in semi-darkness.

She escorts him to the library. Loaded with books, the shelves covering every wall reach to the ceiling. There are books everywhere: piled on the floor, on top of chairs, lying open on the massive work-table. In the empty spaces between the windows (through which he glimpses the Largo do Boticário), three large paintings from Cuzco, and, on a small antique pedestal, a centuries-old statue of Our-Lady-of-Milk, her breast exposed, suckling the Christ Child.

Standing in one corner next to the bookshelves is an easel with a modern painting displayed on it, a portrait of Pérsio Menezes signed by Flávio de Carvalho, in warm colors and violent brushstrokes, his hair disheveled and his long beard intertwining, intermingling with the sun and the stars, his burning eyes, Jupiter brandishing his thunderbolt, Vulcan forging the inferno. On the table, bright flowers in a crystal vase.

The colonel suddenly feels ill at ease, overcome by a painful, unexpected sensation of mediocrity. He tries to fight off the uncomfortable feeling, concentrating on the piano chords coming from the next room. He knows that melody; where has he heard it before? With his co-religionists and classmates at Santa Catarina, at school gatherings, he heard concerts of German music, and he knows of the Führer's admiration for Richard Wagner. Those martial notes announcing the final triumph may well have been composed by Wagner.

"Please have a seat. The professor won't be long."

"And that music? It's by Wagner, isn't it?"

The young girl seems to be taken aback by the question. She waits a long moment before answering, her gaze fixed on the glittering medals—an incredible display!

"Wagner? No. It's Beethoven's Third Symphony, the *Eroica*. Very well known." She adds, perhaps anticipating his next question: "It's Dona Antonieta who's playing. It's a privilege to hear her. Excuse me. . . ."

A servant, a relative, a secretary? Insolent, the professorial tone of someone teaching "c–a–t: *cat*" to an ignoramus. She takes one last look at the decorations on his chest and goes out of the room, leaving him all by himself and feeling even more humbled: very well known music, the privilege of hearing the noted Antonieta Novais Menezes, who has not appeared with an orchestra or in concert for many years. Informed by the foresighted Lisandro, he is aware that she was once a widely acclaimed pianist.

In all truth, there is no real reason for him to feel so overawed, sitting there in the half-shadow in this extraordinary setting where each object betokens knowledge and taste, grandeur without ostentation, austerity without gloom. Having doubtless been told of his visit, the eminent lady, in a most hospitable gesture, has sat down at the piano to grant him this rare privilege. He has come to receive a practically certain vote: Pérsio Menezes has given Lisandro to understand that he wants to deliver it to him personally. In return, to honor the illustrious scientist, the colonel has donned his handsomest uniform, covered with medals and decorations; Pérsio Menezes's vote is worth any five others. But the dress uniform and the decorations are out of place amid the collection of books, the paintings, the Virgin adored in an age long past. Perhaps if he had followed Lisandro's advice—"Go there in civvies, it's better"—he would feel more at ease, less dazed and overpowered.

Beethoven might be well known, but it is Wagner whom the Führer is fond of. There must be reasons for his preference, since he is never wrong; be it in the realm of art or of war, his judgment is infallible. Isn't war the supreme, the most beautiful art? The sound of the piano dies away; the colonel contemplates with repugnance the portrait on the easel: degenerate art. He averts his eyes, in vain; he can still see those burning pupils scrutinizing him. Unbearable.

He hears the sound of the piano again. The rhythm has changed: the cadence of a funeral march. Fleeing the gaze of the portrait, pursued by the powerful music, Colonel Sampaio Pereira raises his eyes and finds himself face to face with Death standing in the doorway, staring at him with the same burning pupils. He shudders.

The terrible vision walks toward him, with such slow footsteps that time stops to wait for him. An imposing athlete before the onset of the disease, the figure before him is now a deformed giant, a skeleton covered with wasted flesh; the long beard and the disheveled mane now thin and sparse; the long fingers nothing but bones; the clothes, now much too loose-fitting, accentuating the destruction of the body. Gaunt features the color of wax, the face of a dead man.

Step by step, Pérsio Menezes draws closer. Terror-stricken, the colonel rises from his chair; the medals on his breast shake. Distant but still audible, the sounds of the funeral march.

"Sit down," the cavernous, sepulchral voice orders.

He does not offer his hand, a shapeless claw—no doubt wishing to spare his visitor the disagreeable contact with bony fingers, Sampaio Pereira reflects gratefully. He sits down in a chair, upholstered in leather with a back and arms in jacaranda wood, facing the colonel's armchair. With an abrupt gesture, he gives the terrified candidate his leave to speak. Forcing himself to overcome his insecurity, Colonel Agnaldo Sampaio Pereira, candidate for a seat in the Brazilian Academy of Letters, begins declaiming his usual speech, to which he appends paeans of praise for the Immortal so close to Death that he has become one with it.

The Professor of Celestial Mechanics listens in silence, his piercingly bright eyes half-closed. The piano chords come and go, mount and descend, disturbing the candidate's delivery. Why hasn't the pianist chosen music by Wagner if she has really intended to offer him a privileged experience? The colonel haltingly reaches the end of his formal request: he hopes to merit the signal honor of being accorded the eminent Academician's vote, and trusts that he has not yet pledged it to another candidate.

"My vote has been determined for some time now." His voice is slow and barely audible; each word costs him an effort. "I shall tell you here and now that I am not going to vote for your adversary, the general who was here a few days ago. I have nothing against him personally, but the literature he perpetrates is of a most inferior quality. For that reason, I shall not vote for him." He doesn't raise his voice, but the tone of it becomes imperious. "I have very little time left to live, but before I die I wanted to see you, for I know everything about you, Colonel Agnaldo Sampaio Pereira."

For the first time since he crossed the threshold of the house in Cosme Velho, the colonel breathes more or less easily. The solemn and glorious moment when Pérsio Menezes will formally pledge his vote to him is at hand. The letter accompanying it, already composed and typed up by his secretary, must be lying on the table. The colonel waits, his nerves on edge, trying not to hear the piano chords, an accursed privilege.

Pérsio Menezes raises his emaciated hand and points his finger at Agnaldo's chest, gleaming with medals.

"Where is the Iron Cross?"

Allowing him no time to reply, the finger rises to point straight at the face of the stupefied colonel:

"The only one that you should wear, over your heart. On a Gestapo tunic, not on a Brazilian uniform."

Utterly perplexed, the colonel stammers:

"What do you mean?"

Leaning for support on the arms of the chair, Pérsio Menezes rises to his feet, Death rising along with him:

"How dare you hope for my vote? You, a Nazi! The precise contrary of culture, the polar opposite of what it means to be Brazilian."

The sound of the funeral march, the sepulchral voice wrenched from those diseased vitals, long pauses between the phrases, deathly disgust in every word:

"All of us have two sides to us, a good one and a bad one. Worse than a robot, you are only half a man, someone who tortures prisoners. Do you perchance have a wife and children, anyone you love? I doubt it. Someone who loves you? No one. Those who serve you do so out of fear or self-interest. Have you ever loved anyone, felt affection for a woman, smiled at a child, had a moment of tenderness? Or were you always what you are now, a miserable wretch? You are rotten, and you smell bad. My vote? How could you possibly imagine that I would vote for the Gestapo?"

His voice, until then slow and muffled, rises, awesomely stern:

"Get out of here, before I slap your face!"

He raises his hand, the skeleton-fingers of Death reaching out toward the candidate's terror-stricken face. Colonel Agnaldo Sampaio Pereira backs out of the room as the chords of the funeral march rise to a crescendo. Death advances toward the colonel, who escapes down the hall at a run, passes through the front door held open by the secretary, falls into the arms of the gorillas of his security unit, collapses on the seat of the car, covers his face with his hands.

▇ THE SECOND LIEUTENANT

On awakening and getting out of bed, Dona Herminia is surprised to see her husband still lying there fast asleep. At that hour, having done his daily exercises to keep himself in shape, taken his cold shower, and swallowed his morning coffee, he should be at the ministry; he is never late. It is only on very unusual occasions, late at night or sometimes very early in the morning, that Dona Herminia really looks at Sampaio. The colonel keeps saying, and repeating with Spartan emphasis, that he is not his own master—his time, his efforts, his very life belong to the cause. Dona Herminia has grown accustomed to this.

Her husband's sleep strikes her as being too peaceful. She goes over to him, feels his face with her fingers. He is dead.

Lying there in his pajamas, his round, innocent eyes half-open, he does not look like a hero fallen on the battlefield, a Manichaean figure symbolizing evil and obscurantism, a Nazi SS, a Gestapo chief armed with a whip. Just a poor dead man, lying in his bed, like so many others.

He reminds her of someone. Dona Herminia searches her memory for a face in the past. She sees in her mind's eye the timid, passionate young second lieutenant she met long ago, in some other time; he used to recite verses that begged for a kiss. Dona Herminia suddenly remembers and begins to cry softly.

GUERRILLA WARFARE ON THE ESPLANADA DO CASTELO

◼ UNPUBLISHABLE OPINIONS

"Let's bury him with great ceremony and without delay. That way, we'll be rid of him as soon as possible and forever," was the advice of the director of the Press and Propaganda Department, whose political duplicity has already been mentioned. He had just released the official government communiqué announcing the death of Colonel Agnaldo Sampaio Pereira, in which he was eulogized as "a brave soldier of our Fatherland, the possessor of an extraordinary service record, whose dedication to the regime constituted an essential factor in maintaining order and extirpating the threat of Communism."

For the news bulletin to be put out by the National Agency, the editor wanted to know:

"Will The Man be attending the funeral? Or will he merely appear at the wake?"

"Who? The president? Are you out of your mind? He won't show up either at the funeral or at the wake. He recognized the usefulness of our late lamented Goebbels, but he detested him. 'That Pereira stinks of the Middle Ages,' he once said to me."

On hearing this confidential bit of gossip, the editor said fawningly:

"The day you're able to write your memoirs, what a book that will be, eh, sir?"

"If I had a memory, I wouldn't be occupying this post, my boy. I'm deaf, dumb, and amnesic. But not impotent. Not yet, anyway."

Why is it I find him so likable when he's such a cynic?

the editor wondered, and ventured a comment often heard in editorial rooms, those nests of agitators:

"Hated as he was, the colonel was lucky. He died in bed, of natural causes. Because if the regime were ever overthrown and he were still alive, he wouldn't have escaped the firing squad. . . ."

"In his bed, yes. But who said it was from natural causes? He died of slow poisoning. Hemlock, as befitted the circumstances."

An astounding revelation, coming from such a source. Ah, what a sensation when the journalist passed it on to his colleagues! People were right to say that in the struggle for power in the New State, dreadful things happened behind the scenes.

"Poisoned? With hemlock? How? By whom?"

"By the little old men in the Academy. Dose by dose, a slightly stronger one each day. It was Pérsio Menezes who handed him the last cupful to drink down."

The director's slightly squint-eyed gaze wandered out the window and fell on the landscape of reinforced concrete:

"A great man, that Pérsio Menezes, a genius. Did you know that at Princeton he discovered and mapped two stars that no one knew of before? He peopled heaven . . ."— he smiled—". . . and hell too."

▩ THE SOLE CANDIDATE

Immediately after António Bruno's death, Lisandro Leite had promised the powerful Colonel Sampaio Pereira the privilege of being the sole candidate. On the death of the colonel, buried with a noisy display of tanks, soldiers, trumpet flourishes, speeches, and artillery salvos, just eight days after the close of the registration period, the one who suddenly found himself the sole candidate was the disesteemed but lucky General Waldomiro Moreira.

The general learned of the demise of his adversary (and

enemy) thanks to a telephone call from the faithful Sabença, a copy-desk editor on the staff of the *Diário da Tarde*, where he spent five hours a day correcting the pidgin Portuguese written by the paper's gang of illiterate reporters and columnists.

"I've good news for you, General! I'd like to be the first to congratulate the new Immortal."

Ah, General Moreira's heart, an old, unreliable machine. Almost anything can make it begin to race. It requires permanent control; powerful emotions must be avoided. Impossible to do so in such circumstances, in the heat of the electoral battle. What had happened? Afrânio Portela had considered it a possibility that that scoundrel of a Pereira might withdraw his candidacy.

"He's withdrawn?" *He*, and not "Goebbels Pereira" or other contemptuous nicknames; a tap had been put on the general's phone once he had registered as a candidate for the seat left vacant by Bruno. A friend had told him about it, and recommended prudence when he—and the rattlebrained Cecília—made calls.

"He kicked off. He's dead."

"What's that? When?"

The general's tachycardia grew worse and worse. Where had Conceição and Cecília gone off to? He needed one of them to bring him his medicine and a glass of water.

"He was found dead in bed this morning. The funeral is set for five o'clock this afternoon. It's going to be spectacular, with a speech by the war minister, a procession of tanks, and artillery salvos. Since the registration period is closed now and you no longer have a rival, you're automatically elected already, my eminent friend."

Luckily, Dona Conceição happened to come into the room just then and immediately ran to get his medicine. On realizing that he was elected, the general had very nearly had a heart attack.

Out of danger, lying on the chaise longue, he euphor-

ically passed on the good news to his wife and daughter—
Cecília had finally appeared, her face smeared with beauty
cream (the preamble to a lengthy makeup session, this
being the day of the week for her tryst with Rodrigo):

"You see before you General Waldomiro Moreira,
member of the Brazilian Academy of Letters, an Immortal!"

Later on, Dona Conceição was to lament: "Why doesn't
a person die at precisely the right moment?"

▓ THE MILITANT

On learning of the colonel's death from the noon news-
cast over Radio Carioca, Maria Manuela called Afrânio
Portela, asking to see him, that very day if possible. After
Bruno's death, they had had long phone conversations in
which the novelist kept her posted on the ups and downs
of the battle. She had asked to meet him both because
she was eager for further details concerning the sensational piece of news and because she wanted to tell him
personally that she would be leaving Brazil very soon—
her bags were already packed.

A discreet bar, the Privé, on the top floor of a tall building on the Praia do Flamengo, with a view overlooking
the bay, very near the novelist's house. Packed to the
rafters at night, when top-ranking stars appeared there—
Silvio Caldas, Dircinha and Linda Batista, Dorival Caymmi,
the Mexican Elvira Ríos, Lamartine Babo, the piquant
Pagas Sisters—in the late afternoon it had practically no
customers: a few passionate unmarried couples whispering together. Seated alongside the balcony railing, Afrânio
and Maria Manuela contemplated the cortege that came
into view on the Russel, preceded by a regimental band
playing funeral marches. Atop a military caisson, the casket draped with the Brazilian flag. Troops on foot and on
horseback; a contingent of the Special Police in their new
German vehicles, powerful cars and ultrafast motorcy-

cles; large black limousines with high government officials. Two battle tanks ended the procession. Colonel Sampaio Pereira had resumed his command post. Maria Manuela watched in fascination. She asked for explanations:

"A sudden death, wasn't it? What caused it?"

"I'd call it an unexpected death. The cause? What else could it have been but the battle we had joined? I confess I didn't expect that; that wasn't the objective I had in mind. But let's give him his due: the colonel died in combat."

"Please, my friend, drop this silly charade. What do you mean, he died in combat? You weren't hoping for his death, but you were hoping for something else—what was that?"

"That he would withdraw his candidacy." He looked away from the funeral procession, preferring to gaze upon that vision of melancholy beauty, Bruno's last mistress. "Sampaio Pereira was nothing but an idiot, arrogant and conceited, taking himself to be all-powerful, convinced that no one would have the courage to oppose his desires. The strategy was to lead him to give up, to withdraw his candidacy; the tactic was to wear him down by means of a mounting series of disappointments and failures. With every blow he received, he grew more and more irritated, gradually destroying himself, gnawed away from within. He thought he was going to be the sole candidate, and he had a rival. He dreamed of being elected by unanimous vote, and the dream didn't come true. Later on, he began to lose votes that he had regarded as certain, to feel the hostility toward his candidacy. Figueiredo mortified him, and let's not even speak of Evandro. Stunned, humiliated, he saw that he had lost."

"He was beaten?"

The procession went on, slowly and solemnly leading the "hero to the trench of immortality" (as the minister said in his forceful oration at the graveside), with traffic stopped to let it through, and groups of curious onlookers on the sidewalks.

"Not at that point, far from it. I don't know if we would have beaten him if we had gotten as far as the election. I doubt it. That's the reason why the entire campaign was planned to make him feel demoralized, rejected; so that, fearing defeat, he'd give up his candidacy. The ploy of the president's dinners, a masterstroke, left Sampaio Pereira in a panic. We obliged him to swallow toads and snakes— all sorts of insults and humiliations—to make him feel sick to death of the campaign and throw it up. They stuck in his throat and he choked to death."

The sounds of the regimental band gradually faded away as the cortege reached the Avenida da Ligação and began to disappear from sight.

"Pérsio was so repelled by the colonel that it was hard work persuading him to receive the man. He did so out of love for Bruno, and out of love for Bruno Antonieta sat down at the piano and played the Funeral March from the *Eroica*. I spoke with Pérsio on the phone yesterday, and he told me that he feared he'd gone too far. When the colonel asked him for his vote, Pérsio flew into a rage and threatened to slap him, and Sampaio Pereira left at a run. The fatal dose, apparently. And so he never got around to paying his formal call on me. . . . In any event, my lovely little darling, the memory of our Bruno has been preserved, safe and sound. I've kept my promise: we did the possible and the impossible. It was worth it."

Maria Manuela took Mestre Afrânio's hand and kissed it.

"I'd also like to kiss Professor Pérsio's hand. What about his health? Is there really no hope . . . ?"

"None at all, unfortunately. I fear that this has been his last contribution to Brazilian culture."

"I can leave with my mind at rest now. Afonso, my husband, has been promoted to the rank of ambassador and is being posted to Venezuela. We'll go directly from here. My father's arranged it so that we won't have to run the risk of traveling back to Lisbon by sea. We're to leave next month, via Manaus."

They contemplated the dazzling landscape in silence: the sea of Guanabara, the islands, the mountains, the beaches, the little town of Niterói in the distance.

"Do you know where I met António? In Niterói. . . . Such a crazy thing. . . . If you have time to listen, I'll tell you about it."

"Today is the first day of rest I've had since Bruno died, and you've had me come meet you at the dinner hour. I've all the time in the world now, and I love listening to fairy tales."

An almost mischievous smile drove away the sad expression on Maria Manuela's face.

"You're right. It was a modern-style fairy tale, involving politics and an unfaithful wife, an absurd fairy." She paused à moment and then asked: "You know I'm a dangerous anti-Salazar militant, don't you?"

"Bruno showed me a poem in which he spoke of a goddess descended from Olympus brandishing a hammer and sickle. A delightful poem."

" 'The Goddess and the Minstrel,' one of the first ones he wrote for me. Well then: I had arranged to meet a comrade in Niterói, an exile who was to give me certain documents to be sent on to Portugal. In my position, I have ways available. . . ."

The daughter of one of Salazar's ministers, the daughter-in-law of the most powerful banker in the country, the wife of the deputy ambassador of Portugal, she found herself in a privileged situation for fighting fascism: inside the enemy's lair, hearing confidential information, knowing the secret agents of the PIDE operating in Brazil, having access to the diplomatic pouch for her personal correspondence. Afrânio Portela listened intently to the woman sitting across the table from him: well-bred, refined, elegant, idolized by the gossip columnists, queen

of the salons of fashionable Rio society and of the diplomatic corps—who could imagine her working hand in
glove with subversives, involved in clandestine activities,
breaking the law? It was a subject worthy of a novel, so
intriguing he felt tempted to go back to writing fiction.

"The contact was to be made in a bar, in the Saco de
São Francisco. I arrived first, as we had arranged, went to
the tobacco shop, and bought some cigarettes. My comrade appeared, almost at a run, looking panic-stricken.
He handed me the envelope and told me he was being
tailed. 'Don't let the PIDE agents see you,' he ordered,
and disappeared. I put the envelope in my purse. What to
do to keep the agent from seeing me? Can you imagine
what could have happened if he'd recognized me?"

Mestre Portela savored the suspense. A scene straight
out of a novel!

"And what did you do then?"

"I spied António sitting at one of the tables inside the
bar nursing a drink, no doubt waiting for a woman. I knew
him from having seen photographs of him and having
read his books; I'd loved his poems ever since I was a
schoolgirl. Without hesitating, I sat down in a chair next
to him, and without any further explanation told him
that I mustn't be seen or recognized by a man who was
going to walk past the door of the bar and have a look
inside. He didn't ask any questions. The PIDE agent might
have suspected anybody but me, since he couldn't even
see my face, which was hidden by António's, our mouths
clinging together in the longest kiss in the world. . . .
António let me leave then, in a taxi, without even asking
who I was. . . ."

Afrânio Portela could see himself composing the novel.
Who could tell: might he not go straight to his typewriter,
armed with reams of blank paper, put aside his note-cards
on the poets of the Inconfidência movement, and try to
recreate those political intrigues, the atmosphere of the
Portuguese embassy under Salazar, the difficulties of the

exiles, the poet's last passion, the enigma of Maria Manuela?

"The following day, I received a book with an extremely formal handwritten dedication, accompanied by the most beautiful orchids I've ever seen. The phone call came later. . . . It was António who taught me what love was. Before that, I was only a militant; he completed me, he made me a woman."

The artillery salvo, far off in the distance. The first shovelful of earth was falling on the body of Colonel Agnaldo Sampaio Pereira.

▪ THE LADY IN BLACK

I

At first she resisted. Not out of consideration for her husband or respect for marriage. She had no ties of affection to her husband, who was lazy, mediocre, and frivolous, avid for honors and distinctions, his greatest aspiration being the papal title of nobility that would be his as soon as he inherited his share of his father's immense fortune, amassed in the colonies thanks to the sweat of blacks and multiplied in the mother country thanks to the complicity of the government. This ambition to become an aristocrat had led Afonso Castiel to pursue a career in the diplomatic service, a noble activity, leaving his brothers responsible for the vulgar management of banks, agricultural holdings, and industrial enterprises; it had also led him to marry Maria Manuela Covo Silvares d'Eça, a blueblooded descendant of an old and distinguished family, with a coat of arms and the motto: "In the hands of the King I have placed my life and my honor." Ah, if only he could have, Afonso would have adopted the illustrious family name of his wife, instead of adding to them his Castiel, a surname with the perceptible smell of the ghetto. Intimate ties of friendship and business linked the filthy-rich Salomão Castiel to the influential Silvares, minister of foreign affairs; both of them enjoyed the trust and the rare esteem of the dictator. As for holy matrimony, Maria Manuela did not consider it worthy of the slightest respect, her marriage being merely a duty, the most onerous one of all. She resisted Bruno's advances in the name of proletarian morality, for ideological reasons.

António Bruno had recognized her in the bar in Niterói. He sensed that her fear of being identified and the need to hide her face that had caused her to throw herself into his arms had nothing to do with any sort of love-intrigue. A political conspiracy, espionage perhaps? He had seen the man slip her the envelope outside the tobacco shop. The woman's beauty and the mystery surrounding her had left him dazed, mad with passion. He couldn't live if he didn't make a conquest of her. He had to possess her, no matter how: pomegranate mouth, swan's neck.

He began his siege of her, using all of the resources he had accumulated in the course of considerable experience. Flowers and books, a tender voice, honeyed words, brilliant and charming conversation, the heat of desire. Polite and reserved, Maria Manuela—a solid fortress— did not succumb.

Bruno contrived to open a breach by way of literature. In exchange for his books, sent to her one by one, each of them with a less formal handwritten dedication, he received in the mail the one volume published in his lifetime by Fernando Pessoa: *To the much-admired Brazilian poet António Bruno, this 'Message' from the greatest contemporary Portuguese poet, with the profound admiration of a reader, Maria Manuela Silvares Castiel.* Bruno knew vaguely of his Lusitanian colleague, whose popularity was to spread to Brazil only after the war. An intellectual oriented toward French culture, Bruno knew very little about modern Portuguese literature, except for the great generation of Eça, Ramalho, Antero. He had read Ferreira de Castro's *The Virgin Forest*, he had heard of

Aquilino Ribeiro, he was acquainted with but not attracted by the melancholy verse of António Nobre, but he liked Cesário Verde's poetry. Apart from that, a total ignorance that stupefied and shocked the patriotic sensibilities of the beautiful holder of a degree in literature from the University of Coimbra.

With Fernando Pessoa and his fellow poets as a point of departure, their telephone conversations grew longer, eventually leading to a first rendezvous at the Portuguese Literary Center, at which she arrived, breathless and beautiful, loaded down with volumes of poetry—titles and authors unknown to Bruno. It had not been Lusitanian poets, however, that had brought her there: she had acceded to the ardent pleas of this passionate admirer because that first kiss, born on a happenstance having to do with politics, still made her mouth burn from the lingering taste of the lips and tongue of the Brazilian poet, sapping her will, awakening repressed desires.

A game of hide-and-seek: Bruno, aflame with passion, speaking of love; Maria Manuela, knowledgeable and platonic, explaining the whys and wherefores of the groups centered round the reviews *Orfeu* and *Presença*, offering him copies of *Seara Nova*. What else could he do except resort to the same weapons? He counter-attacked with Prévert, Breton, Aragon, Éluard, Tzara. Poet by poet, verse by verse, the sense of intimacy between them grew, tender words mingling with the stanzas; the fires of passion set the literary discussion aflame. With García Lorca and his *Gypsy Ballads* they found common ground, a propitious terrain where love flourished. They exchanged kisses, seated on a rustic bench amid the trees on the heights of the Silvestre, reading Neruda's *Twenty Poems of Love and a Song of Despair*.

Maria Manuela ceased resisting, succumbed when Bruno recited, in a doleful murmur, the series of three sonnets in the manner of Camões that she had inspired: "Visitations by Juno to the Royal Villa on the Praia Grande in

Niterói." What did proletarian morality mean, exactly? She had never given him a precise explanation, but it most certainly did not mean being faithful to Afonso, a husband who, moreover, could not have cared less about his wife's love-adventures. Do whatever you please with me, she had said to Bruno, vanquished and happy to be so.

For Bruno, one last love-affair, madness, folly; for Maria Manuela, her first love, the discovery of the other side of life, which brought a new dimension to the humanism that was her ruling principle. A comrade, Fernando Castro, had taught her the meaning of solidarity; with the poet António Bruno she learned what love meant. "António completed me," she confided to Mestre Afrânio on the day of the colonel's funeral.

Her first love had come late; she was nearly twenty-eight years old. She knew days of complete happiness—infinite tenderness, infinite sensual fulfillment; freed at last. The chance encounter in Niterói had taken place shortly before Christmas, 1939, and Bruno had died in September, 1940: ten perfect months, during which there had not been a single moment that was not filled with harmony and beauty.

II

Breaking away from the feudal traditions of the family, when she had completed her secondary studies Maria Manuela refused to confine herself to domestic duties, won the right to attend the university, and signed up for courses at the Coimbra Faculty of Letters. Enthusiastic, gay, intelligent, she began immediately to participate in student life. After a brief and disappointing phase as the object of romantic serenades on the banks of the Mondego, she fell in with leftist groups whose seriousness appealed to her. A law student with ascetic features and a harsh voice, Fernando Castro took it upon himself to indoctrinate her. While her other companions courted her, wasting their time making ridiculous declarations of love, he spoke of politics, of the wretchedness of the country and the people, of the oppression of Salazar's regime, of the injustices of colonialism, whose bloody claws were ripping out the vitals of the Portuguese nation. He gave her forbidden books by Marx and Lenin to read: the *Communist Manifesto*, a résumé of *Capital, Imperialism, the Final Stage of Capitalism*. And she read all of them, along with a number of others: Gorki's *The Mother*, and Mayakovski's poems. He described the saga of the October Revolution, the banner and the hope of the exploited, the crucible of a better world, with neither rich nor poor, where private property did not exist, where everyone had enough to eat and a right to the benefits of culture. Maria Manuela was dazzled.

She asked to join the party, and after a test period, indispensable in view of her background, during which she was closely watched and judged, she was admitted under the nom de guerre of Berta. In a joyous mood, in the wee hours of the morning after a night of daubing slogans on the walls of the university with tar, she gave herself to her sweaty comrade Castro, who, rejecting the rigid principles of proletarian morality, resurrected abandoned theories of free love and put them into practice. Only a saint with a heart of stone could spend entire days and nights in the company of the beautiful Maria Manuela and remain indifferent. Comrade Castro was very nearly a saint. Admittedly gaunt, but not made of stone.

A fanatic out of conviction and natural inclination, he educated her in accordance with the strictest principles of orthodoxy and dogmatism, converting Comrade Berta into a sort of Marxist nun. Maria Manuela abandoned everything that signified luxury, ostentation, refinement, from expensive dresses and shoes to beauty creams and cosmetics, evidence of capitalist rottenness. Free of all artifice, resplendent in the pure beauty of her face, in the incomparable elegance of her body uncluttered by useless finery, she drove students and professors mad, inspired dozens of bad poems, reams of dreadful prose, execrable songs and *fados*. None of this troubled her or touched her heart—they were all stupid expressions of bourgeois decadence. The hard mattress and the parsimonious carnal embraces of Comrade Castro were enough for her dulled sensibilities, since her appetites had never been awakened. Only the Revolution mattered; everything else was secondary. She shut herself off from sentiment and desire.

While attending a leaders' meeting in the Serra da Estrela, Fernando Castro fell into the hands of the police. Maria Manuela wanted to visit him; the party was opposed. She did not understand the reasons, but obeyed the categorical veto. She stayed on in Coimbra, finished her studies, went on with her illegal activities. She sought in poetry a substitute for the political homilies of her absent comrade, whose preaching, though stern and strict, was animated by a spirit of generosity. She was not interested in any of her other comrades, whether fellow students at the university or ideological fellow travelers. Given a long sentence, Fernando Castro did not serve it; he died in Tarrafal prison camp, a few months after his arrest. Maria Manuela was profoundly affected by the death of a comrade, but did not mourn for a lost lover.

On receiving her degree and returning to Lisbon, she volunteered to go underground, breaking completely with her family and her milieu, becoming a professional revolutionary. Not only was she denied that opportunity; when Afonso Castiel asked for her hand in marriage, she was advised to accept the fiancé whom both families, by common accord, urged upon her.

"Advised" is not the proper term. The marriage to the diplomat was forced upon her, a duty to be fulfilled. Having told the leader of the group of militants with which she worked the laughable story of the marriage proposal she had received, adding that she would never agree under any circumstances to become the wife of that fatuous imbecile, she found herself summoned a few days later to a secret high-level meeting. A long trip in a car, with her eyes blindfolded, in total silence, just herself and the unknown driver. For the first time, Maria Manuela was about to meet a member of the Central Committee.

She got out of the car, and the driver took her by the hand and led her, still blindfolded, inside the house. "Wait here," he said, and disappeared. Shortly thereafter, she heard an educated, impersonal voice say: "You may remove the blindfold, comrade." She saw before her a middle-aged man, thin, hollow-cheeked, with burning eyes, the look of an apostle. "I am happy to meet you, Comrade Berta." He held out his hand to her and then pointed to a chair. "Sit down. We have a great deal to talk about. I am Comrade Neves." Maria Manuela felt her heart beat faster. Before her was Comrade Neves, member of the Politburo, a legendary leader, the hero of fantastic stories: two prison breaks, one from Fort Caxias in Lisbon, the other from Tarrafal, braving the open sea in a primitive boat he had made himself. There were also amazing stories about his dazzling talents as a theoretician—he had been through the Comintern School in Moscow. He emanated a charisma that commanded respect and obedience.

For a few moments he seemed approachable and human, speaking almost affectionately of Fernando Castro, who had died in Tarrafal, the victim of the torture to which he had been subjected in Lisbon when he was interrogated. He had behaved heroically, had revealed none of the many things he knew as the leader responsible for the groups of student militants in Coimbra. He had proudly admitted that he was a Communist and announced to his torturers the inevitable downfall of Salazarism. "An example for the entire party," Comrade Neves concluded, again adopting an impersonal, imperious tone that emphasized the distance between the party leader and the militant. "And now, let's talk about you, comrade."

Throughout the interview he treated her with respect

but without warmth, a purely political respect; there was only one bond between them, the Revolution, nothing else. Party comrades, not close companions, since he, a member of the Politburo, made decisions and gave orders, while her duty was merely to carry out the orders she received. The leader knew all about her previous activities, in Coimbra and in Lisbon; he both complimented and criticized her, with neither exaggerated praise nor blame. He explained, professorially and peremptorily, that the party had not taken proper advantage of what she had to offer. In view of both the position held by her father and her family's prestige, Comrade Berta should be assigned special tasks; there were any number of militants available to daub slogans on walls and distribute propaganda leaflets.

The Politburo had arrived at certain decisions with regard to the work the comrade was to do. From now on, taking her orders directly from the leaders of the party, keeping her distance from the group of rank-and-file militants to which she belonged, she would be in permanent contact only with a member of the Central Committee who would supervise her new party activities. The war in Spain was at its height, and as the daughter of the minister of foreign affairs, with easy entrée to official circles, she could be extremely useful. Her assigned task would be to gather information and pass it on; the Politburo had decided at the same time to approve her marriage to Afonso Castiel, since it would appreciably extend her area of operations.

Open-mouthed with astonishment, Maria Manuela tried to argue. These were not the dangerous tasks she had hoped would be assigned her. She made no attempt to conceal her disappointment: she was going to feel more like a spy than a revolutionary. The leader's voice, a cold and sharp-honed steel blade, rose, putting an end to her complaints and disagreements:

"Comrade Berta, you have just shown that you have

not yet freed yourself of petty-bourgeois influences, that you have not yet acquired the Bolshevik mentality. The party is prepared to entrust an important battle sector to you, in the belief that you are capable of occupying it, and instead of feeling proud and grateful, you are endeavoring to dispute decisions reached by the Politburo. What is it you want? To play the heroine, painting slogans on walls and distributing propaganda tracts on market days, holding forth from a platform at lightning demonstrations? The party is assigning you tasks, and it is your duty to execute them."

Even before she realized that it was useless to resist, Maria Manuela had already persuaded herself that she was in the wrong: she was just a stupid, romantic petty-bourgeoise, still very far from possessing the moral fiber and the heartfelt conviction that characterized tried-and-true Communists. Quite obviously, Comrade Neves was a real Bolshevik, trained in Comrade Stalin's school. She was filled with tremendous admiration for him:

"You are right, comrade. I shall do my best to overcome my class limitations, to be worthy of the party's confidence, and to subject my praxis to self-criticism." "In the hands of the party I have placed my life and my honor": her motto.

The marriage of Maria Manuela Covo Silvares d'Eça and Afonso Castiel was the event of the year, still remembered today by Lisbon high society. The bride pale and dazzlingly beautiful; wedding dress, veil, nuptial garland from Paris, signed Coco Chanel; the Wedding March played by the organist Klaus Bergmann, brought specially from Vienna, a little detail that cost a fortune; the sermon by the cardinal of the Church of Os Jerónimos, extolling the alliance of two great and illustrious families, linked now by marriage ties, with God's blessing! And then the reception, grandiose, incomparably sumptuous.

In bed, the pretentious, perfumed Afonso interested her even less than the timid and sweaty Fernando had. On divesting himself of his morning coat, the idiot played the role of the self-assured macho, advised her to be courageous, and promised to be very gentle—"Don't be afraid, you won't feel a thing." Convinced that he was about to deflower her and convinced that he had done so when he penetrated her and crowed in triumph. Maria Manuela knew of Afonso's relations with a popular *fado*-singer from Alfama whom he was supporting—her and her successive cousins, a lighthearted lot, footloose and fancy-free.

The leader from the Politburo was right. Maria Manuela was able to furnish the party with valuable information about confidential, sometimes secret matters, information she garnered in her father's office, at her father-in-law's, in conversations with her garrulous husband. Afonso doted on hearing and passing on the latest gossip, gathering rumors in the corridors of the ministry, in government antechambers. In on everything having to do with Salazar's aid to Franco, Comrade Berta was of real help in furthering the Spanish Republican cause.

With the permission of the party, she accompanied her husband to Brazil, where he had been assigned the post of deputy ambassador, and she became a rapid and reliable means of contact between the exiled Communists and their leaders based in Portugal. A trusted comrade remained in constant touch with her—the one person who knew that she was working for the party. A year after her arrival in Rio, she met António Bruno, on that exciting afternoon in Niterói.

III

She blossomed in the poet's arms. In Coimbra she had discovered a world to transform; in Rio she discovered life in all its fullness. A stunning revelation when finally, after so many refusals, she stripped naked in António's bed and for the first time ever moaned with pleasure and climaxed. It was not long before she was the most complete woman imaginable, the most voracious, thirsty, and hungry, seeking to make up for lost time. Fulfilled and happy.

Fulfilled and happy, she nonetheless did not desert the front lines of the anti-fascist fight. Her loyalty to the party was no less great; she did not neglect her duties, to which she added yet another of her own—transforming the lyric poet António Bruno into a politically committed one, making his verses a weapon of workers striving to change the world. She cited the example of the Chilean Pablo Neruda, the author of the *Twenty Poems of Love* responsible for their first kisses. A consul in Spain during the civil war, he had placed his poetic inspiration at the service of the proletariat in arms.

Apropos of this constant subject of conversation between them, António showed her an article by a critic who, though he praised the "Brazilian atmosphere" of his poetry, accused him of ignoring social problems and of not taking a stand in a "world in upheaval, at a crucial hour, when García Lorca, whom he calls his brother, has been shot to death by Franco, when Thomas Mann has fled his native land so as not to end up in one of Hitler's concentration camps, and when António Machado is dying in exile." An article that happened to have appeared in the last issue of the review *Para Todos* before it was placed on the forbidden list by the DIP despite the prestige and the many influential contacts of Álvaro Moreyra, the owner and publisher. Maria Manuela agreed completely with the author of the article: António was not doing his duty. The beautiful, seditious Portuguese doubtless contributed to the speech he delivered before the Academy on the theme of the crystal tower that had been shattered by the war.

Bruno laughingly announced that he would write an entire volume of poems with social import, but he never fulfilled that promise. On the other hand, however, he did write love poems, verses full of delirious passion: a mad minstrel, a troubadour at the feet of the courageous lady who was risking her honor and her fate for him.

She was not risking anything, Maria Manuela insisted repeatedly; between her and her husband there existed only the formal bonds of matrimony. Afonso continued to keep singers as mistresses—a spectacular mulatta at the moment, a samba dancer at one of the theaters on the Praça Tiradentes who was also surrounded by cousins, amusing rascals—and if Maria Manuela had not had other lovers before António, this was due only to the fact that none of the many men who had paid her court in the fashionable salons had ever interested her. She even threatened to abandon her husband and her social position to come live with him, in poverty and poetry. To keep her from taking such an insane step, the poet was obliged to resort to political arguments. What would the party think? They might even expel her. A decisive argument.

At fifty-four, still in top form but sensing the approach of old age, Bruno felt blessed by fate, having been granted the love of this beautiful young woman, courageous and cultivated, born a great lady and become by her own efforts a daughter of the people. He did his best, in secret, to write the poems of combat that she kept begging him for, but did not succeed—they sounded false. The only one that bore the hallmark of true inspiration, verses full of hatred, loathing, rage, despair, and hope, a bleeding heart and an upraised fist, was the "Song of Love for an Occupied City," written as a lament for the fall of Paris, rewritten as a call to the peoples of the world to fight against Nazi fascism, for the liberation of all occupied cities—Bruno's poem and Maria Manuela's, the first copy of which she herself typed. A heritage safeguarded by the militant dressed in mourning, the lady in black, shared with others at an hour when morale was at its lowest in Brazil, in Portugal, and in the African colonies—read in the jungles of Angola, of Guinea-Bissau, of Mozambique, where blacks in revolt lighted the campfires of the first guerrilla bands.

▓ A BIRD'S-EYE VIEW OF A CONVERSATION BETWEEN ACADEMICIANS

An astute observer, *doyen* Francelino Almeida immediately noted symptoms of a change in attitude on the part of General Waldomiro Moreira. Seated on the sofa next to Justice Paiva of the Supreme Court, Francelino was contemplating the buffet table, where various Academicians were drinking tea, coffee, fruit juices, and eating little cakes, buttered toast, sweet biscuits before the beginning of the weekly meeting, the first one following the death of Colonel Sampaio Pereira. In a low voice the *doyen* alerted his friend:

"He's not the same anymore; take a good look. Something's changed. Something in the way he greets us, the way he addresses us, his manner in general. Before, a humble admirer, eager to please. Now he's less servile; he swaggers. Since that other one waited till the end of the registration period before dying, leaving the general a clear field, he's got the election sewed up. . . ."

"If Sampaio Pereira hadn't died, were you going to vote for him?"

"I was hesitating. The colonel was a powerful man, and refusing him my vote would have been foolhardy. On the other hand, Moreira has a powerful patron. . . . I might have ended up committing an act of utter folly. . . ."

The bone-thin little minister, blinking his eyes because of the bright light, lowered his voice even further:

"Tell me the truth, my good friend Francelino: patron or patroness?"

"Touché! And what a patroness!" Francelino exclaimed with an eloquent clack of his tongue.

"Don't tell me it's the same one . . ."

"You too? You, a sure vote for the late colonel? The secretary?"

"The secretary? What secretary? Whose?"

"The general's, so shy and retiring I've come to think she's a virgin. . . ."

"I don't know that one. Do you mean to tell me that he put his secretary in your clutches? What amazes me is the general's success with women. He doesn't have the looks or the charm. . . ."

"And how about yours? Who is she?"

"Who else would it be? That adorable demon who goes by the name of Maria João."

"The actress?"

"In the flesh. And she managed to get my vote for him, can you imagine?"

The two men laughed, softly and gleefully. Still intrigued, Paiva commented:

"Who would ever have thought that that Moreira had protectresses like those?"

"The truth is that Pereira's death solved our problems. But just look at the general. He doesn't look at all like the poor fellow who called on me. What's more, he can't be poor, judging by the basket of cordials and fancy biscuits he sent me."

"He really is poor, though. He lives on his general's salary. All he has to his name is the house where he lives, which cost him many sacrifices to buy. He must have spent a month's pay on you."

"How does it happen that you know so much about him?"

"Through Maria João, naturally. That little devil never stopped talking about all the general's virtues and trials and touting him as a poor, honest man."

"Can that be true? Those Army officers are economical and monogamous, they have few expenses, they always put aside a bit here and there, they build up their little nest egg. . . . The basket he sent me must have cost him a pretty penny."

"Has he ever come to the tea before? I keep seeing him in the assembly hall, listening attentively to the lectures. But I don't remember having seen him up here on the second floor before."

"I think he came up here once, when Rodrigo invited him. He was very ill at ease, and barely accepted a little cup of coffee. But today he's come up here on his own, and just look at what an appetite he has."

At the tea table, General Waldomiro Moreira was speaking in a loud voice, having a second cup of coffee with cream, making a perceptible breach in the cornmeal cake. Seeing him behave in that fashion, relaxed and quite at home, no one would have taken him for a mere candidate; he had assumed the role of a duly elected Academician. Justice Paiva, a man who knew how to enjoy life, returned to the pleasant subject of womanizing:

"Just between us, the one who's really fared well is our Rodrigo. The general's daughter is a real dish. . . ."

"You say that because you didn't see the secretary. . . . A divine mulatta. . . ."

"A mulatta?" The justice's sensitive pupils dilated, and his voice was tinged with envy. "You lucky dog."

Conversation at the Academy, waiting for the meeting to begin. A meeting during which the president announced the death of Colonel Sampaio Pereira. There now remained only one candidate striving for the chair left vacant by António Bruno: General Waldomiro Moreira. The Academician Lisandro Leite eulogized the deceased prospective member of the Illustrious Company, and asked that an expression of condolence be recorded in the minutes of the meeting.

Left alone at the tea table, the general and sole candidate swallowed a last piece of cake, reflecting on the stupidity of certain rules and customs: since he was practically an Academician, his rightful place was there among the other Immortals. In cases such as his, the paragraph of the official regulations, justified in principle, providing that those who were not Academicians be barred from entering the meeting room, ought not to apply—there was always an exception to every rule.

A MAN DEFEATED

On his return from the cemetery, Lisandro Leite—the only Academician (and one of the few civilians) present at the interment of Colonel Sampaio Pereira, his dear and fearsome friend Agnaldo—felt defeated. Worse still: without a candidate. He had placed all his hopes on an election that had turned into a disaster. On top of his desk, in the margin of the newspaper opened to the page with a long obituary announcing the death of the "illustrious officer and widely hailed writer, a candidate for the Brazilian Academy of Letters," Pru had written in red pencil: *It was high time he kicked off!* The thankless child.

For a few days he was glum, withdrawn, taciturn. On his return from the Academy meeting, he told Dona Mariúcia:

"I called for a vote of condolence and spoke a few words. Portela, Evandro, Figueiredo, the others smiled, gloating over my plight. Triumphant. General Moreira, who appeared for the tea, was beaming with joy. As the old saying goes, the person who enjoys the cake isn't the one who bakes it but the one who gets to eat it. All that hard work for nothing. And on top of everything else, Pru, that ingrate . . ."

"Leave Pru alone, and don't take it so much to heart."

"I was counting on being appointed to the Supreme Court."

"Don't worry. You'll get there someday."

"Nobody ever gives something for nothing, Mariúcia.

174

It's necessary to lay the groundwork, to create precisely the right conditions."

"You'll manage, I'm sure. Come on, buck up! I've never seen you like this before."

"The only way is to wait for Pérsio to give up and die. He seems to be made of cast iron; according to the doctors he should have been dead and buried long ago. . . . Then I'll back the candidacy of Raul Limeira, who's an intimate of The Man. ['The Man' was the head of state.] With his support and Paiva's, who knows . . ."

"See? All you have to do is wait. Everything comes in its own good time."

Lisandro's mind had gone off on another tack:

"There's something I wish I knew. . . ."

"What's that?"

"What happened when Agnaldo paid his courtesy visit to Pérsio. He was to call me immediately afterwards. He never did, and I tried all his phone numbers, but he wasn't at any of them. Then I talked to Dona Herminia, and Pérsio's letter to accompany his vote wasn't among the papers that Agnaldo left."

"Forget all that; it's water under the bridge. I'll tell you something: I'm certain that one of these days I'll be the wife of Justice Leite of the Supreme Court."

"I'm certain of only one thing: I don't deserve you."

"Idiot!"

Where did his consuming ambition come from? From him or from Mariúcia, elegant and serene?

■ HISTORICAL CLARIFICATION

The guerrilla forces were first marshaled on the Esplanada do Castelo, round about the Brazilian Academy of Letters, just after the alarmed and meaningful glances exchanged between the indignant Evandro Nunes dos Santos, pince-nez in hand, and the dumbfounded Mestre Afrânio Portela, on the following Thursday. In other words, one week after the plenary session during which President Hermano do Carmo informed the Academy members of the death of the candidate Colonel Agnaldo Sampaio Pereira, a month and a half before the election.

Contrary to what has been reported by less scrupulous and less trustworthy historians, the guerrilla campaign did not begin on the very day of the colonel's funeral. There was a brief interlude between the dramatic end of the Battle of the Petit Trianon and the beginning of the recruitment of volunteers for the new campaign. Little more than a week, quiet days when everything appeared to be reposing in God's own holy peace. Those who thought so, however, were not taking the mutability of human nature into account.

During the short period of time that elapsed between the aforementioned Thursday on which Ambassador Francelino Almeida, an old hand at intrigue, detected, at teatime, the symptoms of change in the behavior of General Waldomiro Moreira, the sole candidate, and the following Thursday, these vague symptoms had become obvious and threatening signs—sinister ones, Evandro called them. Whereupon the two old sharpshooters agreed to meet in secret to hatch a new conspiracy, immediately following that afternoon's session, at which the Academicians discussed, with their customary politeness, details of the projected spelling reform proposed by the Lisbon Academy of Sciences.

▒ THE FORMER FUTURE MINISTER

The moment General Waldomiro Moreira entered the salon where tea was being served, everyone realized that he had donned, without removing his Army uniform, the full regalia of an Academician. As the candidate put forward to oppose an adversary regarded as unbeatable, he had ripped off his general's stars, demoted himself to the rank of buck private, obscure and obsequious, a submissive dogface soldier, revering the Immortals, drinking in their words, applauding the most diverse ideas and opinions, in certain cases totally opposed to his own. He too had had to swallow his share of humiliations and affronts, of snakes and toads—the biggest one of all, impossible to get down, during the visit to Evandro. The essayist had offered him a copy of his polemical volume, *Militarism in Latin America*, the tenor of which was harshly negative—he held the military responsible for the misfortunes, the backwardness, the dependence characterizing the Latin-American countries' relations with England, the United States, Germany. Most impolitely, he had made it a point to repeat, to the general's face, opinions regarding the role of the armed forces that bordered on the insulting. The candidate had listened in silence, without answering.

Then suddenly everything changed. Two weeks later, after calculating votes with Afrânio Portela and Rodrigo Inácio Filho, he had gone to sleep defeated and awakened with his election a sure thing: his rival had kicked the bucket. The phase of humiliation and of bitter pills to swallow had ended.

He put the Academy regalia on over his general's uniform, on which the stars, the epaulettes, the medals gleamed once more, more brightly than ever, since, envisioning himself as already an Academician, he had now resumed his general's rank and authority. Thus doubly uniformed (despite being dressed in a badly tailored blue cashmere suit), he appeared once again at the weekly Academy tea, behaved as though he were already on intimate terms with his future colleagues, offered opinions, expressed disagreement. As for his appetite, it must be borne in mind that Dona Conceição, following his doctor's orders, kept him on a very strict diet. Whenever he could escape his wife's surveillance, he flung himself upon any sort of tasty morsel; at the tea table lavishly laden with all sorts of delicacies, he stuffed himself.

As it happened, this was the second time in his life that General Moreira, having been bitten by the blue-bottle fly of ambition, and itching badly, had advanced impetuously, taking up positions and assuming command prematurely, freeing himself of the burdensome mask of humility to show himself as God and a military career had made him: arrogant and authoritarian.

During Armando Sales de Oliveira's campaign for the presidency of the Republic, the general's name had been mentioned when assignments of ministerial portfolios were being discussed; if the candidate from São Paulo won, Moreira might be left the post of war minister.

The general never had any doubt that Sales would win: everyone knew that even though the writer José Américo de Almeida was an official candidate, he did not have the support of the president; the government had abandoned him to his fate. Moreover, it was difficult to imagine that a lowly backwoodsman from Paraiba, the representative of religious fanatics and brigands, of exploited, illiterate, starving people, could possibly defeat the candidate of the Bandeirantes and the more recent Paulistas, the owners of great coffee plantations and the new industrialists with Italian names, rich, cultivated, and progressive-minded people. São Paulo, the powerful locomotive pulling along, all by itself, the empty cars of the country's other states: on the platforms at political meetings, speakers tirelessly repeated the proud image.

Sure of Sales's victory, and even more sure of the ministerial portfolio. Not just a run-of-the-mill minister, of education or of public works. Minister of war: to all intents and purposes the second most important government official, just after the president.

He began to frequent the war ministry, where he was seen, on the eve of the putsch that began the regime of the New State, with a black portfolio full of documents tucked beneath his arm. He visited various secretariats, services, offices, in search of information that would be useful to him in his new post. He set up his ministerial cabinet, switched officers' commands, transferred, retired, promoted. All on paper, but making a great public show of the plans he had drawn up, of the program he intended to carry out. He even went so far as to reassign certain officers to key posts in advance.

Since he had very little backing from the military, it is possible that at the beginning of his campaign Armando Sales had thought of General Moreira, whose loyalty to him was beyond question, for that lofty post. But if such a possibility did occur to him he soon thought better of it, and abandoned it well before the November coup laid to rest not only the general's hopes and dreams, but also those of all the others who had devoted their every effort to the campaigns of the two candidates for the presidency. In order to compensate the general for his dedication, Sales planned to give him an excellent sinecure: military attaché in Paris, for example, a perfect assignment for the former top-ranking student of the French Military Mission, an honorary post involving no command decisions, and one located on the other side of the ocean. For besides being pretentious and high-handed, the general was a dreadful bore!

At the tea table, hearing Henrique Andrade complain to the president of the Academy about how far behind the secretarial staff was in sending out correspondence to Academicians, General Moreira spoke up, loud and clear:

"What's lacking in our Academy is a little military discipline. This house cannot function properly without the presence of at least one representative from the armed forces among its members. To impose order, to prevent the authority of the Academy from suffering even the slightest wounds."

Wounds? What wounds? In the silence that followed, old Evandro Nunes dos Santos and Mestre Afrânio Portela exchanged glances. Alarmed, meaningful ones.

The historical errors surrounding the dates and other details regarding the guerrilla campaign led by old Evandro doubtless stemmed from the highly clandestine nature of the various activities that were undertaken. All of the conspirators' plans were conceived and carried out in the strictest secrecy. Even if, instead of being two elderly liberal men of letters, Evandro and Afrânio had been two battle-hardened Bolsheviks with years and years of experience fighting underground, they would not have acted any more effectively or circumspectly.

There was no better place for a confidential conversation than the novelist's car. The chauffeur, Aurélio Sodré, sitting in silence in the front seat, had been in the employ of Afrânio and Dona Rosarinho for more than twenty-five years and was completely trustworthy.

The car heads for Santa Teresa to drop Evandro off at his house. Mestre Portela cuts the latter's indignant grumbling short:

"What precisely was it that you wanted? To have the members of the Academy vote for Sampaio Pereira? Moreira's a third-rate pen-pusher, I grant you, but the other candidate was a Nazi."

"If Moreira were nothing but a pen-pusher, it wouldn't matter that much to me; he wouldn't be the only one. But he's a despot. As I've told you before: this business of electing a military officer is a mistake." Evandro goes on in a rage: "The perfect candidate to take Bruno's place is Feliciano."

"I wouldn't argue with you there. I altogether agree. But in the jam we were in, our only solution was to fall back on a general. What's needed now is to be patient and put up with the situation."

"You can put up with it if you like, but I won't. I'm not one to be patient."

"And what the devil can you do? Moreira's the only candidate now."

"So what? He thinks he's already elected, but there's still more than a month to go before the election. . . ."

"You're suggesting . . . ?" Mestre Afrânio stares at his irate crony. A suspicion has dawned in his mind, and he is beinning to be intrigued.

"Suggesting! Why do you thing such a thing as a blank ballot exists, anyway?"

"But compadre, we went to his house to invite him to run, we urged him to present himself as a candidate. . . . We read his books, we praised them. . . . In all decency, we can't . . ."

"In the first place: I went to his house because you forced me to. Secondly: I've never read a single line he's written, Heaven be praised!" He counted on his fingers: "Thirdly: I chorused your praise of him so as not to leave you high and dry in such a situation. And fourthly: I'm not a decent man."

He removed his pince-nez and absorbed himself for some time in wiping the lenses clean:

"Neither you nor I . . . I've never seen such a wooden expression as the one on your face, praising such piffle and declaring it the work of genius."

Mestre Portela chuckled softly. Evandro went on:

"I've just read a documentary piece published in the United States on the Spanish civil war. During the Battle of Madrid, a fearless little woman known as 'La Pasionaria,' a name that tells you everything, a Communist or an anarchist, I'm not sure which, invented a watchword and confronted the Falangists with it: *No pasarán!* Well, I've just borrowed it. Do as you like, be decent, accuse me of being a scoundrel, remind me that I urged Maginot Line . . ."

"Evandro, that's going too far—a nickname pinned on him by Sampaio Pereira!"

"I heard it from José Livio, and it appealed to me. I

don't care where it came from, whether it's Communist or Nazi, and never mind the fact that Zé Livio is mentally retarded. What I'm trying to get across to you is that I'm totally in favor of civilian power, and am not about to take orders from any military officer. I never served in the Army, and was never even in the reserves."

A wicked gleam in Mestre Afrânio's eye:

"Don't forget, compadre, that in addition to casting a blank ballot, you have the possibility of abstaining." His hand tapped Evandro's bony knee. "A bit of guerrilla warfare never hurt anybody. . . ."

"You mean to say . . . ?"

"I was born to be a guerrilla fighter. . . . I'm at your service, Commander." He thought for a moment: "Given the present situation, the most important thing is secrecy. The enemy must not have the slightest suspicion; the general must feel that his success is assured. The more certain Moreira is that he's already elected, the more stupid mistakes he's going to make."

The car stops in front of the garden surrounding the Santa Teresa house. Aurélio gets out to open the rear door. Isabel spies the two oldsters and shouts to her brother:

"Pedro! Pedro! Grandfather's here! And Uncle Afrânio is with him."

They have not seen the family's closest friend, Álvaro's godfather, since the colonel's death. Isabel kisses the two old men on the cheek and remarks:

"I told Grandfather that everything was going to turn out all right, Uncle Afrânio."

"It's not over yet, my darling. We're taking up arms again."

Pedro arrives on the run and asks:

"What's up?"

"Here we are: Don Quixote, that stubborn old warrior—that is to say, your grandfather—and I, Sancho Panza, his faithful squire, off on another campaign."

"And who is Dulcinea, the damsel you're sallying forth to protect?"

Old Evandro Nunes dos Santos gathers his grandchildren round him. They were the ones who had persuaded him to fight against Sampaio Pereira the Nazi. In his voice permanently hoarse from smoking is a hint of emotion:

"The same one as for the Knight of La Mancha, my children: freedom."

The immense starry night is aborning amid the trees of the garden.

▧ THE SECRETARY LOSES HER JOB

Afrânio Portela sent her an armful of roses and a letter asking her to meet him in the same dairy bar. Rosa climbed out of a limousine with a driver in a chauffeur's uniform and cap.

"You're prettier every day." Afrânio contained his curiosity and did not ask questions about the car parked at the curb waiting for her. "I came to dismiss the general's secretary."

"I had an idea that would soon be the case when I read that man's obituary. I don't rejoice at anyone's death, but in this instance I felt no grief. It made me sick to think that that individual was going to deliver the encomium in Bruno's honor, paying him mere lip service, sullying the name of my beloved."

"We've gotten rid of that one, and now we must get rid of the other one."

"The general? But wasn't he your protégé? Didn't you invent that business about my being his secretary so I'd get him Lindinho's vote?"

"Whose vote?"

"The ambassador's. He insists that I call him Lindinho."

Mestre Afrânio explains the total change in the candidate's behavior, the way Academy elections work, blank ballots, abstentions.

"So I'm fired, am I? It's about time. Lindinho is getting out of hand. He's bent on my coming to drink champagne with him at his place. Not to mention the pinches he keeps giving me. Luckily the marks scarcely show on my dark skin. Otherwise . . ."

Mestre Afrânio mentally calculates the price of the limousine. Bruno's women surprise him and disconcert him, and he is unable to restrain his curiosity.

"Otherwise what?"

Rosa smiles as she sees him staring at the car:

"You know him. He's a friend of yours." She mentions the name of a wealthy textile manufacturer, a Portuguese by birth. "He's going to set me up in a dressmaker's shop of my own, on the Rua do Rosário, on the second floor. I'll be working for myself."

"And his Argentine mistress?"

"She went back to Buenos Aires. When he became a widower, she was determined to get him to marry her; she even put a knife to his chest. . . ."

"A good-looking woman, but bad medicine! 'Señora Delia Pilar, tango singer.' " He smiles, imitating a Buenos Aires accent. "She's the worst tango singer I've ever heard."

"Madame Picq sent me to her house to give her a fitting. That was where I met my present . . . protector."

"The next time I see him, I'll offer him my congratulations. He's gotten rid of that pain in the neck and picked the most beautiful rose in Rio. I congratulate you too. He's a good-hearted, decent man."

"I know. All he wants is a little affection. I think we're going to get along very well together. Affection and respect—those are things I can give him." A smile comes over her full lips, and in her voice there is a note of both sadness and pride: "I've already had the love I wanted; I need only remember those days to feel happy. But tell me, are you letting me go?"

"You're dismissed as a secretary. I just want to know a couple of things. Does he have your address? How does he get in touch with you and arrange to meet you? By phone?"

184

"He thinks that I live in a residence for young ladies run by nuns, where I have to be in before nine o'clock at night. That I came to Rio from the provinces when the general promised to take me under his wing; my father had been his orderly. I made up a few little lies like that. I gave him the phone number of Madame Picq's workshop—with her consent; I told her the whole story and she had a good laugh over it. Lindinho always calls at lunchtime; he thinks it's a French nun who answers the phone, and he says that it's my uncle calling. A comedy routine. He thinks my name is Beatriz, and he calls me Bia. Bia this and Bia that and *whoops:* a big fat pinch for good measure."

"Arrange with Madame Picq to do the following: when the ambassador telephones, she's to tell him that you don't want to see him anymore, that he should stop phoning you. At the same time Madame must give him to understand that the establishment he's calling is not a residence for young ladies by any manner of means, but something quite different, and leave Lindinho—Lindinho, I can't get over that name!—all at sea."

"What is it you want him to think?"

"Nothing that he can pin down precisely. All that's needed is to create a doubt in his mind, the suspicion that everything's not quite on the up-and-up. . . ."

"So as to make him furious at my ex-employer . . ."

"Exactly. And no longer willing to vote for him."

"Poor Lindinho. I've never met such a pawer. When you're least expecting it, his hand starts creeping down the neck of your dress or up under your skirt. He must have been a holy terror in his younger days. . . ."

"Even today, his reputation lives on in Japan and Scandinavia."

"You know what? He's really delightful. He adores telling naughty stories. . . ."

"I put you in a short story, do you remember, Rosa? And I think I'm going to put you in a novel now. All I knew back then was that you were the most gentle, sweet, and tender creature imaginable, and now I know that besides being sweet and gentle, you're bold and brave, altogether fearless."

"That was António's doing. He was the one who made me what I am."

Afrânio Portela remembered the verse: "rose of copper, rose of honey, child-rose." He kissed her hand: Bruno's Rose.

◧ DISAGREEMENTS REGARDING LANGUAGE

"Have you read this?" R. Figueiredo Jr. hands a copy of the *Correio do Rio* to the president of the Academy. "I came by to show it to you." He points a finger at the column entitled "In Defense of the Portuguese Language," advice on grammar whereby General Waldomiro Moreira teaches the ignorant masses how to write in proper Portuguese, in the mother tongue at its purest.

"No, I haven't read it. For the moment, I'm not duty-bound to do so, since the columnist is not yet a member of the Academy, contrary to what he may think. I still have a month left before I'll be obliged to add this trial to all the other tasks incumbent on the president."

"You simply must read it—precisely because the author is not yet an Academician. . . ."

Hermano do Carmo takes the paper:

"In this heat, my dear Figueiredo . . ." He begins reading, then raises his eyes: "This candidate that you people came up with . . . to oppose the one whom God took to His bosom at an opportune moment. . . . Dying was the only useful thing that man ever did. . . ." He goes back to his reading. "What a dolt!"

The president, whose proverbial politeness had become even more noticeable in his exercise of an office that requires sagacity and tact, rarely used pejorative expressions in referring to a fellow scholar, whether an Academician or a mere mortal. He was staggered, however, by the effrontery of this candidate who wasn't even waiting to be officially elected before making public pronouncements as to the proper conduct of Academy affairs. The general disagreed openly with the position of a considerable number of members of the Illustrious House with regard to the explosive question of the spelling reform being studied by the joint committee made up of representatives of the Brazilian Academy and of the Lisbon Academy of Sciences. The Brazilian delegates had not yet arrived at a unanimous agreement reconciling their divergent points of view, thus making it difficult for the committee to proceed with its work.

"The man is unbelievable. Earlier on, there was no one more unpretentious, more respectful, I would even go so far as to say fawning. He's made a complete about-face; being the sole candidate has gone to his head. He never misses a tea, he talks interminably and in a loud voice, gives orders, criticizes. The other day, he grabbed me by the arm and subjected me to a lecture on painting. In his opinion, we hang pictures according to the wrong criteria. We do not give an important enough place to artists that he considers to be first-rate, whereas on the other hand we single out others that in his view are third-rate daubers. You can't imagine how insolent he was."

He reads the last lines and hands the paper back:

"He should have presented himself as a candidate for the Lisbon Academy rather than the Brazilian."

A number of the delegates appointed to the joint committee, among them R. Figueiredo Jr., defended the need to take into account the effect on the written language of certain original features of Portuguese as spoken in Brazil. They were opposed to the view of certain of their Portuguese counterparts, who insisted that strict standards be applied, based on what was correct usage in the Portuguese spoken and written in Portugal, a position unacceptable to the Brazilians. The dramatist used the term "cultural colonialism" to define the position taken by those philologists who insisted upon identical and rigid rules, a unilateral grammar, for the written language in two such widely different countries. In point of fact, both delegations were at the moment divided on this painful and delicate question.

In his weekly column offering opinions and advice on language, General Moreira supported the Lusitanian position unconditionally, and dogmatically outlined the policy that the Brazilian delegation ought to follow, namely "preserving by fire and sword" the purity of the language of Camões as it had been handed down by classic authors. In response to a question from a hypothetical reader, he criticized those whose concessions to the scoundrels bastardizing the language were leading the Academy to abandon its most sacred duty, "preserving the last flower of Latium by keeping its rules intact." He concluded by announcing that within a short time he personally would be participating in the debates, fighting to prevent such pernicious errors. An impatient man, he had prematurely appointed himself war minister in the past, and now he was occupying his chair in the Academy before being elected to it.

"We're really in a fix now. As if we didn't have enough trouble already, what with Alcântara dividing our delegation with his maniacal purism. . . ."

"Your general's going too far. He should at least have waited to be elected before giving us a public dressing-down."

"Why the devil did that unspeakable cop wait till the registration period for candidates was closed before kicking off? What can we possibly do now?"

"Let's see you people who came up with this hot potato peel it now, if you can." And the president adds, with feigned indifference, as though merely volunteering a piece of information: "It would appear that Evandro had some ideas on the subject. Why don't you have a talk with him?"

⚡ THE COMMITTEE IS DISSOLVED

R. Figueiredo Jr. went beyond the president's advice. He not only got in touch with old Evandro Nunes dos Santos; he also phoned the members of the committee that had gone to Grajaú some three months before in order to urge General Waldomiro Moreira—the author of, among other tomes, *Linguistic Prolegomena*—to present himself as a candidate for the Brazilian Academy of Letters, and invited them to his apartment for drinks.

Once he had filled their glasses and passed appetizers around, he showed the other committee members the offensive article. What did they think of it?

Evandro had read it and had had mimeographed copies of it made to distribute to those Academicians who were taking a nationalist stance with regard to the question of language. Figueiredo went off to get a copy of the article out of his filing cabinet. Evandro then informed them of the decision that he and Afrânio had arrived at with regard to the general's candidacy. "We're scoundrels!" he concluded in his usual abrupt manner.

"Since we were already on a war footing," the novelist added, "we planned a guerrilla campaign, along the lines of the Maquis in France. We were going to inform you, but we had already set to work. With great discretion and with impressive results."

"I didn't hear one word about it," Rodrigo said.

"Why didn't you let me know immediately?" Figueiredo complained.

"Despite your discretion, I sniffed something in the air," Henrique Andrade announced. "Paiva is all at sea. Our divine Maria João spent more than a month trying to persuade him to vote for the general, and then all of a sudden she insisted that he should cast a blank ballot. I suspected that Afrânio had had a hand in creating all this confusion."

They discussed the situation. Though they all agreed that the general was an arrogant and annoying nuisance, determined to transform the Academy into a military barracks and the Academicians into disciplined troops, not all of them were ready to form a guerrilla band, and the committee of five was dissolved.

Henrique Andrade apologized for backing out. Had circumstances been different, he would have been pleased to join them to keep that scribbler from occupying an Academy chair. But the country was in the midst of such a serious political crisis, what with the dictatorship of the New State, that as he saw it democrats had a duty to ally themselves with anyone and everyone capable of helping in some way to change the situation. And the general, even though he had been relegated to the reserves and was without a command, nonetheless still had influence in military circles. During the general's campaign for an Academy seat, they had talked together, exchanged opinions, laid plans. Inasmuch as he did not feel that his vote would be decisive, Henrique was not going to change it. He wouldn't mind if the general were blackballed. But he did not want to contribute to bringing such an eventuality about, since he had certain political ties to the candidate. Whatever the result of the election, he wanted to remain on good terms with the general. Furthermore, he would be in Bahia on the day of the election. Before departing, he would leave the letter containing his vote with the general himself.

Rodrigo also asked to be excused. He too would have been pleased to take part in the guerrilla campaign; the Battle of the Petit Trianon had been an exciting experience that he would recount later on in a subsequent volume of his *Memoirs of Another*. But he too had reasons to remain on the sidelines of the skirmishes. They were not civic reasons like Henrique's, but they were equally worthy of respect.

"Domestic reasons," Mestre Afrânio said with a sly, knowing laugh. "Very well, young man, you're excused."

As for R. Figueiredo Jr., his one desire was to be in the forefront of the battle. He was all enthused on learning of the steps that had already been taken.

⚑ AFRÂNIO PORTELA'S VERSION OF THE CANDIDATE'S UNDERHANDED MANEUVERS

Purposely arriving at the Academy ahead of time, Afrânio Portela found *doyen* Francelino Almeida sitting alongside the treasurer, signing the attendance register and thereupon receiving the little envelope with the *jeton* for being present at the meeting. Afrânio and Francelino headed together for the filing cabinets where the mail received by the forty Immortals is kept in private drawers.

"You seem to be looking a little down in the mouth, Francelino. Have you been ill? At our age we must watch our health."

"My health is fine. I don't feel at all indisposed."

"Well, what is it then?" Mestre Afrânio persisted, deeply interested in the well-being of his colleague and friend.

"Certain things are worrying me."

They picked up their mail and returned to the Academy office. The novelist led the diplomat over to a window recess.

"What things?"

"That general, for example. He's changed a great deal, don't you think?"

Having received the cue he'd been waiting for, Afrânio came straight to the point.

"As far as I'm concerned, he's changed far too much. I don't mind telling you, Francelino, that I've been vastly disappointed by that man." He lowered his voice. "As you may have noticed, in the beginning I was interested in his candidacy; I even spoke to two or three friends about it. . . ."

"So I heard."

"Later on, however, on learning of certain . . . how shall I put it? . . . ignoble facts, I changed my mind completely. Strictly between the two of us—something no one else must know, above all the candidate himself—I've decided to cast a blank ballot."

The *doyen* gave signs of being intensely interested:

"Ignoble facts? Of what sort?"

"Underhanded maneuvers. I'm going to tell you the whole story, in confidence. I have an old friend, from my bohemian days, a Frenchwoman who is the proprietress of a most hospitable 'pension' for young ladies, carefully chosen girls who in no way appear to be what they really are. The other day I ran into her and she told me an incredible story. Can you imagine? General Moreira, a habitué of the house, paid one of the girls, with whom he customarily takes his pleasure, to win the votes of certain Academicians for him, by passing herself off as his secretary. . . ."

The *doyen's* face suddenly turned pale:

"That's unbelievable! What a scoundrel!"

"Madame Picq, the proprietress of the pension, had great fun answering the phone calls from a number of our colleagues, trying to get in touch with the girl. The lively *maison de rendezvous* suddenly turned into a most respectable residence for young ladies, run by nuns, and when Madame answered the phone she was Sister Picq, a French nun. A downright scandal."

"A *maison de rendezvous*, eh? . . . Hmmm! Hmmm! The general a habitué, is he? What a reprobate! Paiva told me he was poor, yet he sent me a basket of delicacies, a very expensive one, from Ramos and Ramos."

"He sent me one too. And one to Evandro, one to Figueiredo . . ."

"And where does he get the money to pay for all these things? To hire high-class prostitutes, to make purchases at Ramos and Ramos, at the prices they charge?"

Mestre Afrânio lowered his voice still further, speaking almost in the ear of the diplomat, whose loyalty to the government, whatever regime was in power, regardless of its nature, was notorious—Francelino Almeida had a horror of opposing the powers that be:

"So you don't know, then, that the general is the right-hand man of Armando Sales, of the people who attempted the coup in 'thirty-eight, along with the Integralistas? He didn't take part in the fracas personally because he wasn't in Rio at the time."

"I knew he'd been in Armando's camp."

"He still is; he's one of the most active members of the conspiracy against the regime. He wants to get himself a seat in the Academy precisely in order to have a cover that will enable him to act with impunity. Behind him are Armando Sales's people, the Mesquitas of São Paulo. They're the ones who furnish the money to cover the expenses of his candidacy. The biscuits you ate, my old friend, were subversive."

"But in that case, electing that man to the Academy is dangerous!"

"Once he found himself the sole candidate, he dismissed the girls and stopped sending baskets. In my opinion, the worst thing of all is the attempt to use the Academy for political ends. You know that I'm not in sympathy with the regime, but I don't engage in politics here within the Academy; I think it should remain an institution apart, above political contingencies and controversies of the moment. For all these reasons, I've changed my vote."

"I never intended to vote for him," the *doyen* said with the barefaced lack of scruples of the seasoned diplomat. "I'd pledged my vote to Sampaio Pereira. You're absolutely right: a vote for that man is sheer folly. Luckily you've alerted me to the danger."

There was still one thing he wanted to clear up:

"And how about Maria João? Why was she campaigning for him?"

"That's something else altogether. Maria João is a cousin of the general's wife, and she became involved at her cousin's request."

"I do thank you, Portela. I'm most grateful."

"Above all, don't let the general realize where you stand. He's a dangerous sort, capable of taking violent revenge. Do as I do: I keep on the friendliest of terms with him and let him think he's got my vote in his pocket. When it comes time to deposit our ballot in the box . . . After our votes have been burned, how can anyone guess which of us cast blank ballots?"

❋ THE DOUBLE-DEALING ALLIANCE

Lisandro Leite brooded for exactly two weeks, the space of time that elapsed between the first and the last of the three sessions of the Academy following the death of Colonel Sampaio Pereira. When he returned home that third Thursday afternoon, he didn't seem like the same person: his depression had vanished. Dona Mariúcia was well acquainted with her husband's abrupt mood-swings.

"What's happened? All of a sudden you're not down in the dumps anymore."

"Something incredible. If anyone had told me, I wouldn't have believed it. But I've had proof, concrete proof. The very same individuals who urged the general to present himself as a candidate, the Portela clique, are now trying their best to put the quietus on it. I've discovered things that take my breath away. This time the one who's really up in arms is Evandro. He keeps referring to the general only as 'Maginot Line,' the nickname Agnaldo invented for him."

He recounted all the details to her: phrases with a double meaning, confidences cleverly drawn out, words idly spoken, whispers overheard.

"And what about you? What are you going to do? Back the general?"

A broad smile appeared on the jurist's fat face:

"Who, me? Not a chance. I'm going to join them. . . . The seat on the Supreme Court can still be ours after this election is over. If the general isn't elected, if he doesn't even win a majority of the votes . . ."

He explained, analyzing the situation: if the general weren't elected, he, Lisandro, would be twice as strong as before, in a privileged position to claim the seat that would be left open on the Supreme Court on Paiva's retirement.

For one thing, the supporters of the late colonel, powerful government officials, would be pleased if the Academy rejected the general, a member of the opposition who was an enemy of the New State. They would not attribute the failure of his candidacy to Evandro and Portela, but rather to him, Lisandro, since he was about to immediately inform all those with whom he had remained in contact during the battle for Sampaio Pereira's candidacy, beginning with the minister of war, the chief constable of the regime, of his vast labors to prevent the election of the stubborn enemy of established institutions, having taken this task upon himself in order to honor the memory of his late lamented friend the colonel, who had passed on at the very moment when the country needed him most. Furthermore, the Academy chair having been once again declared vacant, he would sponsor the candidacy of Raul Limeira, the rector of the national university, an intimate friend of the head of state. A physician, Limeira's aspirations did not lie in the direction of a seat on the Supreme Court. Limeira could be a decisive trump card when the triple list of nominees was put forward and the time came to appoint the new justice to sit on the court. You don the full regalia of the Academy, and in return I'll get the robes of a Supreme Court justice.

Dona Mariúcia buried her elegant, well-manicured fingers in her husband's unruly lion's mane:

"Didn't I tell you not to worry, my dear Justice?"

And thus was born the double-dealing alliance between

Evandro's forces and those of Lisandro Leite, whereby the band of guerrillas received unexpected volunteer reinforcements. An informal but active alliance, and in all likelihood a decisive one.

▓ THE MAQUISARDS

As a result of the war, French intellectuals of various sorts and persuasions had sought asylum in Brazil. Writers, publishers, journalists, singers, painters, people from the world of the theater. The most eminent of them, Georges Bernanos, settled in Minas Gerais, and the others made their homes either in Rio or in São Paulo. They joined the prestigious professors who had arrived in 1937 to occupy recently-established university chairs. An outstanding figure among them was Roger Bastide, the writer and scientist.

With the support of Brazilian intellectuals, they set to work organizing aid for the French Resistance, for the Free French forces of General de Gaulle, and for the Maquisards. Conditions in the country at the time were unfavorable to the political activities of the Free French, since the dictatorship of the New State was beginning to collaborate more and more closely with the Nazi-fascist Axis powers; rumors circulated that Brazil was about to adhere to the anti-Comintern pact that had been signed by the Reich, Italy, and Japan, with the support of Franco's Spain; the head of state conferred, without the knowledge of the minister of foreign relations, with Hitler's ambassador, to discuss ways and means of broadening the ideological and economic ties linking the two nations so as to lead eventually to a treaty of alliance between them. Despite this, by exploiting the internal contradictions within the regime and the marked sympathy of Brazilians toward France and its culture, the exiles managed to organize an active movement that, on the one hand, was not entirely clandestine, but on the other hand was not public either. The government kept them under police surveillance, but tolerated their activities. Eminent figures in the intellectual, military, and political life of the country—the aforementioned minister of foreign relations, Oswaldo Aranha, General Leitão de Carvalho, and, according to persistent rumors, the dictator's own daughter, Alzira Vargas—opposed the alliance with the Axis and actively participated in the efforts of the group of Free French, few in number but hardworking and dynamic, who, far from their occupied homeland, were fighting for its liberation.

Among the Brazilian intellectuals with closest ties to the French Resistance movement were the Academicians Evandro Nunes dos Santos, Alceu de Amoroso Lima, Afrânio Portela, R. Figueiredo Jr., the poets Murilo Mendes and Augusto Frederico Schmidt, the actor Procópio Ferreira and the actress Maria João, the writers Álvaro Moreyra, Sérgio Milliet, Josué Montello, Anibal Machado, and the publisher of the literary review *Dom Casmurro*, Bricio de Abreu, who had lived in Paris for more than ten years.

All of them, plus a number of other anti-fascists, met at Evandro Nunes dos Santos's home on the occasion of the arrival in Rio of Professor Roger Bastide, who had come to deliver lectures and establish contacts. A close friendship, born of mutual admiration, united the two essayists. Evandro had gathered together all those friends of France to meet with Bastide and to explore effective ways of helping the Gaullist groups and the Maquis—the Resistance. The young mistress of the house, Isabel, together with her brother and her grandfather, received them, radiant with joy—she was, after all, António Bruno's goddaughter.

Among the decisions arrived at, one in particular took on special interest because of the funds it was certain to raise and, above all, the publicity it would receive: Maria

João proposed that they organize a single benefit performance, on behalf of the Free French and on a Monday evening (the day of the week that theaters closed to give performers time off), of a play written by António Bruno, *Mary John*, in which she had made her debut in 1922 with the Leopoldo Froes Theatrical Company. The pretext would be the celebration of her twentieth year on stage. General enthusiasm: under the patronage of *Dom Casmurro*, Álvaro Moreyra agreed to direct the new production and Santa Rosa promised to design the sets. R. Figueiredo Jr. would write the program, Procópio would play the part of the fake Hollywood star (a role created by Froes in the original production), Afrânio Portela would take on the task of obtaining permission to use the Teatro Fénix from the owners, the Guinles. Everyone, beginning with the ladies, promised to sell tickets, at a stiff price.

A joyous evening, a well-laden table, drinks of excellent quality, brilliant conversation, the adolescent enthusiasm on the part of Pedro and Isabel for the cause of French freedom. Having made their plans, the guests wandered out into the garden to enjoy the sea breeze on the stifling-hot December night. Mestre Afrânio, Dona Rosarinho, and Maria João sat down together on one of the rustic benches beneath a breadfruit tree.

"What a marvelous idea of yours that was, Maria João," Dona Rosarinho said, affectionately taking the actress's hand.

"I learned lots of things from Bruno, one of which was to love France. And besides, you know, I've always wanted to restage the play he wrote for me—my play. It may seem naïve today, but the verses are still wonderful, don't you think? The one problem is that I played the part of Mary John when I was twenty years younger; I'll be thirty-eight soon. . . . "

"Don't spread the news. Nobody would take you for more than thirty . . . ," Mestre Afrânio said, paying her a gallant compliment that happened to be the pure and simple truth.

"I thought of inviting a young actress to play the role, but I confess that I'm dying to play it again myself. It's like going back to those days; Mary John is me at the age of nineteen. But can I get away with that?"

"Easily," Dona Rosarinho answered. "I wouldn't pull the wool over your eyes and let you make a fool of yourself. It's just a question of makeup." The two of them had been friends ever since the long-ago days of the original production of *Mary John.*

Mestre Afrânio changed the subject:

"And what about our Academy electors? How's it going with the right-about-face, *les tournants de l'histoire?*"

Maria João's mischievous laughter rang out among the trees:

"The most amusing cheap farce . . . To think I managed to sew up four votes for that scoundrel of a general, not counting good old Paiva's, and then had to undo everything and make a hundred-and-eighty-degree turn. If you could only have seen the poor dears' faces. . . ."

"How did you explain your interest in the general's cause?" Dona Rosarinho asked.

"Very simple: family ties. I claimed I was a first cousin and an intimate friend of his wife's."

"And what reasons have you given them now for asking them to cast blank ballots or to abstain?"

"I invented a frightful story that scandalized the poor things. Filled with indignation, very nearly in tears, I reveal how intolerably the general has behaved. Lacking all respect for his wife, his home and fireside, friendship, he tried to seduce me in his own house and drag me off to the conjugal bed. A horrendous scene, worthy of the best Italian melodrama: the general trying to rape me, and me heroically resisting. Freeing myself from his clutches only after a terrible struggle, my blouse ripped to shreds, my breasts black and blue, I made my escape as he insulted me, calling me unmentionable names. The effect on my poor darlings was unbelievable. They know that never in my entire life have I ever gone to bed with the husband of a friend of mine, whoever he might be."

Afrânio Portela averted his eyes and looked up at the starry sky: he knew that better than anyone else. Maria João, stubbornly clinging to her very few firm prejudices—my principles, as she called them. When, years after Bruno, Afrânio had presented himself as a candidate, she had ended the conversation:

"It's not possible, my adored Mestre Afrânio. You know how fond I am of you, but I'm Dona Rosarinho's friend. Impossible; don't insist, so as not to make me feel sad."

A sea breeze gently ruffled the great actress's hair as she ended her story:

"The dears were revolted. Who could possibly vote for a monster like that? The poor general. . . . How come he turned into such a rotter all of a sudden?"

"He's not a rotter; he's a general."

R. Figueiredo Jr. came over to them, with a concupiscent gleam in his eye:

"Maria, I've just been talking with Alvinho"—he was referring to Álvaro Moreyra—"and we've had an idea for the performance, a real inspiration."

Maria João rose to her feet and offered her arm to the dramatist who had translated Ibsen for only one reason— to enable her to be Hedda Gabler:

"Come and tell me about it. . . ."

Afrânio Portela's eyes followed their silhouettes as they disappeared in the dark. Maria João must not be a friend of Figueiredo's wife. Vitality incarnate, devouring men and events, garnering fame and fortune, ex-Princess of Mid-Lent, born in a wretched suburb, a great actress. Bruno's loves, his women—he had left his mark on all of them. *A* for António, *A* for *amor*, an indelible brand burned into their hearts.

Mestre Portela had not told Rosarinho the news because he hadn't yet made up his mind to confront the reams of blank paper. But he had been more and more strongly tempted to write the novel he had in mind, in the course of this conspiratorial night during which the Maquisards set up camp on the heights of Santa Teresa, in the city of Rio de Janeiro.

❖ CLOCLÔ AND EXU-SEVEN-LEAPS

Flighty, oh so flighty! And yet she's good-hearted and fair-minded, General Waldomiro Moreira reflects on hearing Cecília's suggestion. The young woman has diverted her attention from the radio, where Stela Maris is singing blues, to say:

"Father, when you're in command at the Academy, arrange for Claudionor to be awarded a prize right away. Cloclô deserves one."

"You're right there; he has many merits. A devoted friend, with a sense of hierarchy. It's hard to believe he's a civilian."

As a matter of fact, Claudionor Sabença seems more like the general's orderly, ever at his service. He had dogged his every footstep, attended the Academicians' lectures and applauded, listened attentively to the general's accounts of his courtesy visits, counted and recounted the possible votes—calculations that have happily become pointless, thanks to the timely death of the colonel.

Moreover, in strictest confidence, the author of the *Descriptive Grammar of the Portuguese Language* (First, Second, and Third Year) has claimed responsibility for the disappearance of Cecília's father's redoubtable adversary. Interested in spiritualism, from time to time he visits a place where voodoo rites are practiced, a *terreiro d'umbanda* where Mother Graziela do Bunokô reigns, a fat, absolute queen who receives, among other less awesome spirits, the powerful one revered under the name of Exu-Seven-Leaps, a devil capable of casting indescribable evil spells. When Exu-Seven-Leaps intervenes, on being invoked by Mother Graziela, it is as though lightning has struck. For matters involving money and love, getting a man and a woman in bed together or separating them, cases of jealousy or the evil eye, the priestess calls upon other spirits. On the purebred Indian Curiboca, the very best one for curing sick people, on Yemanjá Maré Alta, a specialist in lovers' quarrels, and on the old black, Ritacinio, whose forte is the numbers game, the lottery, and everything else having to do with money. Mother Graziela reserves Seven-Leaps for desperate cases, knotty problems requiring special treatment, strong magic.

Sabença requested, and paid for, a powerful spell, one that cost him an arm and a leg, whereby Seven-Leaps would block every path leading Colonel Sampaio Pereira to the Academy. The supplicant's aim was purely and simply electoral; the blood of the roosters and the candlewax were merely intended to close the portals of the House of Machado de Assis to General Moreira's adversary. But Seven-Leaps, as Mother Graziela warned and Sabença later realized, was heavy-handed; he was not content to go halfway. He went all the way—and left the colonel stone cold dead.

A practicing Catholic, General Moreira did not believe in such superstitions. But Dona Conceição and the forsaken Cecília did not have a moment's doubt, and sent an offering to buy cane brandy and cheroots for the blessed Exu. Whether it was superstition or exorcism, Sabença deserved their thanks.

"When the prizes are awarded next year, I'll try to get one for Sabença. He could receive the José Verissimo Prize for the anthology that he's just had published." The general knows all about the prizes awarded by the Academy.

"Wouldn't it be possible this year, Father? It would be a nice Christmas present for Cloclô."

"An Academy prize isn't a Christmas present, you silly girl. But he can set his mind at rest. I'll take care of the matter. And don't use such a ridiculous nickname to refer to a philologist who, despite being a very young man still, has already won a certain renown."

Pleased at his answer, Cecília comments:

"Once you've entered the Academy you're going to be a terribly important man, aren't you, Father? It's only bigwigs who get in there, people from the very top drawer of society."

Taking advantage of this rare moment of interest in such matters on the part of his daughter, the general tells her a number of things in confidence: the basic makeup of the Academy is in need of thoroughgoing reform, a necessarily slow process since its members are appointed for life. In the elections held in recent years, certain principles that had oriented the choice of Academicians since the foundation of the House had clearly been abandoned. In earlier days, priority had been given to representatives of the upper classes of society. Today, preference was given to writers, even when they possessed no qualifications other than literary ones, to the point that the Illustrious Company had recently been without a single representative of the armed forces—an absurdity! Not that he was against the entry of writers, but it was necessary to know how to choose them. Certain of the ones seated there at present—Heaven preserve us!—had no knowledge of the most elementary rules of grammar, and positively murdered the Portuguese language. Some of them lacked even the sense of propriety required to be worthy of wearing the regalia of immortality. With all due modesty, he himself was the example of a perfect choice: a writer and a high-ranking Army officer, a general. He turns toward his daughter, whose attention is now divided between what her father is saying and the music being played on the radio, the divine voice of Stela Maris:

"Don't go telling everybody what I've just said. Don't breathe a word of what I've told you to anyone, do you hear? Above all, not to an Academician," he orders.

If only she wouldn't tell Rodrigo, at those times when . . . Flighty, oh so flighty! But despite everything a good daughter: a heart of gold and a sense of what is only right and fair.

❧ CECÍLIA THE INSIPID

A heart of gold and a sense of what is only right and fair, perhaps. Generous toward those to whom she gives herself, eternally hoping to find a man who won't grow tired of her.

Why does it always turn out like that? When men first meet her, they are inflamed with desire, pay her court, try to seduce her, lay the world at her feet. In the beginning, everything always goes wonderfully well: Cecília is charming, alluring, and gives all of herself, the works.

Why doesn't their interest in her last, why does it flag after only a short time? One of them, good-looking and stupid, had flung a cruel word in her face: "Banal, you're banal, don't you realize that?" Another, less good-looking and cruder still, referring to the hour of truth, used an insulting image: "Insipid, you're as insipid as a tasteless lettuce leaf without a drop of salad dressing." First she cried, and then she dipped into her reserves, because she couldn't live without a man. Whom did she take after? Dona Conceição has never found an answer to that question.

The first and only man on the waiting list (the dental surgeon, a handsome young man who looked like José Mojica, had dropped out when he caught her by surprise with Rodrigo), Claudionor Sabença soon saw his patient and persistent attentions rewarded. Cecília became more human; she began leaning on his arm, peeking at him out of the corner of her eye, and looking away in shy confusion when he caught her doing so. She listened to his poem in honor of her and sighed: "For me? How marvelous! I don't deserve such a thing." The hour of triumph was close at hand.

With Rodrigo, Cecília had reached the very heights of glory: he was noble, rich, had his name in the papers, his picture in magazines, accompanied by extravagant praise of his charms, the very last word in taste and refinement. He would never call her banal or insipid; he was courtesy itself. She nonetheless sensed that he had lost interest in her. Their love-trysts grew less and less frequent: in the beginning they had met every day, then later every other day, and after that every three days, and now just once a week and sometimes not even that. At their last meeting, Rodrigo had informed her that he would soon be leaving for Petrópolis, where he would be spending Christmas and New Year's, returning to Rio in mid-January to cast his vote for the general.

Cecília had suggested that she accompany him: she could stay in a pension. But Rodrigo refused, as usual with the greatest politeness, explaining that the brief separation would make their reunion all the more eagerly desired. But Cecília knew that there would be no reunion.

In any event, he would not be leaving immediately. He wanted to attend the benefit performance being put on by Maria João during Christmas week: the new production of António Bruno's play. During the next week, because before then he didn't have a single free moment, he would bring tickets for her, the general, and her mother. Since he would be delivering the formal encomium of the poet in his acceptance speech, Cecília's father couldn't get out of attending the play, all of it in verse. The very prince of politeness, Rodrigo asked the family's permission to offer them the tickets as a gift. The next week without fail, he repeated. It would be their last meeting, Cecília surmised. So refined, so elegant, so nice, so well-endowed—oh, what a shame!

It was at this juncture that Cecília called Claudionor Sabença "Cloclô" for the first time. In an access of passion, Cloclô answered: "Ciça, my sweet Ciça!"

"The visit is absolutely indispensable. No candidate can arrogate to himself the right not to visit this or that Academician, on any pretext whatsoever. The Academician, yes—he is free to dispense with or even to refuse the visit; but the candidate is obliged to request a day and an hour when he can be received in order to announce his intention and plead insistently for the Academician's support."

In the Academy library, leaning back in an armchair, fingering his cigarette case, old Francelino Almeida is setting forth his categorical opinion to three colleagues who had been discussing the subject when he arrived. The *doyen* of the Academy, an Immortal for forty-three years, the last survivor of the founding members, an indisputable authority on everything having to do with the statutes, rules, and traditions of the Illustrious House, he is listened to with attention and respect:

"I know full well that the courtesy visit is not prescribed in the official rules; it is not a requirement set down in writing. Nonetheless, it is more of a hard-and-fast rule than any of the other provisions laid down in the statutes or regulations. It is the condition sine qua non if the candidate is to be elected. It is pointless to speak of enmity or of disdain. Here in this cenacle, there are no enemies or adversaries, and every member deserves respect."

He could discourse for hours on the subject, since he considered it a principle fundamental to the preservation of the prestige and the authority of the Illustrious Company:

"The fact that an Academician publicly manifests his approval of a certain candidate, promising him his vote, does not free the other candidates of their obligation to pay him a formal visit. On the contrary, in such circumstances the visit becomes all the more indispensable."

He puffs with pleasure on his cigarette—precisely five a day so as to avoid colds and bronchitis—and goes on:

"The Academy is unique, without peer; it must be courted, flattered. And since the Academy is made up of Academicians, logic requires that we be courted and flattered. What would become of us without these visits?"

His colleagues greet his question with exclamations that second the venerable diplomat's statements. He concludes, in a stern tone of voice:

"The general is committing a grave, inexcusable error by announcing that he will not visit Lisandro. Why is he assuming this arrogant position? Because Lisandro did his best to further Sampaio Pereira's candidacy? A right that was his to enjoy, and a right that he exercised. The general is the one who has no right to take offense and break with one of the most longstanding traditions of the Academy. He is behaving very badly."

The *doyen*'s summing up of the situation meets with the unanimous approval of the colleagues who are listening to him. One of them adds:

"As well as being high-handed, Maginot Line is loose-tongued. I don't know which is worse."

He might well have added that, in addition to being high-handed and loose-tongued, the general was ingenuous: he had told two or three Immortals in confidence of his decision not to visit Judge Lisandro Leite, who had demonstrated his animosity toward him in the course of the campaign and was persisting in fighting against his candidacy, doing his best to pressure certain Academicians—former supporters of Colonel Sampaio Pereira—into casting blank ballots. His dignity as a general obliged him to make the insulting decision not to visit the judge. As the sole candidate, he would permit himself certain indulgences; he enjoyed certain privileges.

A confidence shared with an Academician at election time is a secret left for safekeeping in a sack with a leaky bottom. It makes the rounds borne on the winds—on the breeze from the overhead fans on stifling-hot summer afternoons in Rio. Especially when the confidence is revealing of heresy and presumption: since when does a sole candidate enjoy certain indulgences and privileges?

The visit to Lisandro had been the only exception made by the general in his peregrinations as a candidate. He had put up with a train ride to Minas that shook up every last bone in his body, and it had been worth the trouble: he had brought back with him the vote of the hemiplegic author of short stories. He had traveled by plane to São Paulo, where he was received with extreme cordiality by the poet who had composed the *Book of Ballads of the Bandeirantes*. The two of them had recalled together episodes of the revolution of '32, in which the bard had participated as a staff officer of Colonel Euclides de Figueiredo. Instead of the usual twenty minutes, the visit had lasted far into the afternoon. As for his vote, the lyric poet, author of the *Book of Psalms*, had informed the general that he would be sending it directly to the Academy, as was his longstanding habit. An expensive trip on account of the cost of the plane ticket, but despite the expense the general had returned to Rio in a state of euphoria, feeling that he had certain proof that this prestigious vote would be his, and would have been his even if instead of being the present sole candidate he were still contending for the seat against that scoundrel of a Sampaio Pereira. The poet Mario Bueno was a comrade in arms and in the world of letters.

THE PREVIOUS VISITOR

The brotherhood of arms turned out to be a stronger tie than that of poetry. A few days before the general's visit, the guerrilla fighter Evandro Nunes dos Santos, given the name "El Pasionario" by Afrânio Portela, had come to São Paulo, with the sole aim of embracing Mario Bueno and discussing with him various subjects concerning the

Academy. They were old friends—relatives, so to speak, since the poet's wife was the cousin of Evandro's late lamented wife Anita. On his rare visits to Rio, Bueno always stayed at the mansion in Santa Teresa.

The matter of the successor to Bruno's Academy chair had twice brought Evandro to the quintessentially Paulista home of the descendant of the Bandeirantes. He had come the first time to ask Mario Bueno to vote for the general. An easy task, for Bueno detested Sampaio Pereira, who, while still a major, had been the head of the security forces and the intelligence branch of the Army in São Paulo after the revolution of 1932 had been overthrown, and had tarred the vanquished with the blackest of brushes, accusing them of being separatists.

"He's a man who hunted us down like dogs. How could you possibly think I could support him? Don't you know me better than that? He came to visit me, and I received him politely and promised him my vote, as I do all the candidates who come to see me; I'm a well-bred man. But it's obvious that I'm going to vote for your general, who, moreover, played a part in the epic Constitutionalist battle."

Things were more difficult the second time, when he came to ask the poet not to vote for the general, to cast a blank ballot instead. The Constitutionalist epic turned out to be a serious obstacle:

"He may well be a third-rate pen-pusher, a despot, and a bore, I grant you. But he's a brave man; he immediately answered the São Paulo call to arms! Moreover, since I hardly ever go to Rio, I appear so seldom at the Academy that he's not going to bother me."

Evandro had expected him to raise this objection. Everything having to do with the movement in '32 had become sacred for the bard of "On to São Paulo!," a heroic call to arms, the only really dreadful verses in all of his copious poetic production. Evandro, however, held a powerful trump card:

"Well, I thought your greatest desire was to see José Feliciano get a seat in the Academy. . . ." He slowly cleaned his pince-nez and placed it back on his nose. "When I phoned you to tell you that Bruno was dead, we agreed that the perfect candidate to replace him was Feliciano, and it was you who first brought his name up. A great poet, a fine person, and what's more, a man from São Paulo, one of your own kind."

"It's obvious that Feliciano would be ideal, but with this whole business of candidates from the military . . ."

"I was eager to mount a campaign for Feliciano, but Afrânio thought we needed a general to run against Sampaio Pereira, who was a colonel. He was right, and strictly between us, I'll confess that even with a general I don't know if we would have defeated Sampaio Pereira. But that dyed-in-the-wool fascist couldn't hold up under all the uncertainties of the battle, and broke down. So what earthly use is a general to us now? Have you heard the talk going the rounds about there being specially reserved chairs in the Academy? One for the Army, another for the Navy, another for the Air Force? Sooner or later, the military police and the firemen will be demanding theirs. Listen, Mario: we're going to keep that crashing bore from being elected. Then Bruno's seat will still be vacant, and it'll be Feliciano's turn."

"And . . . is there a possibility of that?"

"According to my calculations, it depends on your vote."

Mario Bueno regarded José Feliciano as his blood brother. Comrades since the days of their youth in the editorial rooms of newspapers and in the dark nights of the "São Paulo madness," they had slept with the same loose women, courted the very same girls from good families, taken part in the wild carnival revels in salons decorated by Lasar Segall, participated together in the Modern Art Week, and signed the same violent manifestoes against the Brazilian Academy of Letters. In 1932, José Feliciano was in Campos do Jordão, in a tubercular sanatorium, undergoing collapsed-lung therapy. He did not hesitate for a second: they tracked him down and finally found him, a volunteer on the Minas front. They brought him back by force to complete the treatment.

"You've won me over, you old anarchist. I won't cast a blank ballot, because the general fought in the revolution of 'thirty-two, but I'll abstain. The result is the same, and yet there's a difference. . . ."

"I know."

"I'm saving my vote for José. In the last analysis, if he never got to fight it was because the doctors dragged him out of the trenches. And what a poet, my friend . . ." —Mario Bueno possessed that rare gift, generous admiration—"São Paulo's greatest poet."

"A great poet, I agree, but it's you who are São Paulo's greatest poet."

Mario Bueno possessed the rare gift of generous admiration and, at the same time, the far less rare gift, one fairly common in literary circles, of self-admiration:

"No, Evandro. I'm not the best poet in São Paulo; I'm the best poet in Brazil."

◼ EVENTS PRECEDING THE PERFORMANCE

On the last Monday before Christmas, in anxious and feverish expectation, Maria João presented on the stage of the Teatro Fénix, in a gala performance, *Mary John*, the play in verse by António Bruno, eighteen years after its premiere. Despite the astronomical price of admission, there was not a single empty seat, and there were people standing in the side aisles and sitting on the floor in the center aisle. Till curtain time, people seeking admission crowded around the ticket window, pushing and shoving, despite the sign reading "SOLD OUT" that had been posted there.

All Rio de Janeiro had turned out for the affair, all the

city's notables, from Oswaldo Aranha, the minister of foreign relations, whose presence represented a denunciation of the duplicity of the foreign policy of the New State, to Sténio Barreto, The Creep, for whom Maria João had reserved three loge seats that cost him a small fortune.

The performance had been widely advertised and publicized in the papers and on the radio stations: a gala evening commemorating Maria João's twenty-year career on stage (beginning with her first small roles in reviews starring Margarida Vilar), it would be the high point of the year in the world of the theater and an unprecedented event in the cultural life of the capital.

For some time, the news sections of the papers had reported that the proceeds would be donated to the Free French cause. Before the performance, *Dom Casmurro* published the text of the program, written by R. Figueiredo Jr., and the news was thus publicly confirmed: "To commemorate her twenty glorious years in the theater, Maria João has decided to render homage to eternal France, today trampled underfoot by the Nazi boot, by dedicating her anniversary celebration to the combatants fighting against the cruel and obscurantist occupant of her soil, and by turning over all the profits to the Free French. It should be emphasized that all those who are participating in the staging of this performance, from the owners of the Teatro Fénix to the stagehands and set carpenters, have donated their services, as a token of friendship and admiration for the First Lady of our theater and as a sign of their total solidarity with the heroic struggle of the French people, which is also our struggle. No play could be more suitable for this evening in honor of Maria João and the freedom-fighters of France than António Bruno's comedy *Mary John*, written especially for Maria João's debut in the legitimate theater and staged in collaboration with Leopoldo Froes. To the great and unforgettable poet who wrote *Mary John*, France, the country in which he lived, the country whose culture nourished him, was a second homeland. His heart could not bear to see it humiliated, held in captivity. António Bruno was one of the first victims of the fall of Paris."

Since this weekly had not been suspended or forbidden, the other papers and the radio stations took advantage of this apparent oversight on the part of the censors and praised Maria João's gesture. A deluge of adjectives rained down, grandiloquent and affectionate. The news leaked out that the director of the DIP, a contradictory personality, had personally authorized the publication of Figueiredo's text and had shut his eyes to all the publicity. He did not manage to maintain this liberal position very long. He soon received orders from higher up, issued by the same office in the Palacio da Guerra previously occupied by Colonel Sampaio Pereira, condemning the publication of the text, which was described as seditious. As a result, the DIP forbade any reference, in advertisements or in news items about the performance, to France (either occupied or eternal), to Nazis, or to the Maquis. The distribution of the program was also forbidden.

But the damage had been done. In Rio no one talked of anything but *Mary John,* and the rush to secure tickets very nearly became a pitched battle. Huge sums were offered for just one seat, and even more for a copy of the program with R. Figueiredo Jr.'s text.

It so happened that, as the fight for tickets was going on, another much more serious battle was underway within the government. The most radical sectors of the New State demanded that the performance be prohibited; factions sympathetic to the cause of the Allies defended the staging of it. Rumors of threats and dire predictions spread like wildfire. There was talk of pressure having been brought to bear on the Guinles, the owners of the Fénix, to get them to withdraw their permission to use the theater; nothing came of it. It became known that those responsible for the new production of the play had decided to stage it even if the censors banned it: the doors of the theater would be opened to the public and the curtain would go up at the hour announced. The actors would begin the performance even at the risk of being arrested and brought to trial. The news leaked out that Alzira, the daughter of the head of state, had announced to her father that she herself would be present at the Fénix if the performance were prohibited, and would applaud the actors.

The performance was finally authorized, on condition that at no time—above all after the curtain went up—would there be any mention of its connection with the Free French groups. It was merely to be a gala evening, celebrating Maria João's twenty years on the stage.

The result of all this was that the initial significance of this new production of *Mary John* was vastly transcended. It had now become a confrontation between the forces of Brazilian Nazi-fascism and the country's intellectuals, who had taken to the trenches once again to fight for freedom. This was how it had always been, ever since the days of colonialism and the poetry of a mulatto from Bahia, Gregório de Matos.

MARY JOHN, MARIA JOÃO, MARIANNE

The first burst of applause rang out when the curtain of the Teatro Fénix went up, revealing the set designed by Santa Rosa—a revolution in Brazilian scenecraft, the beginning of a new era. The applause was repeated each time another actor appeared on stage, reaching a crescendo to greet Procópio Ferreira in the role of the con man posing as a Yankee movie-actor, a role created in the original production by Leopoldo Froes. Ferreira, containing his emotion, began to recite the first verses of the play as the applause continued. When Maria João came on stage, a lively, scatterbrained suburbanite girl of eighteen, a giddy youngster whose head has been turned by

Hollywood films, Miss Mary John, the performance had to be interrupted—the ovation went on and on.

After this vibrant beginning the audience settled down, and the comedy, with its subtle composition and its resounding verses inspired by Maria João's beauty and temperament, reached the end of the first two acts in a joyous atmosphere that was not, however, without a slight edge of anxiety: no one would have been surprised if the police had suddenly appeared and cleared the theater.

As the curtain rose for the third and last act, the spectators were astonished to see, standing at the back of the stage, not only the entire cast, but also the entire stage crew, the electricians, the stagehands, the prompter, the author of the text of the program, the Academician R. Figueiredo Jr., the director, Álvaro Moreyra—all those who had collaborated in putting on the gala performance. Only Maria João was missing.

An enormous basket of red, white, and blue flowers, the colors of France, occupied the center of the stage. The audience began to applaud once more, applause that became deafening when Maria João emerged from the wings, dressed as Marianne, in a tricolor skirt and a liberty cap. She waited till the ovation died down, her hand placed over her heart. Finally, with that hint of mystery in her hoarse voice which no one who heard it would ever forget, she announced:

" 'Song of Love for an Occupied City,' a poem by António Bruno, written after the fall of Paris, shortly before his death."

Impossible to describe the audience's emotion: no one had expected to hear the poem that had been denounced as accursed recited on the stage of the Teatro Fénix. It was like an electrical charge. Someone rose to his feet, others followed, and then the entire audience rose, applauding, and remained standing. Silence finally fell, a silence so total that the words of blood and fire, the stanzas wet with tears and shaking with anger, humiliation and rebellion, love and hate, seemed to come from the depths of time, from the four corners of the earth, shattering the walls of the theater.

The lament of the first verses. The poet weeping for the raped city, a river of mud where once the Seine had flowed, the bodies of the victims, the Nazi boot, the mourning and the silence, the despair and death in the deep plainchant of the great actress. Then the tone of the poem rose and swelled to announce the liberation to come, trumpet flourishes, the voice vibrant and victorious, celebrating solidarity, proclaiming the day that would dawn tomorrow, life and love. Each stanza interrupted by a crescendo of applause, unprecedented, unbelievable.

In the orchestra, standing at her seat alongside Dona Rosarinho and Mestre Afrânio, the Portuguese Maria Manuela smiled through her tears, repeating in a half-whisper, word for word, the verses of the poem, her poem. On the following day she was to leave Rio for Caracas, perhaps never to set foot in Brazil again. She would nonetheless have left traces of her passage: at her urging, António had summoned men to join the fight for freedom. Maria Manuela is also rising above her grief and loneliness, Mestre Afrânio concluded. Thanks to Bruno's outstretched hand, to the summons of this song of freedom.

Tears were streaming down Maria João's face too, but her voice remained steady and strong in the final apostrophe against the murderers of entire peoples, each word a grenade and an ovation. Paris was set ablaze by the light of dawn in the hands of Maria João, a Brazilian girl from the suburbs who had suddenly become Marianne, Free France.

Paris, Paris, Paris, a brightly burning, eternal flame! Everyone in the theater on his feet, Marianne's voice, stronger and stronger, repeating the name of the city, written by Bruno with his life's blood. Those who were there that night knew, beyond all doubt, that oppression, violence, death would never succeed in destroying freedom, life, man.

216

Maria João repeated the word *Paris* for the last time, and the immense, endless ovation burst forth; the sea of applause rose in tremendous waves, shaking the very rafters of the Teatro Fénix.

At the end of the third act, as Mary John, the other characters, and the director of the new production of Bruno's comedy were being acclaimed once more, a woman's voice rose from the back of the stage, one that many people recognized immediately, the voice of the poetess Beatrix Reynal, singing the first lines of the "Marseillaise."

On stage the entire cast joined her, followed by everyone in the audience. Far more than a performance or a celebration, Maria João's gala was a triumphant sortie of the Maquis.

▓ REPRISALS

In reprisal, the government refused the Brazilian Theatrical Company, directed by Maria João, the subsidy for the 1941 season for which it had applied. The proposed program consisted of García Lorca's *Blood Wedding*, a new comedy by Joracy Camargo, and *The River*, a first play by a young writer whose prestige was growing, the editor-in-chief of Samuel Lederman's recently forbidden review *Perspectivas*, who had acquired a reputation as a vehement propagandist, an ardent defender of the rights of the people, an extremely dangerous Communist: Carlos Lacerda.

Called to the office of the director of the DIP, with whom she was careful to keep on good terms, Maria João easily guessed the reason for the summons. The director sat down alongside her on the black leather sofa. The cross-eyed gaze of this controversial figure fixed itself on the dreary cement landscape: in the distance a little patch of sea was visible.

"There are times when I feel like handing in my resignation, like saying to hell with everything," he confided. "You might well ask why I don't do so. I don't know what you'll think if I tell you that I stay on because in one way or another I manage to prevent certain things, to make the measures taken less harsh, to leave a little room to breathe. This being the case, why don't they boot me out? I think The Man needs both his fanatic supporters and me, somebody to stand up to them. For the same reason, he won't accept Oswaldo Aranha's resignation. I lose in most cases, but who can win all the time?"

Maria João gave him a sympathetic, almost pitying smile: "Speak frankly; I can take it."

"I tried to back the subsidy; I interceded on your behalf, I can assure you. You may or may not believe it. But the scandal caused by your gala evening—Bruno's poem, the 'Marseillaise'—was too great, and our little Hitlers are beside themselves with rage. If it were up to them, the entire cast, and you first of all, would be in jail."

He looked at the woman sitting next to him—her beauty, her elegance, her defiance—and went on:

"On top of everything else, the repertory that you proposed is hair-raising. You plan to begin with García Lorca; I adore him, but they hate him: a Spanish Republican— a synonym for Communist—shot to death by our good ally, General Francisco Franco. And then *May God Repay You*. Joracy's reputation is no better, and the new dramatist that you discovered, that young Lacerda, has one of the longest records in the police files. I wasted my time and my breath." A pause, his eyes looking far off into the distance through the window. "And what do you intend to do now?"

Maria João's eyes followed those of the director of the DIP; at first all she saw was cement, and then finally she caught a glimpse of the little patch of blue sea:

"I'm going to stage the plays that I programmed for the season, unless the censors ban them."

"Where will the money come from? I know that even

if you didn't go into the red with *Hedda Gabler*, you didn't make a profit on it either."

"I'll find financial backing, don't worry—I know where to look for it." She rose to her feet. "Thank you anyway for all the effort you went to on our behalf. I know it's true you did, and I'm grateful to you."

She held out her fingertips; the director of the DIP kissed them and accompanied her to the door of the office. A job as odious as it was important; a battle lost each day. Nonetheless he clung to the post; he could not bring himself to abandon that small scrap of power. He had been born amid direst poverty, in a hamlet in the northeast that no one had ever heard of. He should have ended up working other people's land, like his father, his mother, his elder brothers. But arrangements had been made for him to attend the seminary as a non-paying student, for his intelligence and his eagerness to get himself an education had touched the parish priest and the bishop. On seeing himself in a cassock, a book in hand, he had made up his mind to be a powerful man, at whatever cost. It had cost him a great deal, too much sometimes.

Once outside on the street, Maria João bit her lips hard. No one had ever managed to make her back down once she'd made up her mind; that was how she had earned herself a place and responsibilities in the Brazilian theater. She would stage the repertory she had planned, even if it were necessary to spend a weekend in Petrópolis with The Creep. After the *Mary John* performance, nothing could sully her; she was now beyond good and evil.

THE NATURE OF THE CHRISTMAS FESTIVITIES

The white-haired attendant is serving coffee. In the president's office, Hermano do Carmo is listening to the arguments of two judicial luminaries: Justice Paiva, of the Federal Supreme Court, and Judge Lisandro Leite, of the court of appeals. They are discussing the details of the Christmas tea, the purpose of which is to permit socializing between the Academicians, accompanied by their esteemed spouses, and employees of the Academy.

This tea is held on the last Thursday before Christmas, the one and only gay, intimate social occasion during the year that brings the Immortals' wives together. The tea table is even more sumptuous than at the already lavish weekly teas. The president of the Academy, with his wife at his side, receives the couples and offers flowers and small souvenir gifts to the ladies. For them, the wives, this festive annual occasion is fascinating and exciting, since they are allowed to go everywhere in the Petit Trianon: the library, the archives, the secretariat, the small reception rooms where their husbands confer with each other and receive friends, territory ordinarily off limits to women—"the most exclusive men's club in the world," according to the journalist Austregésilo de Athayde, who had recently published a lengthy piece, complete and impartial, on the Brazilian Academy of Letters.

When a new Academician is received, the wives appear in the grand salon, majestic creatures in dresses by famous couturiers, dripping with jewels, elaborately coiffed. But the Christmas tea is not as elegant and formal an affair, and there are no long speeches to sit through and applaud. In a relaxed mood, the women chat together about all sorts of things, pass round photographs of their grandchildren, talk of domestic problems, the lack of maidservants, the high cost of living. They go on conversing and laughing as the Academicians hold a short, quick meeting to justify receiving a *jeton* on this Thursday traditionally devoted to the employees of the House. In those days the annual recess of the Academy began on the first of February and lasted till the end of March. Hence the Christmas tea did not mark the close of the Academic year; its purpose, then as now, was to serve as the occasion for a cordial meeting of the wives of the

Immortals, during the principal Christian holiday season, in the guise of a social gathering in honor of the staff employees and the servants of the Academy.

"He appears every Thursday, as though he's taken his seat before being elected. He might well have the nerve to turn up, with his wife on his arm, at the Christmas tea. Inadmissible!" Justice Paiva is unable to hide his disapproval.

Lisandro Leite, who has become even more fiercely opposed to General Moreira's candidacy ever since learning that the general has decided not to pay him the traditional visit, expresses his categorical objection to such an inopportune appearance:

"It is necessary, my dear Hermano, to inform the general of the exclusive nature of our little festive gathering: just ourselves the Academicians, our wives, and the staff of the House. We do not extend invitations, nor do we admit intruders."

Niggling problems of protocol such as this nearly drive the president out of his mind. In accordance with its statutes, the Academy has a set ritual for each event, and the Immortals insist that it be strictly observed. With upraised hands Hermano do Carmo takes Heaven as his witness:

"Believe me, if General Moreira appears, it won't be for lack of hints and innuendoes on my part."

"Hints and innuendoes won't solve the matter. Maginot Line hasn't acquired that nickname by sheer chance: he's impenetrable," Justice Paiva reflects gravely.

"I know. For that very reason I did more than merely hint. Last Thursday, seizing on one pretext or another, I told him, in no uncertain terms and straight to his face, that the Christmas-week tea is restricted to Academicians, their wives, and our staff. If he appears, it's only because he's a boor."

"If he shows up, I'm leaving and taking Mariúcia with me," Lisandro threatens.

"No, Lisandro, you're not going to do any such thing," Hermano says.

"Why not? He's a candidate, and he's announced that he's not going to pay me a visit. . . ."

"For that very reason. That unfortunate declaration of the general's has hurt his candidacy a great deal; it's a mark against him. But if you retaliate by suddenly abandoning the company of your colleagues on this intimate and festive occasion, you'll merely be proving that the general's stand is only right. Do you want him to be right, by any chance? What do you think, Paiva?"

"I entirely agree. Lisandro spoke without thinking; he's hurt, and he has a good reason to be. But he's absolutely not going to leave the party. I'll personally see to it that he doesn't."

The judge doesn't argue with the justice, whom he is hoping to replace when the latter retires in a few months:

"That fellow insulted me. But naturally I'll behave in a civilized manner."

"I don't think he'll come," Hermano do Carmo remarks. "I was almost too explicit; I fear I went beyond the limits of civilized behavior that you've just defined, my dear Lisandro. But if he shows up nonetheless, what's going to happen?"

The two luminaries wait for the president himself to answer:

"On the one hand, we'll be obliged to follow Lisandro's example and put up with him. On the other hand, the general will have another black mark chalked up against him. There's nothing in this world that doesn't have its good side."

"Hear, hear! You're perfectly right," Justice Paiva, a man who could not be said to lack either cunning or sagacity, says approvingly.

▓ THE HAPPY FAMILY

Was it boorishness or the conviction that he was already an Academician, awaiting only the imminent setting of the date of his reception—a mere formality—to begin to bring the Illustrious Company into line (straighten up those ranks, you men)? The general appeared at the Christmas tea, in uniform, arm in arm with Dona Conceição. To cap the climax, he brought along his daughter Cecília and his friend Sabença.

His friend Sabença, a candidate eager to fill the empty place in Cecília's bed, a happy man, just a step away from the altar.

▓ THE EVENTS IN SÃO PAULO AND IN RIO DE JANEIRO

The sudden death of Colonel Sampaio Pereira resolved the problems of conscience of a number of Academicians: an unexpected relief. As for the steps taken, however, by the many police forces of the federal district and various Brazilian states and by specific military units against individuals suspected of subversive ideas and activities— liberals, anti-fascists, diverse leftists, all of them labeled Communists—there was no change, much less a sense of relief.

If the colonel was missed as the head of a vast, active, and well-paid network of repression—which probably was the case, given the ideological inflexibility and the literary prestige of the former candidate for the Brazilian Academy—his worthy successor was soon found, since, as the double-dealing director of the DIP commented, "In Brazil we lack competent personnel in all the branches of public administration with the exception of the police." That branch had efficient and devoted public servants at every level from top to bottom, specialists in multiple fields and, above all, torture experts. The instructors imported from the Gestapo found that they had nothing to teach, and contributed nothing more than a few highly sophisticated torture devices.

The Christmas and New Year's holidays had barely ended when a communiqué issued by the Department of Political and Social Police of São Paulo announced a sensational development, the first of a series that was to shake the country: the destruction of the base where a plenary session of the Central Committee of the Communist party was being held. A fatal blow, according to the police bulletin, to the structure of the subversive organization; the result of patient work, long investigation, complex studies carried out by the efficient security system responsible for the maintenance of law and order.

The police action was not only brilliant but difficult and heroic, according to the communiqué handed out to the press. When the Commies realized that their hideout, situated in the Serra do Mar, on the road to Santos, had been surrounded, they tried to shoot their way out; the casualties that resulted numbered two secret agents wounded and six agitators dead, among them the long-sought Bexiga, a member of the party secretariat. Six dead, fifteen top-ranking leaders put under lock and key, and a great quantity of weapons and propaganda material seized. Other arrests might follow at any moment, since the investigation was continuing as those arrested underwent interrogation. The communiqué made no mention of the participation of military units in this heroic exploit.

A few days later, the São Paulo chief of police called together the journalists who covered his office to announce further spectacular activities by the political police. As their search proceeded and as a result of information obtained during the interrogations, the investigators had located the clandestine workshop where the party's principal publication, *A Classe Operaria*, and most of its literature were printed. Five extremely dangerous individuals had fallen into the hands of the police.

The reporters could see and photograph the material seized in these two major operations: very few weapons— a small number of revolvers, two rifles, one worn-out light machine gun, some boxes of ammunition—and a great deal of printed matter. In addition to copies of the last issue of *A Classe Operaria*, manifestoes, prospectuses, pamphlets, tracts containing watchwords, analyses of the national political situation, accounts of strike movements not mentioned in the press, appeals to workers and peasants, pleas for financial aid to organizations fighting against the regime and for political prisoners. Portraits of Marx, Lenin, Stalin, Dimitrov, and Prestes. And also the "Song of Love for an Occupied City," by A. Bruno, printed in an orange-colored leaflet.

During the collective interview, the chief of police brought out Comrade "Steel," the nom de guerre of Félix Braga; behind his back, his comrades called him "Stalin's Louse" because of his uncouth manner, his blind admiration for the secretary-general of the Bolshevik party— whose nom de guerre he had adopted and whose example he cited at every turn—and his fierce fanaticism. A former medical student with a middle-class background, he concealed his bourgeois origins, passing himself off as a mill-hand. He had dropped out of the university to devote himself to working underground, had rapidly worked his way up in the ranks of the party, the leadership of which had been decimated by the blows it had suffered at the hands of the reactionary forces, and had eventually become a permanent member of the Central Committee and an alternate member of the Politburo.

The chief of police stressed Steel's importance, his titles, and the threat he constituted before allowing the prisoner to speak. He had a statement he wished to make.

In a hesitant voice, Stalin's Louse read aloud a document that he had signed the night before—of his own free will, as the chief of police took care to point out. On finding himself in prison, all alone in his cell, he had had a chance to reflect, to take stock of his life, and had realized that he had sacrificed his youth for an unworthy cause by becoming a militant in the Communist party, a monstrous refuge for murderers and traitors to their country, and that he had become a tool of Russian interests. The party duped students and workers, leading them to conspire and act against established institutions, religion, the family, the Fatherland. Perceiving the error of his ways, Félix Braga had decided to publicly abandon the criminal ranks of the party, as he was doing by means of this document that he had written and signed.

He read haltingly, stumbled over words, started over again; it seemed obvious to the reporters present that he had not drafted the text himself—a Communist, even one deserting the cause, would refer not to Russia but rather to the Soviet Union. The signature, however, was undoubtedly his, since he affixed it then and there to the various copies handed out to the reporters.

Once the depressing reading was over, the chief of police asked Steel to state once again whether or not he had written his statement because of threats or violence on the part of the police. With downcast eyes, he answered no; having repented of his criminal past, he himself had resolved to address this message to Brazilian youth, so that other young people would not allow themselves to be corrupted by the Communists. He answered yet another question put to him by the chief of police: Did he know of any prisoners who had been tortured? No. He had not seen a single one with marks left by torture, nor had he heard any complaints from those who had been taken prisoner with him. Once photographs had been taken, the penitent ex-member of the party was led away by police officers, and the reporters were not able to ask him any questions. What purpose would that serve, since the material given them for publication could not be cut or amended, nor made the subject of doubts or debate?

Front-page headlines, four-column photos, editorials

lauding the competence of the police and calling young people's attention to Félix Braga's moving, heartfelt, and dramatic document. An entire week of praise for the New State, and abuse for the Soviet Union.

There continued to circulate, however—in whispers—less heroic, more believable oral versions of these sensational events. As certain curious reporters verified, it had all begun with the entirely accidental arrest of a young militant who was transporting a bundle of copies of *A Classe Operaria*. He was standing up in a crowded bus when the driver swerved to avoid an oncoming car and crashed into a light-pole. The violent impact sent the boy sprawling, and as he fell he let go of the bundle, which came undone when it hit the floor, scattering copies of the forbidden paper all over. A cop who happened to be a passenger on the bus seized the subversive material and hauled the militant off to jail.

At the district headquarters of the political police, the renowned inspector Apolónio Serafim interrogated him. On the second day, turned into a bloody, limp rag, the hapless youngster revealed the location of the hideout in the Serra do Mar and the print shop in Bras, and also spoke of the meeting of the Central Committee. Beside himself with excitement, Apolónio Serafim went to the chief of police, and the chief of police went even higher up, to the military authorities. A meeting of the Central Committee? They would assume command of operations.

"A Bolshevik must be as hard as tempered steel in order to stand up to the forces of reaction," Steel had continually pounded into comrades' heads in a threatening tone of voice. Taken from his cell to be interrogated, on entering the room and seeing the cops with their rubber truncheons, the lighted cigar in the mouth of one of them, the cat-o'-nine-tails, and the almost cordial smile on the lips of Apolónio Serafim (Félix knew him by reputation and from his photograph), he turned as white as wax and felt his balls grow ice-cold. He became even paler and colder when he caught sight of Bangu and Martins, lined up naked against the wall, in handcuffs, beaten within an inch of their lives, covered with blood. Lying on the floor, also naked and in even worse shape, his face disfigured, unconscious or dead, was Comrade Gato, a well-known journalist. Félix Braga felt as though he were about to piss in his pants. Apolónio walked over to him:

"'We'll see if you're really made of steel!'"

His fist hit Félix square in the chest, knocking the breath out of him. Apolónio Serafim had something of a sense of humor. "My hands are worth their weight in gold," he said, holding up his enormous elephant's paws, his iron fists. One punch was all it took. Steel was nothing but one of Stalin's lice; he very nearly vomited up his very soul:

"Don't beat me, for the love of God, I'll spill everything."

He spilled everything, and signed the document that he read to the reporters. He personally guided the police vans to the various hideouts that he had knowledge of, thereby unleashing another wave of arrests. In order to escape trial and having to live side by side with his former comrades in the same prison cell, he asked the colonel, who had listened to him spill everything he knew every day for a week, to send him to Rio; since that was his usual area of operations as a militant, he could be very useful to the colonel. When he was finally let out of prison, months later, the only vestige of his former political activity that remained was part of the nickname given him by his former comrades; even the cops called him "The Louse."

Such trials and tribulations do happen. The more fanatical and radical an individual appears to be, the more cowardly he turns out to be when he falls into the hands of the police. Anyone who has ever been a militant knows how true this is.

The real name of Gato—"The Cat"—the comrade whom Félix the Louse had seen lying on the floor of Inspector Apolónio Serafim's interrogation room, was Joaquim da Câmara Ferreira, a newspaperman on the editorial staff of one of the major São Paulo dailies. He led two lives, one open and aboveboard and the other clandestine—as an editor on the highly respected daily morning paper on the one hand and as a senior editor on a forbidden monthly on the other. He was an affable, friendly, cheery man. He did not demand that others be men of steel, nor did he call his comrades who were making a show of being Bolsheviks petty-bourgeois. He was tortured for two weeks, yet they didn't extract one thing from him—aside from his fingernails and part of his skin. One morning when they brought him from his cell to be tortured, he ran to the closed window, shattered the glass with his fists, and sawed his two wrists against the jagged edges. They hurriedly dragged him away to keep him from killing himself. The notice of his arrest and the torture he was undergoing went the rounds in editorial rooms. Journalists, their union, the São Paulo Press Association, the owners of the paper on which Joaquim worked all rallied round and took steps on his behalf. He did not die, but was brought to trial, found guilty, and given a prison sentence. He served part of it, and then was freed when political prisoners were granted amnesty in 1945. He was the opposite of Steel, and following his release he resumed his activities as a militant until he was murdered during the next dictatorship.

In Rio, the arrests were not restricted to party members hunted down in the hideouts pointed out by The Louse (with his wrists still in handcuffs). Intellectuals, doctors, engineers, civil servants, bank employees, and even bankers were placed under arrest, and a number of them brought to trial—their names had appeared on the lists of financial contributors to the party that had been found in one of the raided hideouts.

The investigators invaded, occupied, and sacked the office of a law firm in Cinelândia headed by an attorney widely regarded as being extremely clever and capable, a likable individual with an entrée to many important circles, a trial lawyer respected even by the judges of the National Security Tribunal, before which he had appeared to defend political prisoners. He and his law partners had won acquittals and reduced sentences for the accused in numerous trials. His name was Letelba Rodrigues de Brito. He was arrested along with one of the two other law partners of the firm and three of the four law students who were lending him their assistance.

Among these students was Prudência dos Santos Leite, better known as Pru. While still in her fourth year in law school, she had already proved herself to be more competent and clever than many graduates with law degrees. She had inherited her father's razor-sharp mind, his stubbornness, and his good-heartedness, along with her mother's beauty and serenity.

THE FATHER AND THE MOTHER

When he learned of the arrest of his daughter, Lisandro Leite lost his senses. Passionately devoted to his wife, his children, and his grandchildren, he adored his rebellious, flighty, irresponsible daughter, who had become involved with Communists and had never let an opportunity go by to criticize the positions and the actions taken by her father as a justice of the court of appeals and as an Academician. During Colonel Sampaio Pereira's candidacy, for example, Lisandro had wearied of finding aggressive notes that she had written and left on top of his workdesk. Though he protested, screamed at this crazy daughter of his, threatened her, he nonetheless loved her as dearly as always. He positively drooled with satisfaction when his colleagues on the faculty at the university law school, Pru's professors, praised the girl's talent—"like father, like daughter"—her studiousness, and even her laudable contribution (as they saw it) to the cases of defendants being tried before the National Security Tribunal, as a junior clerk in the scarcely respectable law firm (in Lisandro's opinion) headed by Dr. Letelba de Brito.

He moved heaven and earth to get Pru out of prison. He used his influence with the other justices of the court of appeals, with military authorities whom he had met through Sampaio Pereira; he got Hermano do Carmo to take steps in the name of the Academy.

The days went by and the jurist grew more and more apprehensive and dispirited. His lively wit, his cheerful good humor, his extroversion fell by the wayside. He had not succeeded even in learning where his daughter was being held, nor had he obtained permission to visit her. One of the military authorities whom he approached promised to intercede on his behalf, but forty-eight hours later he informed Lisandro that his hands were tied in view of the grave situation of everyone connected with the law firm: "All of them, your daughter included, are in trouble up to their necks."

As they lay one night in their conjugal bed, Dona Mariúcia, seeing her husband unable to fall asleep, tossing and turning, put her arms around him and drew him to her:

"You must sleep, Lisandro."

"I can't. When I think of the insane thing that Pru's done, I feel like killing her the day she comes back home."

"I understand. You're afraid that Pru's arrest will hurt your chances for a seat on the Supreme Court."

"What does the Supreme Court matter to me!" he burst out in a voice filled with anger. "The only thing I want is my daughter back home!"

He lowered his voice, and a fearful, sorrowful note crept into it:

"They torture people, did you know that?"

"That's what Pru told me, and I read in those papers of hers . . ."

"That's not something the Communists have made up;

it's true, I know it for a fact. They burn the prisoners' sides with lighted cigarettes, they tear out their fingernails, they beat them, they mistreat women prisoners. ... Six, seven of them at a time deflower them, rape them. ... When I think of Pru at their mercy, I feel helpless, I can't sleep. ..."

Dona Mariúcia kissed his eyes, his cheek, his mouth: "They're not going to do anything like that to Pru. Aren't you forgetting that she's your daughter and that you're an Academician?"

She drew closer still. Lisandro felt the touch of her breasts and murmured:

"I'm not in the mood. I can't."

"Don't torment yourself so. Pru will be back home soon."

And that was what happened. On being petitioned by the attorneys admitted to plead before the exceptional court, the judges of the Security Tribunal concerned themselves with the fate of Dr. Letelba Rodrigues de Brito and those who had worked with him in his law firm.

When Pru unexpectedly arrived home, set free in the middle of the night, with no traces of having been violently mistreated, elated both at having been let go and at having been arrested, Lisandro greeted her by screaming at her:

"It's all your fault. You got what you were asking for. You're out to disgrace yourself and your family."

"Don't worry, Father. I'm not going to live here anymore; I'm going to move out."

Dona Mariúcia, who had taken her daughter in her arms, let go of her:

"Don't believe one word your father says. While you were in jail, he almost died. He didn't eat, he didn't sleep ... and what's more," she added with a smile, "he even refused to make love to me, for the first time since we've been married. Your father adores you."

Pru smiled at her mother and walked over to her father:

"Do you think I didn't know that? This old reactionary is a softie at heart."

Lisandro ran his fat, sweaty hand through his daughter's hair:

"You're not going to move out, are you?"

"Only if you don't want me here in your house anymore, you monstrous father."

"You crazy girl!"

Pru sat down in Lisandro's lap, just as she had done when she was a little girl.

"Set your mind at rest, Father. I wasn't afraid for one minute."

"The fear was here, at home; we lived with it all during these last days, Pru," the answer came—from her mother.

Dona Mariúcia went over to her husband and her daughter. She could do as she pleased with Lisandro, he was in her keeping and her service. Pru escaped her grasp; it was useless to try to impose her will on her.

"You're dirty; you smell bad. Go take a bath. Your father and I are going to bed and to sleep."

"To sleep? Really?" She was not only a rebel, but cheeky as well.

Lisandro smiled. He felt hungry, thirsty, sexy again: he had come back to life.

▓ THE ARMY CHAIR

From mid-January on, General Waldomiro Moreira began to show up at the Academy every afternoon. Academicians who dropped by the Petit Trianon to pick up their mail, receive a reader or a friend, chat with the president for a few minutes saw the general in the library, taking notes, writing at a desk piled high with books, and were intrigued by this surprising diligence. They came over to speak with him, to find out what he was up to. These interruptions did not bother the general; on the contrary, he was pleased to discuss in detail the work that he was doing. Certain Immortals even encouraged the candidate, a windbag and a braggart, to talk, and he willingly complied.

He was the sole candidate now, he reminded them, and as such he had begun to gather data for his acceptance speech. He was expecting to take his seat immediately after the Academy's annual recess. There was the problem of the full regalia of an Academician, but Altino Alcântara, a friend who cherished the same heartfelt convictions, whom he had invited to deliver the speech receiving him as a member of the Academy, had promised, honored by that mark of respect and esteem, to come up with a solution in case the authorities in Pernambuco, the native state of the distinguished military officer and writer, were tactless enough to break with a longstanding, firmly established, and gratifying tradition: the gift to the new Academician of the uniform, the sword, and the neck-chain, presented by the state in which he had been born as proof of its pride in the native son who had earned immortality. If such a base betrayal of tradition should come about, the prestigious Alcântara would raise funds in São Paulo that would be more than enough to buy the uniform, the sword, and the neck-chain, with a fair sum left over for champagne to celebrate after the solemn reception ceremony. By his heroic deeds in '32, General Waldomiro Moreira had earned the gratitude of the Paulistas, who never forget aid lent them in trying times.

On the days on which he did not teach classes—in addition to his work on the paper he taught Portuguese in a city high school—Claudionor Sabença came to the Academy with his illustrious friend, Cecília's father, and served him as secretary, hunting up volumes on the shelves and copying out references and quotations. When he came by himself, the general devoted his time to composing various bits and pieces of his acceptance speech.

It would be a long one. The chair had had four occupants, three generals and the poet António Bruno. Along with the founder of the chair, that made five figures to be studied for the traditional encomium.

General Moreira took a great liking to the founder of the chair, a classic writer of the eighteenth century, the author of a lengthy epic poem in twelve cantos, *As Amazonas*, in the manner of Camões's *Os Lusíadas*. Unknown to younger generations, but praised and analyzed in manuals of literary history: had he or had he not been a precursor of Romanticism? Anthologies used in schools reprinted, preceded by a biographical note, a passage of the epic, by some strange coincidence always the same one. The founder wrote in the pure Portuguese that so pleased the author of the *Linguistic Prolegomena*, who, moreover, unlike the critics, discerned in *As Amazonas* no signs of Romanticism. The poets of the Romantic school had been extremely careless in their use of the Portuguese language, whereas that of the poet-founder had been admirably correct.

Perusing a venerable and very rare edition, one of the treasures of the library, the general savored the twelve cantos one by one, reciting page after page to the attentive Sabença—oh, the duties love imposes! The general felt guilty for not having read this jewel of our classic literature before. His friend Sabença had undoubtedly read it more than once; the general remembered having seen an excerpt from it in his *Anthology of Luso-Brazilian Literature*. Sabença lied twice over: Yes, he had read it many times, but he preferred to hear the classic verses recited by the general in his imperious, virile, martial voice. The truth was that he had never read it, a scarcely commendable fact in the case of a compiler of anthologies, and in the *Luso-Brazilian* one he had reprinted the same famous passage as many an anthologist before him. If someone in the past had taken the trouble to make a choice, why should those who came after have to make their way through the tangled thicket of two hundred pages written in lofty, unreadable language? As the general's voice, reciting the founder's verses, hammered away at his eardrums, Sabença, in a daze, dreamed of Cecília.

In the general's speech, calculated to cover some thirty-five to forty pages, an appropriate length, taking approximately two hours to deliver, three pages would be devoted to the founder. The new Academician would plead for greater attention to the poet and greater veneration of his memory and his poem. The real heart of the speech, however, would be an analysis of the works of the three generals who had occupied the chair in succession, before Bruno's absurd election. With the dauntless courage that he had revealed in the Constitutionalist trenches, General Waldomiro Moreira attacked the books of the brave military officers, chewed them, and swallowed them down one by one, with great intellectual delectation.

The first general had left only one volume of any length (plus two slimmer ones), 112 pages in large type, under the title *Auspicious Dates in the History of Our Nation*, a collection of commemorative speeches delivered on the anniversaries of important events, almost invariably battles won by Brazilian troops during the wars of the empire. Enough of a book, however, to enable the author, a member of the armed forces, to take his seat as their representative among the founders of the Illustrious Company. He had lived past the age of ninety; though he lacked books to his credit, he had earned more than enough warm respect to make up for it, having been of great service to the Academy in its early days of penury and disesteem.

By way of contrast, he had been succeeded by a general with a vast bibliography who had died only a few months after taking his seat. A prolific historian, he had left eight voluminous tomes on the Paraguayan War, four on the Cisplatine question, and at his death had been working on a series on the campaign against Rosas, the Argentine tyrant, of which only the first volume had appeared, leaving the other two as yet unpublished—and they remain unpublished still. General Moreira knew some of these books and respected them highly. He regarded the general's tract, entitled *Lopez, the Despot,* as being a precursor of his own work, in that both were suffused with the same ardent (and blind) patriotism.

The third general, in addition to being the author of serious and unusual essays on indigenous peoples, published in the Braziliana Series, in which he studied their customs, languages, traditions, and beliefs, was an almost legendary figure. One of the early explorers of the backlands, he had made his way through forests and swamps, crossed rivers, established contact with tribes that had never seen a white man before. Understanding and sympathy for the aborigines of the wilds, a breath of humanism, marked both his writings and his career. In his acceptance speech, António Bruno had discovered a poet in him—if not in the books that he published, beyond question in the saga that he lived.

General Moreira's analysis of the works and deeds of the three generals had suggested to him the title under which he intended to publish his discourse, a brief but substantial essay: "The Army Chair."

He had reserved little more than a page for António Bruno's poetry; being in his opinion saccharine and libertine, it did not deserve even that much. But as the dissolute bard, addicted to French phrases, would have put it: "Noblesse oblige. . . ."

The general had looked through the various volumes of poems and newspaper pieces of the deceased and was not favorably impressed by either the poetry or the prose. Bruno used and abused free verse, abandoning rhyme and meter; and without rhyme and meter there is no verse worthy of the name, the general held. Frequently obscure, incomprehensible, surrealist, what Bruno composed was not poetry but hieroglyphics—not to mention the crude language and the countless Gallicisms.

The play in verse, *Mary John,* the new production of

which he had seen at the invitation of the Academician Rodrigo Inácio Filho, had struck him as banal and frivolous. As for the poem on Paris, Bruno should have sought inspiration in *Os Lusíadas*, or at least in the stanzas of *As Amazonas*, if he had really wanted to compose a war poem capable of rallying the world's peoples. In short, António Bruno was nothing but a mountebank, a vulgar poet. Obviously the general was not about to proclaim this truth from the speaker's platform; it would leave a bad impression. The rites of the Academy prescribe that the successor's formal eulogy of the member he is replacing be an unqualified paean of praise.

He did not, however, hide his scorn for the poetry of the frivolous bard of *The Dancer and the Flower* in his conversations with Academicians during his two weeks of intense work in the library of the Petit Trianon. The important part of the speech was "The Army Chair," whose noble lineage would be restored with his election. Bruno had had no business occupying that chair; he had been elected to it by mistake.

Certain Academicians encouraged him, urged him on to greater heights of long-winded oratory; others listened in silence. General Waldomiro Moreira took both encouragement and silence as signs of approval and agreement. As the sole candidate, he had no reason to keep his thoughts to himself. In the general's acceptance speech, Bruno took on the role of an intruder, a civilian possessed of reprehensible manners and morals amid military officers beyond reproach.

THE BALZACIAN WOMAN

As he sat among the group occupying the cozy armchairs in a quiet corner of the library, to which he had led Dona Mariana Cintra da Costa Ribeiro, Mestre Afrânio Portela spied General Moreira leaning over his desk, pencil in hand. He excused himself, and on the pretext of avoiding having the light fall directly in his eyes, changed chairs so that his back was turned to the candidate. He removed from his briefcase the sheet of parchment paper. At the top were embossed the letters AB, the poet's initials; below them, the words traced in his beautiful calligraphy, almost a design: *The Camisole.* He handed the page to the woman, who could scarcely contain her emotion.

"Here it is. I took it to keep it, a sort of relic . . . Everyone has his own saints."

A tear brimmed over and ran down Dona Mariana's cheek; she did not try to stop it:

"He died thinking of me. Even after all those years, he hadn't forgotten."

At the wake, Afrânio Portela had greeted her as she silently joined the group of Bruno's friends and listened to their praise of him. A faded beauty, with hair turned to silver, she was nonetheless a striking figure still, thanks to her dignified bearing and her immense eyes, limpid as pure water, they too marked by the ravages of age, puffy. Mestre Afrânio heard her sigh. What recollections could she be concealing in the depths of a memory full of remembrances of things past?

He had not seen her again in the last few months, and the evening before he had been surprised to receive a long-distance telephone call, still something quite unusual in that era. It was Dona Mariana, calling from São Paulo, asking to see him. She flew to Rio to meet him at the Academy as they had arranged on the phone. And here she was, the tear running down her cheek, the sheet of paper in her trembling hand, her voice threatening to break into sobs. She controlled herself—something she had learned to do long since—and went on:

"We celebrated his twentieth birthday with a party that lasted twenty-four hours. We went to a jeweler's, and I gave him a watch as my present to him to keep him from arriving late when he was to meet me, as always happened. I was thirty-two years old then, and he called me 'Balzacian,' but not to offend me, quite the contrary." A smile through her tears.

Mestre Afrânio added up the figures in his mind: twelve years older than Bruno, so she was now sixty-six. She didn't look that old. Moreover, she looked younger than she had four months before; the pouches under her eyes had disappeared.

As though she had guessed what he was thinking, Dona Mariana said to him:

"I'm sixty-six years old, and the reason I didn't get in touch with you before was that immediately after António's death I entered a clinic in São Paulo for a little plastic surgery. I only had it done because Alberto asked me to; he likes my eyes, so I got rid of the bags that were ruining the way they looked."

Alberto da Costa Ribeiro, her husband, one of the great financial powers in the country, the coffee king, a ruthless businessman, a great landowner, a major exporter. Afrânio had known him for a long time; Alberto's father and Rosarinho's had been partners in various undertakings.

"I couldn't appear in public before the scars had completely healed, so I hid myself away on the estate in Mato Grosso, where I've been all this time—I like the peace and quiet there. Three days ago, as I was leafing through a back number of *Careta*, I learned from an article by Peregrino junior that when António had his fatal heart attack, he had just written the words *The Camisole* on a blank page. Peregrino thinks it must have been the title of a poem. You can't imagine how moved I was. At the hour of his death, he thought of me, he remembered his 'Balzacian woman.' "

"Was it really the title of a poem?" Mestre Afrânio was both curious and discreet.

"One that in the end he never did write." She raised her head, half-closed her eyes ("Her eyes are like a river," Bruno used to say): "What he proudly used to call his 'studio' was a garret, on the seventh floor of a little student hotel, the Saint-Michel. It still exists, in the rue Cujas, just off the Boul' Mich'. I thought that by meeting António I'd ruined my life, but precisely the opposite happened." She gazed into the novelist's attentive, kindly face. "I'm going to tell you something that's absurd but true, my friend: it was António who saved my marriage and made me a good and faithful wife."

Ah, Bruno's women! They never ceased to puzzle him, to disconcert him, enigmatic figures—what an illogical novel!

"I remember that morning very well because the weather had been bad all week, with no sun. When I woke up and held out my arms to António, he was standing by the bed, contemplating me with a delighted expression on his face. I . . . I was naked, naturally. With his beautiful smile of an innocent child, he said to me: 'You're dressed in sunlight, it's your camisole. I'm going to write a sonnet for you with that title.' I didn't give him time, he put it off till later, and in the hour of his death he remembered. He remembered me."

She could not suppress her sobs. She covered her mouth with her handkerchief, struggled to regain her composure, and succeeded, a great lady accustomed to controlling her emotions.

"I came to offer you an exchange. Let me have that page and I'll give you something that is very valuable but useless as long as it remains in my hands."

She opened her travel bag and took out a school composition book.

"António wrote a 'crown of sonnets' for me in this notebook. They are unfortunately unpublishable, at least in an ordinary edition that would be sold in bookstores. But I thought that you might be able to have a limited, deluxe edition printed, perhaps with drawings. Alberto has many editions of that sort, published in France and England. Di Cavalcanti might do the drawings; he's a very good friend of my eldest son, António." After uttering the name, a slight pause: "He looks exactly like his father. . . ."

Afrânio Portela took the notebook and began leafing through the pages.

"Please, wait till I've gone," she begged. "I don't know how much such an edition would cost, but if you'll agree to make the necessary arrangements, I'll pay the expenses. All I ask is that you send me a copy when it comes out."

"Don't worry, you won't have to finance it; I'll take care of everything. Where is Di now, do you know?"

"In Lisbon with António. They were forced to flee France when the war broke out. Among the things António inherited from his father is his passion for Paris. They're waiting for a boat that will get them back to Brazil."

"And the manuscript?"

"Donate it to the Academy library or to the National Library. I leave that choice up to you. I don't want to keep it in my possession any longer. If I die unexpectedly, I don't want Alberto to find that notebook among my belongings. You're the only one who knows that those sonnets were written for me. Even Sílvia didn't know about them."

They took the elevator downstairs and Mestre Afrânio escorted her to the front door, where a taxi was waiting for her. The driver was sitting reading the war news in an evening paper. Mariana bent over to get in, and the novelist smiled as he admired her ample hips. It was not by chance that she had chosen Di Cavalcanti to illustrate the crown of sonnets, António Bruno's unpublished book, his first one, written before *The Dancer and the Flower*, and, moreover, an erotic one, a collector's item.

Mestre Afrânio did not return to the library. He took refuge in one of the rooms on the fourth floor, amid the archives. He read all fifteen erotic sonnets straight through, from beginning to end. "Initiation to Pleasure." A subtitle: "Crown of Sonnets for a Lady from São Paulo, a Bacchante of Paris." The dedication: "For M. . . . , my Marie de Médicis."

He went back to the first sonnet, reread the verse slowly, in a subdued voice, like someone tasting a wine with an exquisite bouquet:

"O Callipygian Venus with the beautiful behind . . ."

⬛ THE LADY WHOSE BEAUTY HAS FADED

I

The union of two old families, the alliance of two powerful fortunes: the newspapers speculated endlessly in their commentaries accompanying the announcement of the marriage of Mariana d'Almeida Cintra and Alberto da Costa Ribeiro. It was a love-match, however; engaged couples so enamored of each other were seldom seen in high society, where money rules sentiments.

Mariana, tall, fair-haired, with an opulent body— "straight out of a painting by Rubens," the poet Menotti del Picchia, one of her swains stricken with a violent passion for her, had written—those romantic eyes, immense drops of water, their gaze lost in infinity; Alberto, taller still, handsome, broad-shouldered, dark-haired, a widely acclaimed sportsman, a champion equestrian, jumping exceptional mounts over the barriers, owner of a horse-breeding establishment at the Jockey Club, and his father's business partner. The export firm, located in Santos, was the ruling force in the coffee market, the determining factor in the rise and fall of prices, taking in piles of money. The plantations of both families were situated in the most fertile land in the state of São Paulo; on them vast expanses of high-yielding coffee trees flourished. In Mato Grosso they raised purebred cattle and thousands of head of zebu.

Mariana had just turned twenty and Alberto twenty-five when they left on their wedding trip, a three-month round-the-world cruise, but the honeymoon lasted more than four years: receptions, parties, balls, tours, trips to Argentina, the United States, Europe.

Then everything changed. On the death of his father, Alberto took over as sole head of the export firm and manager of the coffee plantations, since he was the oldest brother and his mother did not want to be involved in business matters. He had previously helped his father, had a voice in the decisions that were made, offered advice and suggestions, but it was the old man who had been in charge. Alberto lived for his wife, satisfying her slightest whim, an affectionate and devoted husband. He might have been a little less conventional in bed, Mariana sometimes thought, her body burning with desires whose existence Alberto knew nothing of, since she, out of a sense of modesty and decorum, never allowed herself to betray the least sign of the ardor that was consuming her. They therefore had frequent but banal sex relations, without excesses and without refinements. For excesses and refinements Alberto went to French girls, in the capital and in Santos.

Little by little his endless responsibilities, his hectic life in the world of business occupied him completely, and Mariana found herself relegated more and more to a second place in her husband's life; he no longer had time for her, was never relaxed and good-humored. The days of idling about, of pleasure cruises, were over. Alberto traveled a great deal, hurried business trips that were exhausting. He fulfilled his social obligations, attending the affairs that Mariana was so fond of, protesting, dragged to them by force, overworked and bowed down by the weight of the responsibilities resting on his shoulders. He still engaged in sports on rare occasions, but he was no longer the unbeatable equestrian that he had been; he had lost interest in thoroughbreds and had handed over the horse-breeding establishment to his younger brothers.

Twelve years after their marvelous wedding party, Mariana's and Alberto's married life had reached an impasse. One lonely, rainy day, weary of the abandonment that she attributed to her husband's coldness and indifference toward her, Mariana made up her mind to separate from him. They had no children, and her life had turned into a stupid and pointless sacrifice, bringing her nothing but humiliation and discontent. A month or more would sometimes go by without Alberto's seeking her out; when they had moved to their new town house, a modern-style mansion designed by Warchavchik, they had occupied separate bedrooms.

When she informed Alberto of her decision, the coffee exporter could not believe it. He was stunned. Are you crazy? A separation? Why, when we're living the good life and love each other? Or is it because you don't love me anymore? Yes, she loved him, and perhaps he loved her too, but what was the use of loving each other if they almost never saw each other, rarely went out together to see a movie or a play, to attend a social function? Do you know how long it's been since you've knocked on my bedroom door? Almost two months, do you realize that?

Alberto argued in his own defense. It had been Mariana herself who had wanted separate bedrooms, a fact that in his eyes betrayed disdain, disinterest on her part; he had been deeply hurt. The fact that they had no children had also contributed to their drifting apart; they had both wanted so much to have children, but none had come along. Which of them was to blame? Mariana had undergone treatment, consulted specialists, all to no avail. Alberto had had medical examinations; he was not sterile. They had drifted farther and farther apart, and Mariana had begun to feel bitter. A woman born for love and deprived of it, she suffered in silence, immured within her pride of a great lady, too haughty to protest.

In the beginning she stubbornly held to her decision to separate. But Alberto adored her and refused to accept the idea of living without her; he suggested another possibility. Mariana's older sister, Sílvia, who had been left a widow just a little over two years before, was living in Paris, in an apartment she had rented near the Champs-Elysées. Why didn't Mariana go spend a few months with her sister before making an irrevocable decision? Alberto proposed a six-month vacation from marriage. If the two of them could bear living so far apart, they would separate permanently. But if they missed their life in common, they would go back together and try again. Who could tell?—after those months apart, wasn't it possible that everything would be as it had been in the first years? Moreover, Alberto's two brothers were working with him now, and the younger one was proving to have a good head for business. During this interlude, Alberto would try to hand over to his brothers most of the workload and part of the responsibility that up till then he had shouldered all by himself. Mariana agreed; when all was said and done, she did not want to lose him.

Alberto waved goodbye to her from the pier in Santos, and Mariana wept in her suite on the British liner during the entire crossing. She was planning to stay only a month in Paris; she would spend the remaining five months on their most remote estate, one they had just acquired, on the border between Mato Grosso and Paraguay.

II

Sílvia had left her widow's weeds and her family obligations behind in São Paulo. No one would have taken her to be eight years older than Mariana. She had regained her lost youth in Paris.

"I was the slave of my husband and my children during the whole of my married life, my girl. My husband's dead now; my children are grown up, they've earned their university degrees, they're rolling in money, they don't need me, and *vive Paris!*"

It was Sílvia who introduced Bruno to Mariana:

"You need a man to keep you company, to go for walks with you, to go dancing with, to take you to dinner at Paris restaurants, to escort you to the theater. Two weeks from now, there'll be the Opera masked ball; you must go to the dressmaker's to have your costume made. For all those things and for everything else, a gigolo is indispensable. And I know of one who's exactly right for you. He's good-looking and he writes poetry."

"What about you? Do you have one?"

"To tell you the truth, I have two of them, little Jean and big André. They're the exact opposite in size, and in everything else as well. I like variety."

"The only trouble is that I for my part don't care for variety. The one man in my life up till now has been Alberto."

"It's precisely because you're monogamous that I'm recommending only Bruno to you. His full name is António Bruno, a student, a poet, and a Brazilian born in Bahia. What more could you ask for? And as for charm, there's nobody who can equal him."

"You're out of your mind. I came here to forget my husband, not to be unfaithful to him."

"Who said anything about being unfaithful to him? You're being melodramatic, my dear! Bruno will merely be your escort, go on walks with you, take you to the dressmaker's, to dinner in restaurants: a page. He won't go any farther unless you're willing, unless you're unable to resist."

Mariana resisted the young man's charm, his seductive spell, his poetry for more than a week, but succumbed on the ninth day, on the occasion of the Opera masked ball.

Before that, in the company of António—she never called him Bruno—a young man at once tender and bold, she discovered a Paris that she had never known on previous trips. She visited museums, cathedrals, became acquainted with every detail of Notre Dame, and learned to love the charm, the enchantment of the city, felt the touch of its true breath, far above and beyond the tourist excursions to which she was accustomed. With Jean at times, with André at others, and always with Sílvia, they spent their nights in restaurants, bistros, theaters, cabarets—dancing, laughing, drinking champagne, as António repeatedly declared his love for her and recited love-poems. Was he really passionately in love? He was handsome and charming, irresponsible and unpredictable. His strong dark profile reminded her of Alberto in the days when she had first met him, a young and daring equestrian jumping barriers at horse trials, an Alberto who might have been a mad poet. She allowed António to steal furtive kisses here and there, on dance floors—an incomparable dancer!—on mornings at dawn when he saw her home as Sílvia shamelessly clung to the escort on duty that night. But things never went farther.

Remembering the gallant attentions of another poet, the author of *Masques*, she disguised herself as Marie de Médicis as portrayed on the day of her marriage by proxy in Rubens's painting. A disguise? She was the living image of Marie de Médicis—and the queen of the masked ball. Bruno wore the same Harlequin costume that he had appeared in the year before. The heavy skirts of Mariana's gown kept her from being the ideal partner for the maxixe, but Bruno was such a virtuoso that the other couples stood aside and applauded. Sílvia took advantage of her sister's triumph to disappear with André.

As dawn broke, Mariana found herself half a queen, half a slave, stripped naked from the waist down in the bed of the young dancer, a bohemian and a gigolo, a François Villon from the tropics, as he laughingly called himself after having climbed, drunk and devil-may-care, the six steep flights of stairs to the garret on the seventh floor of the Hôtel Saint-Michel.

On possessing the splendid body of the lady from São

Paulo, Bruno was dying of a desire he could scarcely contain. No other woman had cost him so much time, so much talk, so much charm. Mariana had taxed his patience, responding to his advances by uttering the name and citing the virtues of her husband and putting him off as no woman ever had before; the consummate conquistador had felt that he was on the brink of failure. Humiliating. And so, this first time, he possessed her fiercely, in a rage almost, ripping the magnificent royal skirts (made to order at an ultra-chic dressmaker's, the costume had cost her a small fortune), tearing off the starched petticoats, leaving her naked except for her bodice and her great stiff ruff. A whirlwind.

Once the initial onslaught was over, feeling the neophyte adulteress tremble at the moment of possession and stifle a moan, Bruno realized the drama of that woman's body made for the wild revels in bed of which she had been deprived, knowing only the paltry pleasures of the marriage-bed of a rich businessman. Her husband, whose name and equestrian victories were constantly on her lips, might be an outstanding horseman, a champion of sensational tourneys, exceptionally handsome, a multimillionaire, distinguished, likable, and all the rest, yet in the essential domain that determines everything else he had never gone beyond the banal, as Bruno could easily verify.

After having ravished her with the fury of an Apache, he began to undress her slowly, garment by garment, unhurriedly, for as he did so he took possession of her body detail by detail, lingering over every little particular, making her quiver all over with excitement and wonder at the revelation of sexual pleasure. An expert in this art by inclination and by profession, Bruno transported her from Alberto's routine lovemaking to the realm of delicious refinements, opening her eyes to uses and practices entirely new to her, subtle tonguings and tactile sensations, when on that first dawn he touched her hips and breasts modeled by Rubens, her fully opened flower flowing with honey. Finally he looked upon her completely naked, her erect breasts, her ample thighs, her immense eyes of limpid water. He turned her over: the magnificent backside, the croup of a mare, a mount that Alberto had not known how to ride. In the champagne foam he slowly, slowly savored her.

Mariana responded with an eager, urgent explosion, revealing at the same time both ignorance and the willingness to learn. A sleeping volcano, suddenly erupting: flames rose to the sky, and streams of lava flowed down the hills of the queen's body. The little studio, the miserable garret moaned with the music of the sighs of love in the hour of lust; was perfumed with the scent of a woman, the sweat of a man, the smell of sperm, of satisfied sex, satiated and insatiable; was illuminated by the light born in Mariana's eyes of limpid water, larger still now, for they were filled with tears.

That was how the bacchanal began; it lasted three months. Three months during which Mariana gave and received, making up for the lost years. She wanted only to be in the garret of the poet, of the young man, of the boy from Bahia that the *bon Dieu de France* had sent her by way of Sílvia's sisterly hand. She showered him with presents; she drank in his words and verses. Nipped, bitten, licked, sucked, penetrated, ridden, riding, each night a new discovery, a new sensation, the many flavors, the differences in bouquet—and all in French, the language in which no love-word is obscene: *le beau vit et le gentil con, la verge et la chatte, la rosette et les feuilles de rose, les nichons et les cuisses, la motte, le cul.* Bruno recited to her erotic poems by Baudelaire, Rimbaud, Verlaine, Apollinaire—". . . tes fesses lourdes comme des fromages de Hollande . . ."—and put them into practice: ". . . ma queue éclatait sous tes lèvres/comme une prune de Juillet." Mariana learned and repeated, in the accent of the nuns of Les Oiseaux, where she had studied French: "Mon cul s'éveille au souvenir/d'une inoubliable caresse." Marvelous, falling asleep in Bruno's arms, awakening to the touch of that eloquent tongue: "Ah, comme c'est bon."

The bed of a gigolo and a Balzacian woman, of a bohemian and a bacchante, desire and rut, hunger and appetite. Not content with the poetry of others, Bruno composed for Mariana a crown of licentious sonnets in which he celebrated, detail by detail, her magnificent body, putting into libertine rhyme and meter the Parisian love-affair of François Villon of Bahia and Marie de Médicis of São Paulo, lived on the Boul' Mich.'

III

The love-affair was not limited, however, to the mornings and nights of caresses, the tremendous bacchanal. It was complemented and enhanced by afternoon walks, by endless conversations on the banks of the Seine, in the bistros of Saint-Germain, in the Jardin du Luxembourg, "your gardens and your palace, my Marie de Médicis." Mariana told of her joys and sorrows, marched her entire life past in review. The fantasies of the pupil at Les Oiseaux, the first balls, the demanding heiress rejecting suitors, the meeting with Alberto, their inordinate love, the happy marriage, the trip around the world, the honeymoon that had lasted for more than four years, and then the gradual abandonment, the indifference, the lack of children, the separate bedrooms, the husband out to earn a fortune, dividing his time between São Paulo and Santos, and finally the despair, the proposal that they separate, the stay in Paris before making a final, irrevocable decision. And in Paris she had found Bruno, happiness.

Happiness? Or merely pleasure, the frantic excitement of the marvelous love-adventure, immoral and very sweet? Whichever it was, the separation had now become inevitable; whether or not she missed Alberto was no longer the question. She had been unfaithful to him; it was all over.

Bruno listened with the affectionate solicitude that very early in his life he had learned to accord women. He took her in his arms, changed the subject, kissed her on her immense eyes of limpid water to banish her sad thoughts:

"You have two things, my queen, more beautiful than those of any other woman: your eyes and your backside."

He talked to her of chansonettes and paintings, he recited to her a poem that he had written recently, but she went back to the eternal subject of the husband now lost forever. One night, after they had climbed the steep flights of stairs leading to the seventh floor of the Hôtel Saint-Michel, Bruno asked:

"Why are you so upset? What's happened?"

Mariana opened her handbag and fished out the cable: "Here, read it. . . ."

In it Alberto announced that he was boarding a French ship and would be arriving in Paris within the next two weeks. He could not bear to wait out the six months that they had agreed on, and had turned the firm over to his brothers so as to have time for his wife: *I can't live without you,* the Western Union cable said.

It was going to be an unpleasant moment; no, not unpleasant, much worse than that, it was going to be awful. But she had to tell him that going on with their life as a married couple had become impossible; she had been unfaithful to him. . . . Bruno took her in his arms and began to undress her as she spoke:

"You're not going to do anything of the sort, my Marie de Médicis; you're not going to tell him anything. You love your husband. That's the only thing that counts— why do you want to hurt him?"

"Do you think I still love Alberto? If I do, why have I been unfaithful to him?"

"You never stop talking about him; Alberto is there at your side the whole time. If I weren't a good kid, I might have felt offended. I'm not the love of your life; I merely gave you something you needed, the discovery of what sensual pleasure is. You weren't loved as you should have been, something that was surely as much your fault as your husband's. Who knows, my queen—didn't you perhaps wall yourself off behind your hauteur, your imperial dignity? I was able to break your pride because you were dizzied by passion and I took you by force. When I ripped your dress away, I bared your heart. Isn't that so?"

"I think that's true. . . ." So young still, did António know or had he guessed?

"Well then? Go back to your husband and make your marriage-bed the proof of your love. Give Alberto everything I gave you, everything I took from you and will now return to you. But only on the night that he arrives. Until then you'll be mine, only mine. Mariana Marie de Médicis da Costa, I'll never forget you. In the hour of my death, I'll remember you. Now come on, hurry, we've only a few days left to celebrate our parting."

"Even if I love him, it's impossible to go back to him now, António. . . ."

Bruno was suddenly afraid. Could she be thinking of living with him, of transforming their joyous, exciting, passing affair into a concubinage worse than marriage?

"I've already told you—remember?—that I don't intend to settle down with any woman. I'm not a permanent love-partner, only a temporary one."

"You needn't be afraid. I'm going to go back to Brazil. . . ."

"I want to tell you something else: you were born to be a married woman, to be faithful to your husband. I don't see you passing from hand to hand; you wouldn't be happy."

"That's quite beside the point, António. Listen: besides everything else you've given me, verses and pleasure, you've made me pregnant. I'll tell you straight out that I won't have an abortion. I've always wanted to have a baby. But I won't be a bother to you; I'll have my baby in Brazil. He'll make me remember you, my temporary António."

Bruno smiled, his face aglow:

"A baby? Why *your* baby? He's as much mine as he is yours. He's *our* son!"

He was pensive for a long moment, then took her in his arms and kissed her on the eyes and mouth. Then he spoke, suddenly serious and thoughtful, as knowledge-able at twenty as only poets are, possessing as they do the gift of divination:

"Your husband also wants a child, isn't that so? What's more, the two of us look alike; you yourself have told me so. Don't think that I'm abandoning our son; I know that it's going to be a boy and that you'll name him António. But think with me for a moment: why do you want to bring up a fatherless, illegitimate son? He'll pay dearly for that, his whole life long. For our António, the best thing that could possibly happen is for him to be born the son of Alberto Ribeiro da Costa; and I want only the best for my son. Don't let your feelings get the better of you; don't take me for a worthless wretch. Think things through slowly, calmly, and you'll see that I'm right. I want to give you more than pleasure and a son; I want to give your husband back to you. You and António will be happy with him."

And that was how it was. On the evening of Alberto's arrival, when it came time to say goodbye to Bruno, she thanked him, in tears, and Bruno remembered that he owed her a poem. One day he would write it, because there lingered in his mind's eye the image of Mariana's body clad in a camisole of light, the light of dawn.

The baby boy conceived in Paris, in a bacchant's bed in a garret on the seventh floor of the Hôtel Saint-Michel, was given the name of António, in thanks to the blessed patron of marriage to whom Mariana had prayed for a son. The miracle happened on the night that Alberto ar-rived, when she undressed for her husband in her sister's apartment and, putting decorum aside, gave herself to him eagerly, with unbridled passion. Dazzled, Alberto said:

"I've given you a son tonight; I'm certain of it, my love."

Later on, in São Paulo, another son and a daughter were born, Alberto Jr. and Sílvia, the latter so named in honor of her aunt, who was still in Paris and had no intention of coming back to Brazil. Taking the place of little Jean and big André, however, were Bob, a slight, blond American—Yankees were all the rage—and the Frenchman Georges, a Frenchman being absolutely indispensable.

In São Paulo high society, no one knew of a happier couple, as Mestre Afrânio Portela discovered on seeking more information, material for his novel. A dedicated and attentive husband, a faithful and loving wife, growing old together—in four years' time they would be celebrating their golden wedding anniversary. Mariana and Alberto proved that even among the crème de la crème of society and multimillionaires, filthy-rich and frivolous, love can thrive and be eternal. That is magic owed to poets, who in matters concerning love work more miracles than saints enthroned on altars.

▓ THE FINAL STRETCH

In the final stretch, during election week, in that torrid January of 1941, with the sultry heat weighing down on the city of Rio like a cement slab, two pieces of good news, both due to the efforts of the Academician Altino Alcântara on his behalf, opened up pleasing prospects for the sole candidate. The first, having to do with the Academy regalia, was of economic interest above all. With its jacket front, cuffs, and collar embroidered in gold thread on very expensive green velvet, the uniform costs a fortune, a fortune and a half counting the indispensable accessories: the two-cornered hat with gold trimming and white plumes, the chased ceremonial sword, the gold neck-chain. Altino Alcântara, surprised and flattered by the invitation from his old campaign buddy to deliver the welcoming speech (he had thought that the Academician chosen would be Rodrigo Inácio Filho, one of the sponsors of the general's candidacy and, it was said, an intimate family friend), had promised to launch a fund-raising drive in São Paulo to finance the sumptuous regalia of immortality. It was going to be an enormous and lengthy task, though the idea of public recognition of his heroic war exploits by the inhabitants of the great state did not displease the veteran of the battles of '32.

Repenting of having made this promise, Alcântara chose to act behind the scenes by asking a mutual friend to approach Pernambuco's governor *pro tem*, who proved receptive, pledging himself to sign a decree providing state funds to pay for the uniform of this native son of Pernambuco. State pride had won out over political divergences. Furthermore, as the governor had assured the chief of police, General Waldomiro Moreira, relegated to the reserves, with no troops under his command, installed in an Academy chair, did not represent a threat to the New State. The official gift would neutralize him completely—money well spent.

Besides this welcome news, the illustrious Alcañtara opened up before the general the prospect of a unanimous election. The latter discounted the possibility of one blank ballot, that of Lisandro Leite. He presumed that the judge was the only one thinking of so voting, even though just one such ballot would be sufficient to deprive him, the general, of the pleasure of receiving a unanimous vote, a rare occurrence in Academy elections. The number of Immortals so elected could be counted ⁀n the fingers of one hand.

Withdrawn from politics, an eminent attorney who was head of one of the largest banks in São Paulo and looked after the legal interests of the Banco Português do Brasil and of great industries after the national legislature was closed down following the coup of '37, Altino Alcântara seldom came to Rio, and even less often to the Academy.

Of the same political persuasion as the general, openly in favor of his candidacy, chosen to receive him into the Academy—the general had made no secret of the invitation he had extended Alcântara before he had even been elected—he had not been informed either by Evandro and his cohorts or by Lisandro and those loyal to Colonel Sampaio Pereira of the possibility that the general might not be elected. A sheer waste of time, not worth the trouble. However, on one of the rare occasions when the less-than-assiduous Academician turned up for a meeting, president Hermano do Carmo had mentioned to him the deplorable attitude of the candidate, who had so publicly proclaimed his decision to disregard protocol and skip the ceremonial visit to Lisandro Leite: a development that had been not at all well received.

Before returning to São Paulo, Alcântara had met with the general to give him his vote, inasmuch as a court hearing that he could not possibly fail to be present at, scheduled for the day of the election, would prevent his coming to Rio. He apologized for not being able to appear at the house of his esteemed friend after the balloting to personally extend his congratulations to him, to his wife, and to his charming daughter. He took advantage of this meeting to advise the general to be more flexible in his dealings with Lisandro, first of all by reconsidering the stand he had taken with respect to the courtesy visit to him.

"You'll excuse me, my illustrious friend, but as a high-ranking officer of our armed forces, a general of the Army, I feel I can do no other. My honor is at stake . . . ," Moreira had replied.

A skillful politician, Alcântara found a middle path leading to conciliation. He was an expert at finding middle paths:

"I appreciate the fact that you don't want to go there in person. Do the following, then: write a word or two on your calling-card and leave it with the concierge of the building where he lives. There exist precedents for this in previous elections. By so doing, it may be possible to keep Lisandro from casting a blank ballot and get him simply to abstain, thereby enabling you to be elected by unanimous vote."

His argument carried weight, and General Moreira weakened:

"Would you have a word with him on the subject, my dear friend?"

"I'll write him a little note, from São Paulo."

"In that case I'll leave my card. Tomorrow."

Following Alcântara's advice, he dropped off his call-ing-card at the concierge's, adding to the name engraved on it, General Waldomiro Moreira, a few words in his own hand: . . . *presents his respects to the Academician Lisandro Leite.* He hoped that the scoundrel would re-ciprocate this delicate gesture by abstaining rather than casting a blank ballot. A unanimous vote would crown his victory, placing him among the two or three privileged members of the Academy thus elected, all of whom, nat-urally, never let an opportunity to mention this rare dis-tinction go by.

▓ HURLY-BURLY

Hurly-burly! An expression that General Moreira is fond of, it is used by him to characterize the agitation that reigns in the house in Grajaú on this last Thursday of the month of January, 1941, the date of the meeting of the Brazilian Academy of Letters, beginning at five P.M., at which the thirty-nine Immortals are to elect the succes-sor of the poet António Bruno, who has passed on more than four months before. In very hotly contested elec-tions, it has sometimes happened that no candidate has obtained the indispensable majority vote. In cases where there has been only one candidate, this has never oc-curred.

258

Hurly-burly! Dona Conceição is not familiar with the expression, but on hearing the meaning of it explained by the nearly-Immortal linguist she finds it apt: she has never worked so hard in all her years as a slave to her sister-in-law and brother, and later as a married woman. An infernal amount of work to be done, a frightful responsibility, everything in an uproar. She scurries about the house like a mad cockroach—"You're like a mad cockroach," the general has commented on seeing her rushing about in a panic—giving orders, assigning tasks. She pops up in the pantry, where Cecília and Sabença are peeling fruit for the punch—pineapples, apples, pears, oranges, grapes—and, when they are by themselves, giving each other little kisses: a happy day!

"Do you think more than fifty people will come?"

"Fifty? Far more than that, Dona Ceição." Sabença is fond of diminutives and abbreviations, signs of esteem and intimacy. "You haven't yet realized the importance of the Brazilian Academy. Being a member of the Illustrious Company is the greatest honor a man of letters can aspire to. You can count on a hundred people at the very least."

"Then we'll have to order more vol-au-vent and meat pies from Seu Antero's bakery. Phone for twenty more of each, Cecília."

"Don't worry, I'll take care of it, Dona Ceição."

That Senhor Sabença was the most helpful person imaginable. If Cecília was going to take up with somebody—even if she wanted to go back to her husband, he wouldn't have her, and he was right—let it be Seu Claudionor: he wasn't a youngster, he was going on forty; he earned good money as a newspaperman and a teacher; he was separated from his wife, who'd run off with another man, an old flame of hers, three months after they were married (Cecília had at least waited a year). Not to mention the fact that even though he was not yet forty, Seu Claudionor was already a member of an Academy. A second-rate one, according to Moreira; but that was what he said now. Before he'd received that visit of the committee of Immortals he would gladly have accepted a seat in the other one, and had kept pestering Senhor Sabença to propose his name.

But this is no time to think about Cecília's future or the virtues of Seu Claudionor; the matter is in God's hands! Sabença comes back from phoning: mission accomplished. Before leaving for general headquarters in the kitchen, Dona Conceição exclaims:

"Such expense! Will it be worth it?"

In the kitchen, mountains of codfish balls and croquettes are frying. Three helpers, two cousins and a sister-in-law, on being offered substantial gratuities, have come to lend a hand to Eunice, the faithful maid-of-all-work who has been in the service of the Moreira family since time immemorial. One of them, whose specialty is Portuguese-style sweets, has taken on the job of preparing *quindins, fios-de-ovos, olhos-de-sogra, bom-bocados, brigadeiros*. Dona Conceição, in passing, nibbles on a *quindim:* delicious. In the oven, the enormous ham; already roasted, the turkey and the leg of pork. Seu Arlindo is taking care of the drinks. A bartender recommended by a neighbor who loves to give parties, he arrived immediately after lunch; he charges a lot, but he's efficient. Dona Conceição doesn't know whether or not she should deduct from his pay the cost of the crystal goblet he's broken while washing the glasses. A material and sentimental loss: the goblet was part of a set of twelve that had been a wedding present and is now no longer complete. In addition to the punch, two soft drinks and beer— two small-sized kegs—three bottles of Scotch and two of French cognac that had cost an arm and a leg! Cecília, well acquainted with the vices of Academicians, had insisted:

"There has to be Scotch and cognac on hand. . . ." They were always on hand in Rodrigo's bachelor apartment:

imported brands. "And Brazilian whisky and cognac that tastes like tar won't do. . . ."

Dona Conceição threw up her hands in horror, but what else was there to do? Their bank account, where the savings they had accumulated over the years brought good interest, suffered serious inroads. Cecília had demanded that their dresses for the night of the election, when they would receive people's congratulations, and for the grand ceremony the night the general was received as a member of the Academy three months hence be designed and made by Dinah Amado. Extremely well informed as to what went on behind the scenes at the Academy, Cecília had chosen her because she knew that she was the dressmaker of the wives of a number of Academicians. Four dresses, two hats. A bundle of money; Dona Dinah mercilessly fleeced her customers.

Dona Conceição leaves the kitchen, gives instructions to Cosme, the general's former orderly, now retired from the Army and practicing a less noble but better-paying profession: a runner for the illegal numbers game. His services had been requisitioned two days previously for all the heavy work: carrying crates, fetching tables and chairs borrowed from the neighbors, waxing all the floors in the house.

"I want the reception room to gleam like a mirror."

She must not forget Moreira's medication. On the general's last monthly visit to the cardiologist, the doctor, noting that his blood pressure had gone up even more, had prescribed another pill in addition to his other medication. Though he appears calm, her husband is tense. She knows him like a book—dictatorial but not rude, at least not to his wife and daughter. But today he has called her a mad cockroach, a sign that his nerves are on edge.

Dona Conceição suddenly appears in the pantry, thereby very nearly surprising Cecília and Sabença locked in each other's arms exchanging a long lingering kiss on this festive day.

"Cecília, never mind that fruit, hand the job over to Seu Arlindo and go help Eunice in the kitchen so the girls can do the bedrooms. And you, Seu Claudionor, go talk with Moreira so as to distract him for a while."

Sabença casts a passionate glance at Cecília; Ciça returns Cloclô's gaze, her eyes full of promises. Dona Conceição sighs: God grant that this be a lasting affair, that they stay together, that this whole thing not end suddenly like all her other passing affairs; oh, Cecília, capricious as a weathervane!

Unable to lie relaxing on the chaise longue, the candidate is pacing up and down the courtyard with a martial stride. Sabença, a clumsy recruit, has trouble keeping in step, but nonetheless walks up and down alongside his friend and possible future father-in-law. They go over the details of the solemn election-hour once again. Sabença is to remain in the corridor that separates the reception room where the teas are held from the assembly room, remaining close to the telephone located atop a commode. The moment the balloting is over, he is to telephone the final result: a blank ballot or a triumphant unanimous vote? Perhaps, in view of the calling-card, Lisandro Leite will not resort to casting a blank ballot. In that case, the general is prepared to "forget the affronts of the past and extend his right hand to his immortal colleague"—as he confides to the faithful Sabença.

Glass of water and pill in hand, Dona Conceição approaches:

"Your medicine, Moreira. Don't you think you should take two pills instead of one today?' "

"I don't see why. I feel perfectly all right." He downs the pill, drinks a swallow of water. "I want everything to be ready and in order by the time the Academicians arrive."

He allows a smile to cross his habitually stern face and, a rare gesture, pinches his wife's cheek:

"Tomorrow I'll go to Pena, the official Academy tailor, to have my measurements taken for the uniform."

The general's reception as an Academician is going to cost me a new suit, Claudionor thinks, but it will be worth the money: Cecília's hand, the José Verissimo Prize, and, in the future, who can tell what else. . . . With his father-in-law seated in the Academy, working on his behalf . . . Dreams people the house in Grajaú as Dona Conceição scurries back and forth amid the frightful hurly-burly.

▉ THE MINISTERIAL CANDIDATE

Renato Muller Vieira, the Brazilian Ambassador to Mexico, arrived in Rio on vacation leave on the very eve of the election. An Academician awarded his seat five years before on the fourth ballot of a hotly contested election, for the first time he would have a chance to cast his vote in person. His trips back to Brazil had not coincided with the two previous elections, and he had submitted his vote by mail. For the chair left vacant by Bruno he had likewise sent a letter with his vote to the deceased candidate Sampaio Pereira as soon as he had received the latter's lengthy, cordial cable.

He knew the colonel only by name: he had never set eyes on him, nor had he read the polemical political studies he had written. But he had hastened to send his vote and congratulations, since the colonel was an influential figure in the government and had great prestige in military circles. He could play a decisive role in fulfilling the ambitions of Muller Vieira, who was on the list of possible replacements for Oswaldo Aranha as foreign minister, if and when the latter actually resigned, as he had announced he would. The fact that Muller Vieira had held a post in Germany after Hitler took power seemed to him to be a factor weighing heavily in his favor: he had had good relations with the Nazi authorities and had left a favorable impression behind him, useful in the present circumstances when Brazil was leaning toward an alliance with the Axis.

A poet and a novelist—hermetic poetry, kabbalistic fiction—with half a dozen published books, highly esteemed by certain critics who, in their praise of him, cited Dostoevski, Joyce, and Kafka to explain the anxiety and alienation present in his works: in his novels Brazil did not exist, and in his poetry not even the most sensitive readers could perceive the slightest trace of love. He was not even read by the critics who thought so highly of him, according to R. Figueiredo Jr. (and a number of other backbiters)—critics who, moreover, the acid-tongued dramatist claimed, had not read Joyce or Kafka either, and at best had merely leafed through translations of Dostoevski. The truth was that, whether he was read or not, an aura of genius had come to surround Renato Muller Vieira: in the opinion of these literary theoreticians, his novels and poems reflected the pathos of the contemporary world, the violence that had been unleashed, not that of war—"universal and necessary surgery"—but that within man himself.

He had received a cable from General Moreira as well, a short one; the general paid his own hard-earned money for those he sent, while the colonel used the government anti-Communist budget. He had answered by thanking him for the cable and informing him that he had pledged his vote to Sampaio Pereira. After the death of the powerful colonel, Muller Vieira's tone turned more affable on acknowledging the receipt of a letter from the general, now the sole candidate, calling his attention to the new state of affairs and asking him to send him his vote. The ambassador informed the candidate that he would be in Brazil at the time of the election and would be pleased to cast his vote for the general in person. He did not mention how much he regretted the colonel's death. A man who wielded enormous power, Sampaio Pereira would have paid Muller Vieira back for his support, with interest. The merits of the sole remaining candidate were limited to the stars on his uniform jacket. However, even when he is a member of the opposition, a general is always a general.

The ambassador had arrived in Brazil prepared to take advantage of his holiday to find out what truth there was in reports of Aranha's imminent resignation, and to see that the proper steps were taken to put forward his own name. He had friends he could count on in the office of the head of state. He spent the morning and the early afternoon at Itamaraty, and from there went directly to the Academy. Received with friendly embraces and words of welcome, he dropped by the secretariat and pocketed the check covering the *jetons* he had not yet received— even when he was not present at Academy meetings, he received them by courtesy of the president—and in the tea salon certain Academicians addressed him as "Minister." Not contenting himself with a friendly embrace and words of welcome, Lisandro Leite dragged his colleague over to a window recess:

"Before they mention another name to you, I want to tell you that our Raul Limeira will be a candidate. . . ."

"The rector of the university?"

"Himself. Rector, and even more importantly, the intimate friend of The Man. For someone who already has one foot in the stirrup on his way to becoming foreign minister . . ."

"But a candidate for what vacant seat? Has someone died in the last two days while I was on the plane?"

"For António Bruno's vacant seat."

"But that one's about to be filled today."

"That depends. . . ."

"Depends on what?"

"On your vote, for example. It may be decisive. I've been authorized by Raul to speak with you in his name. He'll find a way of showing his gratitude."

"I have no idea what all this is about. Tell me straight out."

"Let's go into the library. We'll be more comfortable there."

▩ HUMAN NATURE

On getting out of his car in front of the main door of the Petit Trianon, having come from Petrópolis for the election, Rodrigo Inácio Filho finds himself held fast in the bony embrace of Evandro Nunes dos Santos:

"You lucky dog, enjoying the delights of the mountains while the rest of us suffocate here in this furnace. . . ."

As they head for the secretariat arm in arm, Rodrigo asks for information on the march of events:

"Well then, how's the guerrilla campaign going, El Pasionario? The one who thought up that nickname for you was your compadre Portela, that great joker."

"The guerrilla band is going to make its last sortie very shortly." Evandro halted in the middle of the foyer and removed his pince-nez, grinning broadly. "The enemy has his back to the wall. We're going to annihilate him."

"Human nature is loathsome," Rodrigo said in a confidential tone of voice.

"Do you think so?"

"I was the one who discovered the general when you and Portela were looking for someone with the necessary qualifications. I was a member of the committee that went to his home to invite him to present himself as a candidate. . . ."

"I went too. Afrânio forced me to."

". . . I read a book the general sent me. . . ."

"I didn't go that far."

". . . I had a passing affair with his daughter, a wanton young lady but rather vapid. . . . And finally, I'm a friend of the family, almost a relative. However, I'm going to vote for him merely to be at peace with my conscience, and what's worse, I'm pulling for your victory against the poor man. There's no doubt about it—human nature is loathsome."

"Poor man, you say? He rules the roost around here already and claims that Bruno was an unmitigated ass. Imagine how things are going to be if he manages to get himself elected. . . . Look, we may badly need your vote. If you think things through logically, you'll vote against your conscience, and not in accordance with it. Use your head. . . ."

Rodrigo heads toward the secretariat once more:

"*Vade retro!*"

"Wanton and vapid! All right then, pay the price for your licentious ways. But I beg you, don't promise anyone your vote four months from now: our candidate is Feliciano. You already knew that, didn't you?"

"I'll vote for him with the greatest of pleasure, if you people win."

"Do you still doubt it? As long as I have anything to say about it, nobody's going to trade a military uniform for Academy regalia. Neither a uniform nor a cassock."

"You're the last anticlerical left in the world. . . ."

"I'm not anticlerical; I'm a materialist. I have many friends who are priests; what I don't want is for them to come preaching religion here."

". . . and the last antimilitarist. . . ."

"I'm a partisan of civilian power, I grant you. I also have friends who are in the military, but I won't stand for them elbowing their way in here to order us to form ranks. . . . The Army chair—who ever heard of such a thing?"

▧ THE BALLOT BOX

As usual, the *doyen* of the Academy, Francelino Almeida, poses for the photographers, his hand extended toward the ballot box as though depositing his vote in it. After the reporters have left, the doors of the assembly hall are closed.

Dressed with all the elegance of an English lord, the ancient chief usher, a "double-dyed" black with snow-white hair, presents the ballot box to the president, the first to cast his vote. He then presents it to the distinguished Academy members on the platform, then goes down onto the floor of the assembly hall.

There are relatively few Academicians present at this last session before the annual recess. Most of them have fled to cities in the mountains to escape the heat, and some have gone back to their native states for the holidays and have not yet returned. The aged chief usher goes from seat to seat, and each Immortal deposits a bit of paper in the ballot box. The president has officially read off a list of the letters from those absent, accompanied in each case by their votes in sealed envelopes.

Once the chief usher has returned to the platform, the ballot box is emptied. The counting of the votes is about to begin. As soon as it is finished, the ballots will be put back in the box, and the venerable chief usher will pour alcohol over them before scratching the match to light the fire that will consume them. Thus the secret of the vote will be forever buried in the ashes.

In the tea salon the reporters and photographers are polishing off what remains of the food and drink on the well-laden table. During close elections, the reception rooms, the library, the lobby are always jampacked with people—supporters of the various candidates—and buzzing with a confused murmur of voices. An election with a single candidate promises no battle and no surprises; it has no appeal. Nonetheless a number of curious bystanders have shown up, among them the old bookdealer Carlos Ribeiro. They are awaiting the close of the session to catch a ride to the home of the newly-elected Academician, to congratulate him and to get in on the eats and drinks. Standing next to the commode with the telephone on top of it, Claudionor Sabença is awaiting the moment when he will be able to inform General Waldomiro Moreira that he has won immortality.

▦ THE TELEPHONE CALL

Sitting in an armchair next to the phone, General Waldomiro Moreira is awaiting the call from his friend Claudionor Sabença informing him that he has won immortality. Dress uniform, a grave countenance, he is the very picture of dignified serenity. At his side is his daughter—a frivolous creature, yet devoted to her father. Dona Conceição comes and goes, taking care of last-minute details. The two of them are dressed to the nines.

A few visitors, come to await the happy news in the candidate's company, are scattered about the room: neighbors, his closest friends, a number of old barracks buddies, officers who have served with him. They admire the bountiful buffet tables, platters and plates full of canapés and sweets, trays of ham, leg of pork, turkey. The intimate friends are well acquainted with Eunice's consummate culinary talents. In the patio, Seu Arlindo has set up the bar: the kegs of draft beer, the brimming punch bowls, the soft drinks—and, hidden out of sight, the bottles of whisky and cognac, reserved for the Immortals and other Excellencies.

The time has never passed so slowly. The general waits, the guests converse in subdued voices, and every so often a burst of laughter is heard. Dona Conceição appears at the door, bringing one last platter from the kitchen:

"Still no word?"

At that precise moment the phone rings. The general reaches for it, a smile appears on Cecília's face, Dona Conceição halts in her tracks.

"Sabença? Yes, it's me. Well, then? Is it unanimous?"

He listens, his eyes widen in surprise, his mouth gapes open, and he says in a choked voice:

"What's that?"

The blood rushes to his face, a thread of spittle appears between his lips. The general lets go of the telephone, his body doubles over in his chair. Dona Conceição drops the platter; codfish balls roll about the room. She runs to her husband's side, takes him in her arms.

Distant repeated sounds, almost inaudible, on the phone: "Hello! Hello!" Cecília answers, in a broken voice:

"Come right away. Something's happened to Papa. . . ."

He died at the wrong time, Dona Conceição said later. He had let the right time go by, the moment when he received that other phone call. When he learned that he was the sole candidate and considered himself elected.

❖ THE NEWS

Afrânio Portela sets down his hat and cane. The maid is waiting for him with a message:

"Dr. Hermano wants you to telephone him immediately. It's very urgent."

On his way to his study, Mestre Afrânio smiles at Dona Rosarinho as she hastens to his side, eager to hear how the election turned out. As he waits for the president to answer the phone, he kisses his wife and promises to satisfy her curiosity:

"I'll tell you all about it in just a moment." He answers the voice on the other end of the line:

"Yes, Hermano, go ahead, I'm all ears."

He listens, his hand resting on Dona Rosarinho's shoulder. His hand contracts; an exclamation escapes his lips.

"Good Lord!"

He hangs up, stands there motionless, not saying a word. Dona Rosarinho takes him by the arm:

"What's happened, Afrânio?"

"We've killed the general!"

❖ THE SECOND ONE

The grandfather enters the house. His two grandchildren hasten to his side.

"Tell us what happened, Grandfather."

"Tell us this instant, my darling. We're dying to know."

Evandro Nunes dos Santos sits down in his favorite armchair, lights a cigarette. As he speaks, he toys with his pince-nez.

"He had sixteen votes, four short of the majority required. Twelve abstentions, eleven blank ballots. This business of a specially reserved chair in the Academy is over and done with. Bruno will have the successor he deserves: Feliciano."

"Don't you think that poets could have a chair specially reserved for them, my darling?" Isabel, an insatiable reader of poetry, suggests.

The phone rings, and Pedro answers.

"Your president, Grandfather. I think he wants to congratulate you—he's all excited."

Evandro picks up the phone:

"We're . . ." He does not finish the sentence, and sits there listening. "I can't believe it! Regrettable, to be sure. Sad, I agree. But, in the final analysis, war is war."

He hangs up, tells his grandchildren what has happened to the general.

"When he heard the news, it was as though he'd been struck by lightning. He died instantly."

"A heart attack?"

"You can call it that if you like, Isabel. I for my part prefer to think of it as death by violence."

"The second one, Grandfather. Don't forget the colonel. . . ." Pedro reminds him. "You were willing to fight a battle, and I must say, Grandfather, it turned out to be quite a battle!"

▉ TWO ELDERLY MEN OF LETTERS

Two famous, elderly men of letters, democrats—one of them, Afrânio Portela, merely liberal, the other, Evandro Nunes dos Santos, with anarchist leanings—are having a little nip together at the Colombo, in the late afternoon on the day after the election. Mestre Afrânio glances up at the balcony of Madame Picq's workshop, where, in bygone days, Rosa flirted with António Bruno. She no longer leans over the balcony railing; she has opened her own shop, an upper floor on the Rua do Rosário. She sent a card to Dona Rosarinho offering her services.

"I've begun writing a novel, compadre. Day after tomorrow I'm going to go up to the little country place in Teresópolis and sit down at my typewriter."

"It's about time."

"I thought that *The Woman in the Mirror* would be my last novel. I'd lost all interest in the intrigues of the sort of people who frequent fashionable salons and live in bachelor apartments, and Lençois lies far in the past—it couldn't give birth to another Maluquinha now."

"But I read a short story of yours not so long ago. . . . Even the Colombo figured in it, I remember very well."

Mestre Afrânio feels flattered on hearing Evandro mention that story. He hadn't known that his old friend had read it and remembered the details:

" 'The Five O'Clock Tea,' published some four years ago. Inspired by an affair that Bruno had with a little seamstress in the workshop opposite, on the third floor of that building. I'm going to go back to her."

"To whom? The seamstress?"

"Yes, to her. I know her well now, and in the story I wrote I invented her personality out of the whole cloth. She and three other mistresses of Bruno's will be the characters in the novel. All four of them were at his wake. What's more, the novel begins at the wake."

"It was there that our battle began too, when Sampaio Pereira made his entrance, do you remember? He stood at attention for the deceased. The photograph appeared in the papers so that everybody would see." Evandro raised his glass. "And what the devil am I going to do now? You have your novel that's going to occupy your time in Teresópolis. I for my part am going to miss the guerrilla campaign."

"Weren't you planning to begin writing your memoirs?"

"The guerrilla campaign has the makings of a good chapter. . . . The general's funeral was this morning, wasn't it?" Evandro raises his glass and drains it.

Afrânio Portela also drinks the last drop in his before answering. With their two glasses raised, they look as though they are proposing a toast.

"Yes, that's right. He was buried at eleven o'clock. Rodrigo appeared at the graveside ceremony, and they made him leave."

He calls the waiter over and asks for the check. With his characteristic wicked smile on his lips, he looks at his compadre Evandro Nunes dos Santos.

"Murderer!" he says to him in a macabre, affectionate tone of voice.

The two elderly men of letters stroll down the street at a steady, leisurely pace, happy to be alive. They head for the bookstore, to indulge in their vice of leafing through volumes, having a look at the latest books just off the press, commenting on successes and failures, buying under the counter foreign publications whose sale is forbidden by the dictatorship.

■ THE MORAL OF THE FABLE

The moral? Let's see: everywhere, throughout the world, the shadows have descended once again, war against the people, totalitarianism. But, as has been proved in this fable, it is always possible to plant a seed, to kindle a hope.

Pedra do Sal, Bahia,
January–June, 1979.

PEN, SWORD, CAMISOLE

has been set in a film version of Trump Mediæval,
a typeface designed by Professor Georg Trump
in the mid-1950s and cast by the C. E. Weber
Typefoundry of Stuttgart, West Germany. The
roman letter forms of Trump Mediæval are based
on classical prototypes, but have been interpreted
by Professor Trump in a distinctly modern style.
The italic letter forms are more of a sloped roman
than a true italic in design, a characteristic shared
by many contemporary typefaces. The result is
a modern and distinguished type, notable both
for its legibility and versatility.

The book was designed by Janis Capone and
composed by NK Graphics, Keene, New Hamp-
shire. The paper is Glatfelter Offset, an entirely
acid-free sheet. Haddon Craftsmen, Scranton,
Pennsylvania, was the printer and the binder
for this book.